SEAVIEW HOUSE

PAULA HILLMAN

Enjoy!

Paula Hillman

First published in 2023 by Bloodhound Books.

www.bloodhoundbooks.com

Print ISBN: 978-1-5040-8331-7

Part I

Chapter One

AUGUST 2018

There isn't a windier island than Walney, according to its locals. They cling proudly to the notion that theirs is the lowest-lying, the narrowest and the most weather-worn island anywhere in the world. It lies, a beckoning finger of sandstone and salt marsh and dune, in the shallows of the Irish Sea. And central to it all is Seaview House. The place shimmers in the island's collective memory, with its squared-off air of importance and its huge bay-windowed eyes.

Every family has heard about the fish gargoyles, entwined around pillars on the stone porch. Many have admired the shell motifs cut into its red-brick façade. Most know it was a vicarage during its best years; some were even invited into its draughty office for youth groups or the preamble of weddings and baptisms. Jill Francis remembers every room, each memory lodged as a tribute to her survival.

Today, as hot as any other in this drought-ridden August, she holds her breath as she runs past; the place is on her route around the island and hard to avoid.

It's just a house… it can't hurt you.

That's the kind of thing she would say to her pupils. But Jill isn't convinced. Trapped inside Seaview is her story, woven into the fabric of Victorian brick and white marble, a story of sea-blue and washed-out skies. She has never told it; to do so would be the end of everything she has worked for. Lucky then that no one else has access to her story. Apart from the other player. She shakes his image away. Most days she can run past Seaview and keep him at bay. Today, the heat-soaked breeze drags him out.

Her black running vest sticks across her shoulders and she pinches at the fabric to free it. Sweat-drenched hair falls across her face. She turns to the sea and lets the wind do its work. Gulls shriek, catching at the warm currents of air. Her days are her own now school is over; there is nothing more pressing than thoughts of teatime and television. Passing Seaview every day allows control. It is just a house, after all, though boards cover the windows and a necklace of warning chains have surrounded the gardens for years. But the view it gives across the island's channel can always pierce Jill's heart.

Bright rays of sunlight beat down, giving a texture to the water, jade at its high point, black at its deepest; through squinting eyes this could be the Caribbean. Jill has never travelled there, or anywhere else much. Travel unravels her, like an unfamiliar touch.

On she runs.

The bridge swings into view, straddling the channel in its gallant way, on thick, concrete legs. Jill is no longer an island person, saltwater mingling with her blood. It's a good place to run, is all; running away is something different.

A motorcycle chugs past, all cherry-red gleam and the rider's blue jeans stretched out towards the front wheel.

Nice, she thinks. Wind in your hair, patchouli in your nose, the past. Headteachers can't be bikers. Her staff are still shocked she has her licence, never mind turning up on a bike.

As she turns her head to look, her toe catches on an uneven

paving slab. She lurches forward, trying to right herself but the momentum from her speed is too great. Her knees hit the ground first, then her left hip and thigh. A moment passes. She feels the burn and sting of grazed skin, the pain of jolted bone. Then the humiliation of falling in a public place. But no ordinary place. She is lying opposite the gates of Seaview House. Fear puts her on high alert. The control is shattered.

'Do you need some help?' A youthful voice, coming from somewhere above.

She squints into the sun and sees a tall and slim outline. Then another.

'I think I might,' she gasps, then tries to sit up.

'We watched it all happen. One minute you were running, the next, you'd hit the deck.'

Two young men are standing over her. One holding out his hand, the other shielding his eyes and firing up his mobile phone. 'Shall I call 999,' he says. 'I've always wanted to do that.'

'Don't be such an idiot,' the other young man growls. 'There's no blood or owt. Well, maybe just a little bit.'

Jill takes his hand and hauls herself up. Though some of her muscles are painful, her bones seem to be intact, and she can stand without too much pain. Each of her knees has a dirty graze, her left elbow the same.

The young man leads her over to a stone bench at the edge of the promenade. 'Rest for a minute,' he says. 'Shall I call someone for you?'

'Thanks,' Jill replies as she sits down. 'I think I'll be okay by myself. I don't live far away.'

'You sure?'

'Sure.'

He runs his gaze over her legs then smiles. 'Good job the paparazzi never caught you on camera, hey?'

'I'm not famous,' she says, puzzled now.

Both young men are staring across the road towards the gates of Seaview. 'You're not,' says the taller of them. 'But that place is. The house.' He turns to his friend. 'Come on, Matty. Let's go and have a nosy. You take care, love.'

And before Jill can ask anything else, the pair walk away, leaving her with nothing more than a view of their T-shirt-clad backs and a sharp drift of cologne.

She looks down at her bloodied knees, and the world tilts. A high-pitched whistling starts up in her ears and she thinks she might faint. Why would anyone be interested in Seaview House? There's no access to it anyway. As far as she can tell, these two young men wouldn't have been born when the place was finally closed. For many years it has languished in the shadows of unpruned trees, accepted but ignored. Exactly as Jill wants it to be.

She should move off the bench. Once before, she sat here, but that memory mustn't be dredged up. She gets to her feet, grateful for the distraction of stinging knees and jolted muscles. She needs to be home, to feel safe again. She walks carefully, creating a rhythm that will break through the pain. Getting off the island is all she can focus on now.

On the bridge, a judder of wheels against wood takes her from her thoughts, and she stops for a moment. From here, it is possible to see the majestic fells of West Cumbria. Jill looks across the water. This place: the pull of the sea, the soft smudgy yellow of the distant dunes. How can a landscape carry you through time? Break open your capsules of memory and leave you exposed? Her heart thuds against her ribs. Through the slats under her feet, the tide rushes by. A rush, turbulence, gone.

There is a herringbone-brick path on the other side of the bridge. It winds between thickets of rosemary and sea-holly. Jill shuffles her way through a group of dog-walkers, who smile and nod and huff. A young girl glides by on a bicycle, all wild hair, and shorts with a frayed hem. She remembers those days.

The path runs alongside a brand-new boatyard. Its wall is low enough to give a view of white yachts with half-painted hulls, balanced and awkward as fishes out of water. A group of men stand around, talking and smoking, hands resting on fibreglass, revisiting the drama of their high-seas lives. Jill limps past, keeping her eyes fixed on the glitter of tide curving away into the distance, until she has cleared any sight of Seaview. *Out of sight is out of mind*, her mother would say. There is no way of enjoying a waterside run without the loom of the house. She has tried running in other places, but there is something about the feel of sharp sea air on hot skin; she craves it.

When the path ends, she stops for a moment. Her face is burning, sweat runs between her shoulder blades and her knee wounds throb. These sensations help her focus on the present moment, on the life she has now. She cannot allow Seaview House to creep its way back inside her head. The place is dead and buried. If the two young men on the promenade had a bizarre interest in it, that was nothing to do with her. She shrugs and checks along the road for traffic, then hobbles across. The steep hill in front of her will take every scrap of energy she has left. But at the top, she will be almost home.

Her garden smells of honeysuckle; the thick sultry-sweet scent of August. She leans against a brick pillar at the top of her drive and tries to steady her breathing. The front door swings open. It's her husband. Long dark hair now replaced by sharp-cut grey. A camera hangs from his shoulder on a thick strap.

'I'm off, love,' he calls. Then, 'Oh, Christ. What happened to you?'

Jill stumbles towards him.

He stretches his mouth. 'Why didn't you ring me?'

'I took a tumble, that's all. These things happen. I've managed to get myself home.'

The last thing she wants is any fuss. Keeping herself alive and functioning is at the heart of how she lives her life. Battening down her emotions is something she has honed to perfection over the years.

'You get off to work,' she tells him. 'I'll patch myself up and drink lots of sugary coffee. That's what you'd do anyway, isn't it?'

'I'm not leaving you like this.' He looks at her bleeding knees.

'Like what?'

'All dishevelled and—'

'What?'

'Oh, I don't know. Did you bang your head?' Stevie takes her face in his hands. 'Poor thing.'

'Nope. No head injury, honestly. I'm more embarrassed than anything. Falling over in the street.'

He hugs her lightly. 'Let me at least make you a drink,' he pleads.

'No. Honestly. You get to your wedding. Phil's here if I need anything.'

Jill steps towards the house and shoos him on his way. The last thing she wants is someone prodding and poking at her wounds, least of all her husband. Watching him climb into the Land Rover makes her smile. This is what happens when the ordinary is transformed through hard work. Years of terrible schooling, then the discovery of a talent for photography and people. If only she were ordinary. And she is, except at her core, but at this moment she feels like that could be starting to bleed out.

The front door clicks behind her. A silent house. Phil must still be in bed. She gathers her hair into a bunch, lifts it from her neck and wonders again if she should get it cut. Into a neat bob, perhaps. That would be an end to her connection with days spent listening to Neil Young or The Eagles.

'Phil, you out of bed yet?' she calls up the stairs. 'Phil?'

There is a loud groan.

'Come on, up you get,' she continues. 'Half the day's gone.'

They've never been a family to sleep in: even in her teens, it wasn't allowed. A shake of her head flicks the memory away. There has been enough *remembering* today.

In the kitchen, she sets the kettle to boil, then searches the cupboards for a Ziploc bag of first-aid materials. Above her head, the ceiling creaks. A door slams. Phil is up, finally. This is her normality, her stability. She sits down on a stool and digs around for an antiseptic wipe. She notices *The Westmorland Gazette* lying neatly on a creamy granite surface next to her. The front-page photo catches her attention immediately, strikes like a fist to the stomach.

It's Seaview House.

She peers closer. Her heart jumps as she reads the headline. The place is coming down. There will be piles of local brick, crumbles of mortar and jagged shards of glass, crushed marble, and splintered wood. When a house is reduced to raw materials, where do its memories go? Are they silenced forever, or do they fly free through broken walls, seeking out a new home? Jill can't allow that to happen. Even if it means standing with open arms, waiting to trap them, like a bluebottle in a glass. And trap them she will.

April 1976

Seaview House.

That name again, carved into a pair of sandstone

gateposts. It tugs at Jill's imagination. She rests her head against the window of the bus and wonders what might lie behind the gate. The collar of her school blazer feels coarse and itchy against the back of her neck, and she tries to shrug it away. Afternoon sunlight scatters her thoughts along with the seagulls spinning in the open sky. Coming to live on the island, after years of concrete-grey houses and crisp bags clogging every gutter, feels like the best kind of gift. The new house is all magnolia paint and carpets fitting right to the walls, like the ones in her friend Susie Craig's bungalow. Brown lino covered the floors in the old place, so the rugs were always slipping; great for playing magic carpets with her brothers, not so good under bare feet on cold mornings.

Jill's sister, Bonnie, is sitting just behind, heads together and giggling with a freshly-gleaned friend. Though they've only been at the new house for a few days, people drop into Bonnie's lap like it's all they've ever wanted. This one is called Livvy. She has mean eyes: narrow and suspicious, like the cats hanging around the back streets of the old place.

The bus bumps its way over a slatted road-bridge, and Jill cranes to look across the wide expanse of water known as Walney Channel. Glassy and green, and as clear as today's sky, it stretches away as far as she can see. In her head is a picture of herself in this landscape, hair at half mast, drifting with the ebb and flow of the tide.

Like one of those girls in the Athena posters, she thinks, then spits out a puff of laughter.

Boats swirl on their moorings. Below the road are wide mudflats the colour of her brothers' soldier suits. They are almost covered by the water. Small groups of birds dig with pointed beaks, some flying upwards as the bus comes to a thudding halt.

A shuffle of feet tells Jill someone is walking down the aisle. A boy is getting off. He is clad in the Boys' Grammar School uniform, black, and a match for her own, and he has a large Adidas bag on his shoulder. Long auburn hair tumbles down, and she sees a face full of freckles. Striding his way along like he owns the world. And in the pocket of the bag, one of *those* magazines. The ones with women spread wide, lips pursed but eyes dead.

She watches as he jumps from the back of the bus and saunters towards the gateposts. Keeping him in her sight as he climbs up a long flight of stone steps, she wonders for a moment. Is there a house at the top of the neat lawns? And does he live there? As the bus starts up again, she glances over her shoulder. Between some large trees is a glimpse of red brick and dark windows, a stone porch and the boy pushing with his shoulder. A red painted door and something carved, then he disappears inside.

Seaview House? A mansion more like.

August 2018

Jill lifts the newspaper and runs a hand over its front page. The photograph of Seaview is an old one. There are no boards over the windows, only neat curtains, and smooth lawns; she remembers that time. Someone would have climbed the stone steps to capture the place close-up. She shivers a little at the thought, wondering how *The Gazette* came by the grainy snap.

She remembers that day. When her family left the mainland and moved over to the island. The weight of it – the freshness of the new house, the soft hair of her brothers, bent over a picnic tea, and Bonnie's easy friendships – it sits like a rose amongst hooked thorns. Protected, beautiful but lethal.

Jill was an innocent, wishing only to take her dog and find the sea, to gain relief from the long, heated days of school,

11

stretching into nights of air so heavy you could hardly breathe. There had been tension too: talk of mortgages, and her mother going out to work. It had been only a generation of years away, but the values came from another era entirely. And there had been freedom. Children were safe to roam, to discover themselves. The thought hits Jill's brain and she looks over her shoulder in alarm. Freedom always comes with a caveat. While she was watching the tide and the upwards flight of wading birds, someone had been watching her.

But the sea had been such a draw, back then.

April 1976

With Lucky scampering by her side, Jill jogs along the main road through the village, heart thrumming, following the smell of the sea. There is less rain now, the heavy morning clouds replaced by a thin layer of washed-out grey. A dodge between two sandstone barns, and she finds a tarmac path, winding downwards onto a patch of shingle.

Lucky, unclipped, shoots away.

Jill follows him, the shingle crunching beneath her plimsolls. Around the corner of the barns, she finds what she has been looking for: a wide expanse of sea. Lucky is away, enjoying his freedom, black-and-white head trained on smells and sounds, tail wagging and lost in a world of his own. Jill blinks at the view. To her right is the road-bridge, far enough away to resemble a faded painting of itself. The tide, jade-cool and glittering, stretches towards Black Combe – an extinct volcano her geography teacher has told her. She doesn't much care about geography now, just wants to linger. Everything is here. Water, sand, the endless sky. And no sound but her own breathing.

A sea-wood looms up from the beach, a knotted mass of shadows and enticing pathways: a world without end. She shivers and turns back to the scattered water. Lucky has climbed onto a crumbling footbridge stretched out across the flats. She watches him for a moment, chasing the gulls and making them screech.

From behind her come crushed-shingle footsteps. She watches the dog lift his head at the sound. Turning slightly, she calls to him. 'Lucky. Lucky-boy.'

Two figures, matching in height, are walking towards her. She steps out to the mudflats, willing the pair to pass without the need for interaction. The dog comes bounding over. He ignores Jill and runs to investigate.

Bloody dog, she thinks, sliding her gaze sideways, flushing at the sight of two young men carrying large canvas bags. *Fishing gear* flashes through her mind.

'All right,' one of them says. The auburn-haired boy from the bus.

Jill is good with faces, and she remembers him. The other seems more man-like somehow. A practised broody scowl, and the hint of something mean in his eyes. Long dark hair, and a lurcher on a piece of rope; Jill knows her dogs, too. Lucky growls low in his throat. She reaches out and grabs his collar. He snaps at her hand. The dark-haired boy mutters something under his breath, and they both snigger. Jill holds firmly to Lucky's collar and watches as they stomp past. Like they are adults, like they own this bit of beach.

Idiots.

The catch on Lucky's collar clicks shut as she hooks his leash back on. Better not chance him running off and taking on a lurcher. They can be savage, she knows.

Once the boys are out of sight, she moves with the dog firmly by her side, scanning the beach for any other activity, but there is only the oily glister of the bladder wrack tideline.

Lucky's nose twitches. She leans her weight against the strain of his leash and lets him take charge. Five minutes, and the path ends with two choices. Back into the housing estate or up across a patchwork of green and yellow fields. Like her life, they stretch temptingly into the unknown; vivid or muted, shorn or luxurious – it is hard to tell until she's walked on them. On family Lakeland treks, her dad says they should respect farmer's fields and not cross them unless there is a permitted path. She can't see one, but the fields beckon her with their flash of bright colour. As does a gap in the hawthorn and bramble hedge, so she squeezes through, dragging Lucky behind her.

She makes her way across the wet grass. It soaks her plimsolls and the hems of her jeans and feels delicious. Walking in an open field, hair flowing out behind her, salty breeze on her face: this is her.

At the gap in another hedge, Lucky starts to whine; softly at first, but then his shoulders tremble, velveteen ears tracking something. The soft hum of voices, and a rubbery, earthy smell. Her nose twitches. Cigarette smoke, but sweeter.

'Mick. Pass us another cartridge. Mick.' An urgent tone.

Jill creeps forward, peering through the tangled brushwood. She can see the same skinny lurcher, with something trapped between its jaws. A small bird perhaps.

'Get the thing out of its mouth, Stoney.' A deeper voice. Older.

The same auburn-haired boy comes to crouch down in front of the brindled dog. Snatching the bird, he lays it on the ground and yanks the dog away, out of Jill's view.

Two loud clicks and the air explodes.

Adrenaline shoots through her, and she races away. Lucky runs with her, yelping and panting, streaks of black-and-white lightning mixing with her blue and green. Jill is a good runner. School running, or sport of any kind, holds no interest for her, but she loves to walk – and run. Now, she sprints across the wet field, not stopping to look back, with no idea if she has been seen. Mixed in with her fear of the gunshot is the tiniest tinge of excitement. Jill Holland, escaping from danger, and for once, with no parents or brothers or sister hanging off her.

Once back at the estate, she allows herself to rest, panting and gasping and watching Lucky's pink tongue lolling from his mouth.

August 2018

A loud knock jolts Jill away from Seaview and her thoughts. From the hallway, behind the frosted glass of the front door, she can see two dark figures. She puts her hand on her chest for a moment and sucks in a deep breath, then pulls open the door. A young man and younger woman are standing on the step. They are wearing police uniforms. Jill's stomach drops into her feet.

'Mrs Francis?' Hollywood-white teeth.

Jill nods. 'Yes?'

'Miss Jill Holland, I think you were?'

'Yes.' Her heart is thundering.

Who has died? she thinks.

'Can we talk to you about Seaview House?'

Chapter Two

A s Jill steps back from the front door, the heat slides in. She allows the police officers to slide in after it. They follow her to the kitchen. A hand is extended, so smooth and damp it catches at her breath. The core of her bubbles; the inside of a dormant volcano.

'PC Rose Atherton and PC Adam Pickthall.'

The man looks no older than her Phil. His cheeks are smattered with acne, but his smile is pleasant enough. Her eyes fall to the newspaper again. Seaview stares back.

'I saw the place was being pulled down. I haven't read the article yet. What are the plans for the land?'

No answer. Dare she look back at them?

'It'll be strange. The old place going.'

She is talking too much, words coming from a place she doesn't trust. Instead, she paints on a smile for the young policewoman.

'Can I get you a drink? Coffee or tea? Something cold.'

Jill wants to be busy, doesn't like the eyes of the officers following her around the room.

'Something cold would be nice, madam.' Taking off her

hat for a moment, the female officer dabs her forehead with a clean white tissue. 'Cool kitchen. I like all the gadgets.'

'Sit down. Please.' Jill gestures towards the other bar stools, tucked neatly away under the kitchen counter. 'It's hot out there, isn't it?'

Pickthall pulls out the stools, and they settle themselves down, elbows on the granite, heels hooked.

'I'll just–' Jill stumbles over her words, falls head-over-heels into the Seaview of the past. What can be said when she has waited so long and practised so hard? Not truth, surely? She turns on the tap, running her hand through the stream of water until it feels cold enough to hurt, then fills two glasses and adds a splash of Ribena to each.

'Hope this is okay. My son's twenty-eight and he still likes his blackcurrant.' She hands over the drinks, before returning to make one for herself.

Pickthall glances at her grazed knees. 'Did you have an accident, madam?' he asks, frowning his concern.

Jill's attention is dragged back to her injuries. The half-open sachet of antiseptic wipe lies right next to the newspaper. She brushes it up with the side of her hand.

'I fell while I was running. Nothing very exciting.'

'Do you need a moment to clean up?'

'No, it's fine,' Jill says. 'So, Seaview House. What did you want to know?' Her back is to the sink, and she is conscious of her salty smell, her straggles of hair. And the throbbing in her elbow.

The glasses clink down onto the granite, and Rose Atherton takes a notebook from her breast pocket. 'We have the last residents of the house listed as the Reverend Mr and Mrs Brownstone,' she says. 'Did you know them?'

Jill gulps down her reaction. 'I did. Slightly. Nice people. I think they're both dead now, though.' No explanation has been given about these questions, no reasons as to why these two have turned up on her doorstep. It's more than thirty years since she'd had anything to do with the Brownstones. Or him. If she lets that thread be tugged at, who knows what will unravel.

Pickthall is speaking again. 'They had a son, I believe. Do you know anything about him?'

Who has been talking to the police?

Jill hesitates. 'I did know him, a little.' Gritted teeth; lie number one.

Atherton is flipping through her notes. 'You're not in contact with him now, are you? Do you know anyone who is?' She cocks her head.

Jill shrugs, rearranging her expression to one of practised disinterest. 'Haven't seen him since we were at the grammar schools together in the seventies,' she says, swallowing down the acid wave from her stomach.

Lie number two.

What is she doing, lying to the police? It's been her mission, for so many years, to draw no attention to herself. But she can't help it. 'Has something happened?'

Pickthall shakes his head. 'Nothing for you to concern yourself with, madam. We're just trying to track down this—' he looks at his notes, 'Andrew Brownstone.'

'He didn't – doesn't own Seaview though, does he? It belonged to the church. As far as I remember.'

Jill watches as Adam Pickthall gulps down his drink. He passes her the glass, then uses three fingers to wipe his lips.

'Very welcome. Thanks.'

'That's okay.' She looks at Rose. No sign of any softening there, but Jill searches anyway. She must. Becoming normal will mean they trust her. And she needs their trust. They can't be allowed to take even the top layer from her story. She imagines them peeling it back and clapping their palms together in gleeful triumph, Rose Atherton's nostrils flaring in disgust.

'Top up?' Jill is determined to win over at least one of them.

'No.'

Rose sends a frown across to her colleague. 'You remember correctly, Mrs Francis. Seaview was a vicarage. Which means it has been rather difficult to find *speedy* answers to our questions. I do wonder if the Church of England has even heard of the digital age.' She huffs. Ever so slightly, but Jill hears it, and says a silent prayer for the crusty old C of E.

'Why the rush?' Jill chews at her bottom lip.

Give me something. Anything, she thinks.

But Rose Atherton is smoothing back her damp hair and placing her hat back on her head. She tucks some strands carefully behind each ear and swallows down the last of her drink, then stands up and turns an inscrutable brown gaze on Jill.

'If you do remember anything which would help us to contact Mr. Brownstone, be sure and let one of us know.' She holds out a card, and Jill takes it from her hand. 'And get those knees cleaned up.'

'No problem,' she says, letting out a small laugh, then wondering why. Any fun and laughter that might have been part of her day, has gone. The policewoman takes down Jill's telephone number, biro held in stubby hands with chewed-down nails. There it is, written in a small black notebook.

Walking with the officers to the front door, she wonders why, when she has tried to answer their questions, they haven't answered hers.

'Is there a reason you came to see me?' she blurts out, causing Rose Atherton to look at her with cool regard.

'No, madam. We'd just heard you knew the Brownstone family.'

God, she's infuriating, Jill thinks. But she must remain aloof.

'Oh. Okay. Well, good luck.'

She lets the door click behind them and rests her head there for a moment. The core of her is supposed to be invisible. Now, she feels it as a stone. That story, *The Wolf and the Seven Little Kids.* A boulder sewn into his belly when the baby goats had been released.

Then, footsteps behind her. Phil.

'Who was at the door, Mum?' His gruff, morning voice.

'Just someone looking for number thirty-six,' she groans, blinking away the spectre of auburn hair clouding her vision.

Lie number three.

'Okay.' He stretches the word. A technique he uses to avoid conversing in sentences.

She waves him away, needs to get her thoughts together. Who would have pointed the police in her direction? Who would remember little Jill Holland?

May 1976

At the grammar school gates, Jill waits for her father. Bonnie stands alongside, pulling at the buttons of her blouse, wafting out sweat-soaked air.

'I stink,' she wails, nose towards her chest. 'Where's Dad? I need to get changed.'

Jill sighs. Like nobody else but her sister is hot and sweaty. The heat, cheered in at first, is fast becoming a kind of monster, sucking up water instead of blood, shrinking everyone's mood.

Groups of girls drift by, on a breeze of Super-Dry Sure and Bazooka gum. Lena Clarke, strawberry-blonde siren whose word is law, wiggles past with a sneering glance at Jill's flat sandals, ankle socks and family values.

When their dad finally turns up, Bonnie gives a small and breathy cheer. He leans out of the window of the Lada, looking cool in a white shirt and epaulettes, and waving cans of Tizer at them. They clamber in and slide themselves across the vinyl seats.

'You look hot.' He laughs as he drives away. 'Never mind. Home soon.'

Jill gulps down breaths of air and sips her drink. The sugary fizz finds its way straight into the thickness of her blood. Evens it out, somehow. Bonnie begins talking about her part in the school birthday celebrations in June. The gym display, her moves, the ribbons – the words knock against the pain in Jill's head. She stares out of the car window, wishing for silence.

'Even the boys are allowed to come and watch.' Delight from her sister.

'But not parents, I'm guessing.'

'No. Miss Young says it's just for the grammar kids. But the boys' school isn't even the same age as ours, so why are they invited?'

'Perhaps she fancies the headmaster.' Dad is using words he thinks teenage girls might say. The thought of their headmistress slobbering over the dour-faced head of the boys' school, makes Jill's stomach feel slightly queasy. She takes another sip of the Tizer.

Buses and cars crawl across the bridge to the island. The turquoise stretch of tide and white-hot sky make Jill think of the photos in her gran's holiday albums. She and Grandad have travelled abroad many times, mainly on cruise ships, and they like to pose for holiday snaps with glorious views behind them. Gran would look chic in floral sleeveless frocks and large sunglasses and Grandad, in pale chinos and a cigarette between his fingers, was the archetypal club singer. The sea was always a vivid blue slash at the back of their photos, the sun always shone.

They were coming to the *Costa-del-Barrow* this summer, they said, to see the new house. Jill likes it when they visit, though the family have to play musical beds, and she'll probably end up top-to-tail with Bonnie. With her grandparents here, the mood is always lighter, the treats plentiful. And Grandad loves dogs as much as she does. She will show him her beach; picturing herself crunching across the shingle with him makes her smile.

The Lada pulls round onto the promenade. At the gates of Seaview House, two people are climbing out of a white Wartburg; the auburn-haired boy, and an older lady. Though her hair is short and silver, the faces match, with high cheekbones and tall foreheads. His gran? Surely not his mother? Whoever she is, Jill sees a simmer of something between them, and she gawps. Are they arguing? He looks like a man in boys' clothing, the grammar uniform short on the sleeves and the legs, and too tight at the waist. Her face freezes as he catches her eye, then the Lada passes by. She swings her gaze back towards the tide and wonders what their story is.

At the house, Lucky flings himself at Jill, whining and barking and begging to be set free. She whips upstairs and changes into a pair of shorts made by cutting off the legs of her old jeans, and a stripy T-shirt which had belonged to her aunty. It almost fits, pulling across her breasts, and making her laugh at herself. With a flick of her hair, she bounds down the stairs and grabs the dog's leash.

'When's tea?' she calls to her dad. Judging by the crashing sounds coming from the kitchen, it will be ages yet.

'An hour,' he replies. 'Where you off to, love?'

'Just taking Lucky to the shore.'

'See you in a bit, then.'

But Jill is already out of the door and down the path,

inhaling the tangy island breeze – never absent, even on the hottest days.

August 2018

How can the police tell you are lying? Jill is sure they must learn something secret at police college, something never to be divulged. She imagines Rose Atherton spreading her hand across her heart, mouth straight and shoulders pinned back, taking an oath. There are secrets taught at teacher training college too: children are never to be your friends and are the world's best liars.

Not quite the best, she thinks.

In her opinion, those with the most to lose tell the most untruths. Easy to be honest when your world is like pristine-white washing strung out on a day in summer, clean cotton smells filling your nostrils.

Panic sets in.

Yesterday, she'd been the ordinary version of herself, one created over the years, one that would be recognised by her family, friends and colleagues. Today, she has police knocking on her front door, asking about a time in her life she has managed to obscure, using everything good she's ever done.

She steps down the hallway. She will go after Rose Atherton and Adam Pickthall, will tell them everything, make them believe she's just had a momentary lapse of memory. Perhaps Adam might believe her. There had been an openness to his face, a wish to be liked. But Rose would be on her instantly, eyes narrow and asking exactly what Jill had failed to disclose.

And one of those things had been her first encounter with Andrew Brownstone.

May 1976

A squint across the glare of the water and sunlight glitters back; nothing else is needed, as far as Jill is concerned. And no one else. Here, she can be completely herself. A small boat chugs by, trailed by a circle of shrieking gulls, and she lets her thoughts float onto its deck and drift away.

Jumping back to reality, she catches sight of a figure to her left, just in front of the sea-wood. The auburn-haired boy. How has he got here so quickly? He must do what she does, escape as soon as possible. Pretending to be focused on the water, she listens to the crunch of his feet on the shingle. It stops.

Just behind her.

She waits. Something pulses from her belly to her feet. Fear? Who knows about her standing on this beach? The warm coat of childhood peels away from her shoulders. Here is Jill Holland, exposed to the world.

A stone plops down beside her. Another. Then another. The boy is throwing stones. She spins round, can't decide if this is a game or something more dangerous.

'Do you mind?' she sneers.

'No. Do you?' His voice matches.

'Stop chucking stones then.' Her legs are shaky.

'Stop chucking stones then,' he mimics.

Jill turns back around and calls to Lucky. The dog is a hazy silhouette, shimmering his way across the flats in blissful ignorance. She waits to hear footsteps crunching away again. Instead, she senses the boy's presence across her shoulders, like the gentlest brush of fingertips.

'Soz,' he calls, 'I was being a twat.'

Now, he is standing next to her. A prickle of anticipation makes Jill shiver, despite the heat.

'Nice dog.' He tries again. She nods, not trusting herself to speak. Boys don't usually approach her, not on their own. The nearness of him makes her feel dizzy. A clean smell, soap and cotton.

'See that.' He points over the mudflats, to a solitary bird with red legs and a black head. 'An Arctic tern. Rare, they are.'

Jill looks, though she doesn't see.

'I'm Stoney, by the way. Andy Brownstone, but nobody knows my real name.'

'Now I do,' she says, smiling up at him.

'Yep.'

They stand in silence for a moment, watching the little tern take flight and skim across the surface of the tide.

'You new round here?' Questions again.

Jill wants to get away. She's heard of the phenomenon, *getting chatted up*, and is sure it's happening to her, right now. But she's a kid. Isn't she?

'I've just moved to the new estate. Coniston Road.' What is she doing, telling him where she lives?

He smiles slightly. One of his front teeth is chipped, a small triangle missing. 'Oh yeah. The new estate. People weren't happy when it was built.' He tucks a hank of reddish hair behind his ear.

'Why not?' She is suddenly interested.

'Used to be woods and fields. Me and Mick did lamping there of a night-time. There's still long-lining off the end of the island, though, but no lamping.'

As always, Jill covers her lack of knowledge with other questions. Bonnie is good at asking outright when she doesn't understand something, but not her. Better to cover your ignorance, in her opinion. Perhaps it is why people think she's the clever one.

'Can't you do lamping on other fields?'

His expression changes. Heavy eyebrows meeting, and a

25

wink. 'We do. But Chapel Field had hundreds of rabbits. We could get ten on a good night.'

Jill frowns. 'For what?'

'Dogs eat some of them. Have to pick the shot out first, though. And The Old Queen makes a good rabbit pie.' His laughter sounds like a sneer. It has a nasty edge. Jill turns away from him and calls again to Lucky. The dog lifts his head.

The boy moves to stand in front of her.

'So. The dog's called Lucky. Who are you?'

'Jill.'

'Well then, Jill, I'll walk a bit of the way with you.'

Then Lucky is there, submissive, tongue lolling. Stoney kneels to grab hold of the leather collar. Jill runs her eyes along the pale skin of his reaching arm; gingery hair and more freckles. The novelty makes her blush.

'Give us the lead,' he says.

She does as he asks, though more than anything, she wants to be rid of him. Something feels wrong.

Once Stoney has clipped Lucky onto the lead, he lets the dog tug him forward. Jill tries to take it from him, and her arm brushes against his wide chest. His eyes slide downwards, just for a second, and a shiver spreads across her shoulders. She turns away. Together, they stumble across the shingle, Lucky tugging them forwards.

'Seen you at school,' he suddenly says. 'And on the bus.'

'I'm in the third year,' she offers. 'You?'

'Fourth.'

'Exams next year then. What are you taking?'

He pauses, seconds filled with the call of gulls. Then, 'Fuck all if I can help it. I like rugby, but nowt else. Teachers are all bastards.'

As far as Jill understands, you just *do* school. You don't question it or refuse anything or have extreme views about anybody. She has her likes and dislikes, but Stoney's words cause a wave of anger. Who does he think he is?

'My mum says you shouldn't be cheeky about teachers.'

She tries to bite back the words, but they spring from her lips like a fizz of Tizer bubbles. Stoney kicks up the shingle with his Doc Marten's; they are a velvety red like his hair.

'Ever thought your mum might be wrong?' he asks. 'You are allowed to have your own thoughts, you know.' A cool, glittering stare.

She tuts, then folds her arms around herself. Another preachy lecture on how to behave. Lena Clarke all over again.

'Soz,' he mutters. A flick of his fringe. 'Just sick of school. Hate it.'

She walks behind him up a short concrete path and back onto the road. Lucky strains against his leash.

'Calm down, you daft thing,' she whispers, putting her hands against his soft ears, wondering if those words are for her dog or for herself.

Stoney turns his head towards her. 'I like the way you talk,' he says, 'not from round here, are you?'

'I am.' Her face burns. She looks down at her toes, sandy and peeping out from her navy sandals. What is he saying?

'You've got an accent. How come?'

'I was born in London,' she shrugs. 'But we left when I was three. I guess I could talk by then.'

He grins. 'You're a bloody southerner. I knew it. A holidaymaker.'

He is talking as though she should understand what is being said. But she has no idea. Is this an insult?

'And you're an idiot,' she mutters. 'So, we're even. I'm going home now.'

She tugs the dog with her and steps away. If this is the sort of talk used to engage boys, they can keep it; some things she will never get her head round. Like hurling insults as if they are handfuls of gravel, splattering their damage, hoping to hit a target. Talking with Susie is never like this. Perhaps it happens once you get to fourth form. But she is sure of one thing: her need to get away from this Stoney character, though he makes her legs feel weak and her words stick in her throat.

Yet here he is, calling along the road to her. 'Hey. Jill. Jilly. Don't run away. I'll see you around. Won't I?'

Chapter Three

Through the glass panel in the front door, Jill watches the police car drive away. Then she pushes down the chrome handle and steps out into the white-hot air. If any of the neighbours are in their front gardens, they will have seen her visitors, will be craning to find out what is going on.

She walks down the driveway and onto the street. Everywhere is quiet. Not even a breath of wind. But from somewhere deep inside her head comes a sound. The cry of a herring gull. It makes her look upwards, though the sky is empty. And she is transported to the summer of 1976. To sunlight splintering the surface of the tide. To glistening, wet rocks, barnacle-sharp. To the weave of golden days and deep blue nights. The soft cotton smells, and the taste of salt on the tip of her tongue.

Jill remembers many things about that summer. But mostly the heat, the stifling, dragging heat. People would gather on the streets after dark, furtive and gulping down cool air as though it was being rationed. Those with pale skin were burned pink: noses and ears peeled, then scabbing over. Older folk died, as did many of the island's wild birds. And she'd become all too aware of her measure compared to other girls. Not in terms of her schoolwork, which had always been a strength. But there had never been enough money for clothes or shoes; she and Bonnie, and her brothers, had exactly what they needed and no more. Which meant hanging around with friends who looked fashionable, cleaner somehow, with outfits to match occasions. When she thinks about this now, Jill can empathise with every teenage girl who has ever wanted to fit in.

'Hiya.' Di from over the road.

Jill blinks her way back to reality.

The older woman shuffles her way across the tarmac, in big slippers and even bigger shorts. 'You were miles away, there,' Di says. 'Is everything all right? You look like you've been in the wars.'

'Fell over while I was running, didn't I.'

Di tuts. 'Wouldn't catch me running,' she snorts, then realises what she has said and slaps Jill on the arm. 'You won't be catching anybody, either. Not with those knees.'

They enjoy the moment, then lift their faces to the sun.

'Beautiful today, isn't it?' Jill sighs, wondering how long it will be before the police are mentioned. But she is ready; honest deceit is her speciality. It is, after all, what the craft of a teacher is based on. And it has served her well.

'Did I see a couple of young PCs? Coming out of your house, Mrs Francis?'

'I've told you to call me Jill. God knows we've been neighbours for long enough.'

A small giggle, but there's no distracting Di from her mission. She has caught the scent of something. 'They looked like they'd been to your house. Are they doing leafleting again?'

Jill lifts her shoulders. 'It was a survey of some kind,' she says. 'They looked so hot and bothered, I thought I'd better ask them in.' She pauses to watch Di's expression slide. 'Should have sent them over to you, shouldn't I? Tea and scones then, eh?'

'Are they doing everyone?'

'I think so. Better make sure you haven't got anything illegal going on in number thirty-six, hadn't you?'

Di slaps her arm again. 'You're a cheeky one,' she laughs. 'Anyway, how's that boy of yours? Everything okay with him?'

This woman should be a detective, Jill thinks, and her stomach flips over. Imagine her glee if there was a jar of real gossip to serve up with those home-made scones.

'He's fine,' she replies carefully. 'Spends most of his time in bed while he's with us. Hotel of mum and dad.'

'Tell me about it,' says Di. Then she fills the gap in her invitation with stories of her own children – long gone now – and their terrible youth. Jill is glad of the distraction. She listens, focused on Di's face but allowing a drift of thought. That summer had felt like a breathing space in her life, a moment captured, like the silence between kisses.

June 1976

Hundreds of French words lift silently from the collective pages of the textbooks and fly through the open windows and ill-fitting doors. Chairs creak and breaths huff, and eventually a loud bell signals the end of Jill's lesson and the start of the school birthday celebrations. The atmosphere fizzes with excitement.

Jill gives Susie a small wave, and mouths *I'll see you in a min.* But their teacher, all grey plaits and cashmere shawl, has risen tall and is commanding a straight and silent line. They follow sombrely, heads bowed and waiting. Jill can hear the thin

sound of amplified music and voices, then she and Susie burst
through the front doors and into the sunshine.

'You look nice,' offers Susie, as they walk. 'Did you get
those clothes for your birthday?'

Jill nods. 'Thanks. I did. I like your shirt. Suits you.' The
compliments friends give each other. Today, they only serve to
make her feel worse.

'What do you want to do first?' Susie flicks her ponytail,
eyes wide. 'Shall we get a drink?'

What Jill wants is to go home. Her arms and legs feel heavy
with fatigue. Perhaps a drink would help. 'Yes. A drink,' she
says, through gritted teeth.

'You okay?' her friend asks.

'Course. Let's go before the queue gets too long.' She takes
hold of Susie's soft arm and leans her head against it, then
leads her towards the drinks tent. Not letting her friend down is
more important than any miserable mood. But she can't shake
it off any more than she can shake off her terrible choice of
clothing.

Jill's head throbs with the frenetic energy of the day. She
and Susie find a grassy bank, and sit together, paper cups in
hand, people-watching as much as keeping an eye on
Bonnie's gym display. Boys and girls mix, wandering between
white canvas tents and strings of bunting in the school
colours. But freedom has its downside. It is making Jill feel as
though the edges of her could be snapped off at any
moment.

'The best thing about today,' she mutters, 'is finishing at
two o'clock.'

'Look on the bright side.' Susie turns her face to the sun.
'We're missing double chemmy.'

Jill looks at her friend. 'I like double chemmy.'

'You would.'

'What does that mean?'

'What does *what* mean?' Susie isn't smiling, and she always smiles.

Jill hugs her knees. 'Saying *you would*, like you hate me or something.' Her throat feels tight. Silence hangs between them for a moment, thick with heat and misunderstanding.

'You are in a mood today, aren't you?'

'I know.' Time to tell, Jill thinks. 'We all got up late. Dad was shouting. Mum didn't get home until—' But Susie isn't listening. Instead, she is staring at the approaching figure of Lena Clarke. Envy of every male and female in the grammar school, though their reasons are quite different. She's managed to tie her blouse high, midriff like a gold medal, and is wiggling towards them as the world looks on with a dazzle of admiration. Jill blinks, gulps down her Vimto. Wherever Lena goes, trouble follows. Her bright hair is caught back in an embossed leather clip, and she totters in the wedge sandals every girl wishes she owned. Susie has rolled away and is getting to her knees, brushing grass from her jeans, and pulling down her shirt.

Jill frowns up at her. 'Suse. Where are you going?'

But Lena is already there, pushing into the space between them. 'Like your outfit, Jilly Jill,' she simpers, flicking a hank of hair back from her small shoulder. 'I've got the same skirt. You get it in Zeds?'

Here is confusion. Lena being friendly? Or is this a trap? It's difficult for Jill to decide, especially with a pounding head and a rumbling stomach. Standing with Lena is the usual entourage of adoring girls and drooling boys. Susie is caught, all red-and-black checks, at the edge of her vision; this is Jill's situation to handle. Only hers.

'Yep.' It is all she can think of to say. She squints at Lena. 'Zeds.'

The air crackles. With tension. With heat. With Lena Clarke's brash perfume.

'What's wrong with your face,' she hisses. 'You been sucking lemons?'

There is a collective intake of breath. For a moment, Jill shrinks away from Lena's insulting words. Then out tumble her own. 'Better than having a face like a flat-fish. And a brain to match.'

Lena's head jolts forward and she over-bites her top lip. 'You fucking snooty cow,' she spits, and the watching crowd sniggers.

A burst of adrenaline shoots through Jill. Her heart thumps, pulsing red at the back of her eyes. Laying her hand at her throat, she sucks at the air, but it won't go in. Susie. Where is she?

Lena Clarke is snarling towards her. 'Think you're so clever, don't you? Clever little Jill.'

'I don't think I'm clever,' Jill manages to gasp. 'And you don't even know me anyway.' But Lena is up close now, lips shiny, eyes flinty.

Suddenly, a group of boys burst onto the scene, a blur of long hair and Levi's.

'Lay off, Clarke, you slag.' Andy Brownstone.

'Stoney. Get you.' Lena swings her head towards him.

Jill steps backwards, but Lena is already fluttering. Jutting one hip and laying her hand across it.

She's forgotten me, Jill thinks as she glances at Stoney. He tilts his head, green eyes in a face flushed with heat, but grinning anyway. Lena spins between the two of them, flicking her hair out with the backs of her hands.

'Worried about your little girly, are you? Got to save her *reputation*?' The simpering laugh, again.

They move into each other's space, and Jill sees a flare of his nostrils and a dart of heavy brows. She holds her breath.

'You wanna watch yourself, Clarke,' he snarls. 'Shit-stirrer.'

A treacly shudder runs down Jill's spine. She hunches over,

hugs herself. Is she Stoney's *girly*? How can she be? And what the hell is a *reputation*? But Lena is already eyeballing one of his friends, looking upwards, flashing her lashes.

The brain of a kid in the body of a woman.

This is Jill's last thought. A tinny voice cuts across the flaring heat, springing from the end of a loud hailer. Back to school for lunch. Do or die. She moves to catch up with Susie, watching her blonde ponytail swinging as she strides across the grass.

'Suse. Susie Craig. What's up?' she calls, catching at her arm.

'Nothing. Just want my dinner. I'll see you after.' The arm is shaken free, leaving Jill to wonder what she's done.

August 2018

The afternoon is fading to gold, as Jill walks into her garden. At this time of year, the back end of summer, autumn begins its creep, encouraged by the receding water supply. Her lawn is crisp and yellow. Summer bedding plants have become twiggy arcs with hard dead flowers begging to be gone.

She needs to sit down, needs to think.

She is sure people like her neighbour would be supportive if they knew the truth. They may not even believe it. But this visit from the police is causing every muscle in her body to tense, and her thinking to turn black.

There is a wooden bench at the end of the garden, placed directly beneath an ornamental cherry tree. The spring sees the bench covered in a froth of pink, but now it is almost hidden by dense green leaves, just starting to turn. Jill lets herself sink down into the cool shade and she covers her face with her hands.

She thought she was safe.

Twenty years ago, long after she'd visited Seaview House for the last time, she went back. It was probably at the tail end of 1998; there had been snow on the ground and ice in Jill's heart. But she'd needed to see.

She'd been married for almost ten years by then. There had been a career and a small child. And a head full of dark depression which she couldn't shake. If she could just find out the truth, she figured, there could be an end to the fear living in her stomach, tangible enough to be felt if she pressed hard enough.

The place had been so quiet. Panels of fibreboard had been nailed across the windows and doors, and the garden gate had been padlocked. There was no way of getting near, never mind peeping inside. And inside was what she needed. In the end, she'd gone home and given herself a telling off. As though she was one of the teenagers she taught. There were two choices, as far as she could see: climb onto the guardrails of the bridge to the island, and jump, or take another kind of leap, one that would allow her to keep the life she had and polish it until it shone. She would never again think of what happened inside Seaview House, would lie to herself, and lie and lie, until her body could no longer tell the difference.

The fibre of the lie had held up well for twenty more years, like a scar healing over twice as thick. But now, something was picking it away, and she was thinking about what happened in Seaview House all over again.

June 1976

'Jilly. Wait up. Come and have a drink if you like. I live just up there. In Seaview House.'

Jill is surprised to see Stoney just behind her on the bridge. Another victim of the overfull buses after the school birthday celebrations. There had been no sign of golden-girl Bonnie, so she'd decided to walk the three miles home. And the heat is almost killing her.

She waits for him, then wonders what she's doing. Her parents would not approve of Stoney's offer, but for the first time in her life, she wants to do something of her choosing. And it is enough, on this wearying summer's day, to make her say *yes*.

'Great,' Stoney says, pale lashes winking. 'The Old Queen is at work, but Nana won't mind.'

He leads her across the road and through the gate she has seen before. As they walk up the stone steps, the sight of his back draws Jill into a whole new world; wide shoulders and dark auburn hair, spread thickly, demanding attention.

Demand away, she thinks, as they step onto the carved porch, then a red front door is pushed open to let her in.

Seaview House.

Jill follows Stoney as he steps into the cool gloom of the hallway. She catches the scent of old books and lemon Pledge, sees the gleam of polished wood and smear-free glass. Her sandals slap softly against a floor of orange and black tiles.

'The Old Geezer's in his study,' Stoney mutters over his shoulder, 'better not disturb him. Don't see him much anyhow.' He nods towards a heavy door with a brass handle, closed and solid.

Jill stops walking and stares upwards, following the dark wooden handrail and white painted staircase. The ceiling height alone makes her feel dizzy. She longs to have a nose around on the shadowy landing, but Stoney is moving along the hallway and opening the furthest door. A small dog comes clattering out, growling deep in its throat. It stops. Then turns cloudy eyes in her direction.

'Good boy.' She holds out her hand, letting him use his other senses.

'Mac. Stop it, you daft thing.' Stoney comes towards her and lifts the squirming dog away. 'He can't bite,' he grins, 'he's got no teeth.'

She scratches at the wiry hazel fur. 'Poor thing. Is he blind, too?'

'Almost.' That laugh again. Warm. Just for her. 'He doesn't get out much.'

With the dog trapped under his arm, he ushers Jill into a room which she thinks must be a kitchen, though it has a fireplace and shelves stacked with books on either side. In a large tweedy chair, an elderly lady dozes, chin down and lips parted. Jill moves back into the doorway.

'Nana,' croons Stoney. 'Nan. Take no notice of us, we're just having a drink.'

Jill shivers a little. Here she is, the uninvited guest.

Stoney puts down the dog and it climbs back into a basket next to the empty fireplace, circling a few times then settling itself. Despite the heat of the day, his nan is wrapped in a billowy green cardigan, a crocheted blanket across her lap. The hands resting there are rough and gnarled, fingertips the same shade of yellow as those of Jill's chemistry teacher.

'Come in,' he says. 'She's flat out. Don't worry.' But Jill can't help it. Worry is her middle name. Worry feels safe. So does the dog. If there is a dog and a Nan, she'll be fine, won't she?

'We've got lemonade or Sass,' he calls, stepping into an open cupboard. She can hear glasses clinking, and he reappears, looking at her quizzically. 'Which one?'

'Erm. Lemonade, please.' She wants to say *Sass* because she's never tried it but doesn't want to seem greedy.

If you don't ask, you don't get, her mother always says, but Jill isn't fond of asking for things. Bonnie would've asked for Sass.

Stoney emerges from the cupboard with two glasses, full to the brim with lemonade, and hands one to her. She sips gratefully.

'Thanks.'

There is a glint in Stoney's eyes. It makes her think of the wolf in the Ladybird books she loved to read as a child. She takes another sip, watching the bubbles popping across the surface, trying not to remember what happens between small girls and wolves.

'Let's go out the back,' he says suddenly. 'I need a fag.'

The back garden surprises her. Where Seaview's front garden is mown and clipped and cosseted, this one is overgrown, tall dry stems of grass falling in on themselves in a parched and tangled mess. Huge trees crowd the borders, their branches laced together, forming a cool green canopy. Some are hung with half ripened fruit – apples and plums she thinks – and an old wooden shed stands with its door hanging off. Stoney leads her to a garden bench and gestures for her to sit. He reaches into the pocket of his jeans and pulls out a green-and-gold packet, and a cigarette lighter.

'Want one?' he asks, opening it and taking out a small box with *Rizla* written on the top. She shakes her head.

He holds up the packet. 'You don't mind, do you?'

Not knowing how to respond, she says nothing. Feels foolish. But she doesn't smoke and has no intention of smoking, so why shouldn't she say no? As if the fact of her minding matters, anyway.

As he lays flaky brown tobacco along a paper, she watches his fingers. They are pale and thick and seem used to rolling cigarettes. There are freckles on the backs of his hands, and the faintest trace of gingery hair. She leans into the clean cotton smell of him and stares as he runs his tongue along the edge of the paper and rolls it up. He fires up the lighter and holds it to the cigarette, then takes a deep inhale. One second passes. Through pursed lips, he blows out a long plume of fragrant Old Holborn-tinged smoke.

'All right?' he says, much older than his years. When she doesn't answer, he snorts. 'Don't talk much, do you?'

Jill isn't sure what she is supposed to say. But she needs to say something.

'I like the house,' she tries, and he nods.

'Goes with the job. The Old Geezer's the vicar of St Mary's. Hadn't you worked it out?'

'Oh. I didn't realise.' Stoney's dad is a vicar. It doesn't make sense. Not in her world, where vicar's daughters have a tight-mouthed dislike of everything.

'Nana.' He grins. 'She's The Old Queen's ma. Got nobody else, so she lives with us.'

Jill thinks about this for a moment. Time stretches. 'Thanks for the drink,' she settles on, holding up the glass.

'S'okay.' He leans back on the bench and blows more smoke rings. They float outwards into the chilled shade and disappear. Her nerves jangle. How is she supposed to behave?

'I'll have *Sass* next time,' she says, trying to mimic the flirty voice she's heard Lena use. He flicks the half-smoked roll-up onto the paving stones and turns his body towards her. Sparks of burning tobacco scatter.

'So, there will be a next time?' And, reaching out, he runs two fingers down her bare arm.

The jump of her heart makes Jill's eyes hurt. What is she supposed to do? Lena Clarke has deserted her and the shy fourteen-year-old is back, going with her gut instinct. She gets up from the bench and moves away quickly, trying to ignore the place where his touch burns raw.

'I… I'd better get going,' she babbles. 'The drink was nice, thanks.'

Without waiting to be asked, she walks into the kitchen and puts her glass down on a wooden draining board next to the deep square sink. The old lady is still sleeping, but Mac growls weakly from his basket. Stoney is at her shoulder. He follows her down the hall and out onto the porch. They stand together in the earthy shade, looking out across the tide. It is as flat as glass.

'Bye, then,' she says finally.

Stoney watches as she steps lightly away.

'Might see you later?' he calls. It doesn't sound like a question.

Chapter Four

Back in the house, Jill sits down at the kitchen counter and scans the front page of *The Gazette* again. *Seaview House to be pulled down.* The headline makes her flinch. Why now? The place is a monument, a touchstone. And for her, a witness. Perhaps the townsfolk will object. Then she'll be safe.

Phil is in the kitchen. The fridge opens and closes.

'Whose are all the glasses, Mother?' he is asking.

'Oh. They're–'

Stop talking. I need to concentrate, she thinks.

'You dehydrated?' He laughs. 'You always moan at me for using too many glasses. I'll mention this next time. What happened to your knees?'

'Oh, nothing much. I'll wash them in the shower later.'

She can hear metal clinking, cereal rushing out from its box, milk being sloshed. Her eyes scan the words quickly, reading ahead. A teacher trait. Reaching the end of the text before the brain has registered the beginning and spoken it.

Empty for thirty years?

She calculates. 1988. When she'd pushed her way inside

the house through an open door. The revulsion she'd felt snags at the back of her throat, the catch of a long-forgotten smell.

The article suggests the place was boarded up in 1998 because of its unsafe structure.

She has seen those boards, close up. They represent security, especially for her. A flash of worry zips through her body, icy, despite the heat. She mustn't put words to it.

'Are my running shorts clean, Ma?' Phil is reading over her shoulder, the crunch of Frosties down her ear.

She gets up. Nudges him playfully. Tries to find her other self. 'They're on the pile, but they'll need ironing.' It's a good distraction.

'Will you do my blue T-shirt while you're there?'

'Yep,' she replies, digging it out from beneath her husband's clean shirts.

While she unhitches the ironing board from a tall cupboard, Jill takes some deep breaths, but her ears are beginning to buzz. Passing out in front of Phil is something she wants to avoid. The iron hisses and steams, filling the kitchen with clouds of wet flowery perfume.

'Mum. You okay?' Phil is looking at her, a lopsided grin on his face. 'You've gone white.'

Seaview and its story have been locked away in a strongbox allowing life to be lived with no toxic effects. It's not the whole truth, but it's what she tells herself. Everyone has things they'd prefer to keep hidden. She's not special. She thinks about Tutankhamun's many coffins. Every kid she ever taught, loved the creepy idea that entombed within a sarcophagus and three solid gold caskets was the truth of who he was. Her truth is just the same. And she doesn't ever visit the core, the mummy, the body.

'I'm fine,' she tells him. 'I fell over on my run. I think the shock is just starting to hit me, that's all.'

'You sure?' he asks, hovering.

'Sure. Just let me get on, will you?'

When she is done, Phil takes his ironed clothes and bounds up the stairs. Jill hears the bathroom door close, so she will have a long wait before her shower. As she stands at the sink to rinse the glasses and the detritus left by her son, she looks across the garden, wondering when the rain will finally come.

Drought-ridden summers, one in particular. An image comes to her. Concealed beneath a layer of shingle and heat. A swagger and a stare, and a lurcher on a piece of rope.

She rushes out into the hallway and grabs her keys. She needs to look at Seaview properly. Running past most days doesn't count as seeing, and she never turns her head towards the place, anyway. There are warning chains at the front, she knows, but the back is easy to access.

Inside her car, the trapped air is murderously hot. Even with the windows down, it takes until the bridge before she can bear anything more than small breaths.

The Saturday traffic is heavy, queueing at the lights. Being suspended just above the water, squashed between cars, is sending a trickle of sweat across the back of her neck and down between her shoulder blades. A thought comes from nowhere; of standing in exactly the place she is now, watching waves criss-cross the high tide, her stomach full of fear and lemonade. Familiar tunes wind their way into the picture. They drag with them more memories. Lying on a sea-coloured carpet and wondering who she was. A dazzle of sun, or the cool of white moonlight, and Jon Anderson's hypnotic voice lifting her away. She fiddles with the car's digital control panel, trying to find some music to drown them out, or wash them clean.

The traffic lights change to green, and she crawls ahead with the heat haze of other vehicles. A sharp left turn, an over-rev of the engine, and she is driving uphill, along a quiet street leading to the back of Seaview. This is the closest she's been to the place for many years. But the body never forgets. She is suddenly assailed by the smell of sweet almond. Warm in her nostrils and on her tongue. And the sharp taste of uncertainty. How can the sight of a crumbling slate roof provoke the gut-punch she is feeling right now?

The back street isn't quiet. Two police vans and another, smaller and dark grey, are parked, nose-to-tail along the pavement; a uniformed officer in a fluorescent jacket stands at Seaview's back gate. Jill keeps driving. Turns her head away. Focuses instead on her hands, gripping the wheel. Greenish-white knuckles, the colour of old bones.

June 1976

Jill stands at her bedroom window, letting the breeze dust her face and shoulders. She has the urge to walk by the sea this evening, to gulp down the salty freshness coming in with the high tide. But she isn't allowed to be out late. If she is careful not to alert Bonnie, perhaps her dad will make an exception just this once.

Beach walking gives Jill a sense of herself. Every shard of pink and blue shell, every whistle and toot from oystercatchers and sandpipers, are for her alone. Not for her family. Not for school. Not even for Stoney. Here, she is her best self: skin touched by the salt breeze, nose sensing the tide, gaze flying across the wide horizon.

Occasionally, on the beach, she would catch sight of Stoney and a group of other boys, the one named Mick included, all wide shoulders and tobacco smoke. She wishes they would leave the beach to her; they have each other. Sometimes, she hides herself in the sea-wood, wandering the paths under the cool green canopy; other times, she steps out across the width of the mudflats, trying to avoid catcalls that make her cheeks flare red.

'Stoney fancies you.'

'Nice arse.'

'Smile, darlin'.'

Words that fall, jagged and brittle, against her landscape. In truth, she had felt completely out of her depth at Seaview House, hadn't even told Susie about going back there with Stoney; she's seen the horror in her friend's eyes on finding out Jill even knows him slightly.

Her dad is seated in the lounge, holding a can of Castlemaine against his forehead.

'Okay, love?' he asks as she walks in. 'Done your homework?'

'Didn't have any. Too near the end of term.' She blows upwards, moving her hair away from her sticky forehead. 'Can I take Lucky round the block? It's cooler out there.'

Her dad shakes his head. 'No. It's too late. I don't want you on the streets after six, I've told you before.'

Jill doesn't argue; there is little point. Her shoulders slump, and she sits down in the armchair nearest the bay window, legs across the buttoned vinyl. They stick immediately.

'Oh, go on,' her dad says suddenly, pulling the ring on the can. It pops feebly. 'But don't be long.'

She unpeels her legs and skips through to the kitchen. Lucky hears the rattle of his leash, and appears, panting, from the hallway. 'See you in a bit,' she calls, then she is out of the front door before her dad can change his mind.

The air on the beach is coolly fragrant. Honeysuckle grows wild in the sea-wood, amongst tangles of hawthorn and holly, and straight rowan trees: raw nature and the sea.

Jill picks her way through the hollows of brushwood between the lapping water and the wood itself. The breeze has a salty bite, making the hairs of her bare arms stand up. The chill is sweetly painful after the long days and nights of intense heat, and she shivers with delight. Lucky has disappeared into the shadows. She can hear him scratching around. There is a patch of shingle where the tide has retreated a little. Jill jumps onto it and sits on one of the large rocks holding the wood back from the sea. It is so quiet. Just the tide and an occasional *squawk*. The heat of these long days is slowly draining the life out of everything. School feels impossible, and her teachers are snappier than they ever have been.

Roll on next Friday, she thinks.

She is suddenly aware of a movement to her left. A figure. A person, walking across the shingle towards her. A thump of her heart and she stands up. A heavy crunch of feet. Stoney. Who else could it be? She relaxes a little.

'All right.' It is almost a whisper. A match for the evening's hush. 'Just on my way home.'

Lucky comes scrambling out of the brushwood, and she grabs him quickly, snapping on his leash.

'Me too.' She begins to move away.

'Wait up,' he says lightly. 'I'll walk with you.'

She agrees, then watches the step of his boots, speckled with sand and crushed shells.

'Haven't seen you for a while?'

It is a question, but Jill can't answer. She is a schoolkid, walking her dog on a hot evening in the middle of an endless summer. He's acting like she is something else. And she so wants to be something else.

'Doing anything in the holidays?' More questions. She shakes her head. Telling him about her grandparents' visit will give voice to her worries. What would Lena Clarke say? Or would she just wiggle?

'Wanna come for a walk round the top of the island, one of the days?' Stoney sounds keen. She steals a sideways glance. He catches her eye.

'Want to?' A raised eyebrow. A flick of auburn hair.

'Yep. I could bring Lucky.' There is no way her parents will agree to her going on what they would class as a date. But the *yes* slips easily from between her lips and now hangs in the air, waiting for further words to join it.

'Saturday tomorrow. Walk him up to Seaview.' He lifts his chin towards the panting dog. 'The Old Queen will be there.'

This last added to make her feel more comfortable, she thinks.

'Might do.'

The evening light is slowly draining away as they walk together through the housing estate, each house silhouetted grey against the fading sky. Glancing into lounges lit up with family life, sends a wave of regret through Jill. And just the tiniest bit of excitement.

At the end of her path, they stop walking and turn to face each other. Lucky is straining against his leash. Jill glances up. A swish of net curtains. Bonnie.

'Coming tomorrow then?' Stoney again. She lifts her eyes to his and nods slightly.

'Great. 'Bout eleven?'

'Uh-huh.' What is she supposed to do? In the same moment she decides to turn and walk up the path, he puts both of his hands along the sides of her face and his mouth on hers. It is soft and wet, and he flicks his tongue against her lips for a moment. A strange feeling streaks through her. She steps backwards and puts her hand to her throat. Her cheeks burn. Trembling legs carry her up the path, and at the front door she turns and calls a weak, 'Bye.'

He lifts his arm and gives her a small wave, then disappears around the corner and into the briny darkness.

August 2018

Pinpricks of white light flash in front of Jill's eyes: she'll have to pull over. Imagine the fuss if she crashes her car this near to Seaview. There will be questions eventually. But not yet. She's not ready.

Why is there a police presence at Seaview? Perhaps it's nothing to worry about. Her breath is forcing its way out of her lungs at an alarming rate. It is remembering, and there's nothing she can do to stop it. She pushes open the car door and jumps out. She can see the stone bench again, the place where she fell. Her hand is on her chest, and she flings herself down.

He has sat here, too. Andrew Brownstone. Waving at her, as she walked towards him with her dog. How would he look now if he was a modern fifteen-year-old? Boys today have crisply cut hair. And they get their sports-chipped teeth fixed. They certainly don't need magazines to teach them about girls. They have the internet. They know everything.

God, what wouldn't I have given to have had the internet. I knew nothing, back then. Nothing.

The tide is high today, and full. She can see its surge, heading towards the bridge and dragging boats tightly against their mooring chains. The landscape on the other side of the water has changed dramatically over the years. Gone are the old sailing sheds and rusted boat hulls. And the graving dock has been built over with glass and steel, like the New York skyline, she thinks, though she's never travelled to the place. But world travel is possible with a few clicks of a mouse these days. Information moves quickly. She thinks of her sister. Bonnie might be hundreds of miles away, but nothing escapes her; it never has. She was the one who'd first alerted their mother to the presence of Andrew Brownstone in Jill's life. She's bound to have seen the news reports about Seaview

House. Which means she'll be sending Jill a message anytime soon. Lies will come tumbling out again, and each will have to be offset with a gold bar of good behaviour. Her shoulders slump, her thoughts as heavy as a thundercloud on a summer's day.

There is a briny wind coming from the surface of the water. It burrows its way into Jill's brain, opening the file marked 1976, breaking its padlock. And out tumble more images. Her brothers, brown-skinned, hair full of golden highlights, chasing around outside, shirtless and free. Her mother and the pub job. The one which had almost killed her. The way a heated guilt had taken over Jill's usual cool-headedness. All these things evoked by the smell of salt and the wide-open sky. She needs to get home. To escape Andrew Brownstone's clammy presence, his hand in hers.

July 1976

'Need any shopping this morning, Mum?' Jill asks, worries about her mother's tired face niggling away. 'I could walk up to the Co-op if you like.'

Her mother scowls. 'Actually, we could do with some bread and a bag of potatoes. If you don't mind, love. What would I do without you?'

'I'll take Lucky as well. Give him a walk.'

Bonnie darts a look.

Don't say it, Jill thinks. But she does.

'Can I go with Jill?' Bonnie smirks.

Their mother is quick to respond. 'I thought you were going swimming with Livvy's family. They're picking you up soon.' A glance at the clock. 'Have I got it wrong?'

'Oh. Yeah.' Bonnie waits, ever the queen of perfect timing, then adds, 'Jill wants to be alone with her boyfriend, I bet.'

Weary exasperation creeps into her mother's voice. 'What is all this talk of boyfriends? Jill?'

With absolute certainty, Jill knows lying comes back to bite. Perhaps not straight away, but it always does. There is power in the truth, though her sister has yet to learn this fact.

'I've made a friend. It happens to be a boy.' She treats Bonnie to a lift of her chin. 'Troublemaker.'

A raised eyebrow, and her mother looks at her. 'As long as that's all it is.' The smallest smile flickers across her lips.

Back in her bedroom, Jill lets her thoughts wander across the alien landscape of the previous evening. A boy had kissed her. Was it normal? Other girls in her form talked about going out with boys, but she doesn't belong to the group of worldly types. So, what is she doing? To walk up to the front door of Seaview and ask for Stoney, seems impossible. Even knocking for her friends, on the old estate, had been difficult. Parents got in the way. Answering the door with questioning eyes and stone-slab bodies. She could never think of what to say.

Is Lisa playing out?

Clearly not, as she's in 'ere. The lifted-thumb gesture.

Jill dresses quickly, one glance in the mirror answering her musings. She's a kid.

She gathers her hair back into a ponytail and pushes her feet into plimsolls.

Lucky is already whining at the front door. With the shopping list and money in her hand, she steps outside.

Along the main road, the blistered tarmac is melting again. Cars crawl lazily, and Jill smiles. She is glad to be on foot and not stuck behind panes of glass in stifling metal boxes. A hot wind lifts the small wisps of hair around her face, a tickle of sweat forms around the back of her neck.

The tide is coming in, adding its salty flavour to the heat. To dive into the sea would be bliss, but people don't swim here. The estuarine mudflats are dangerous, the trapped water unpredictable. Her shoulder tops are already crowning red, and she rubs her free hand across them. Lucky is panting heavily and tugging at his leash. Heading in the direction of the Co-op means she can't let him run free. Her mind is full of Stoney and Seaview. Yes, she will pass on her way to the shop, but she can't walk up those steps and knock on the front door. His friendship is welcome, but it makes her feel like a piece of her middle has been rubbed away by one of those pink erasers Susie has in her pencil case, and he's about to draw something new there.

Stoney is a friend with influence, who likes the same things as her, but he comes with a heavy price tag. The kiss had meant something, but she isn't sure what.

He is sitting on one of the promenade benches. Auburn hair alight with sunshine, and a white three-button T-shirt. Jill's legs tremble slightly, across the thighs. Her control of the situation is slipping away, and she is letting it. The turn of his head means she can hear the sound he is making. A cross between the clicking of the tongue to call a pet, and the cocking of a rifle.

He gets up. 'You came, then?'

Silly question when she's standing right here. 'I'm going to the Co-op for my mum.'

There is a flash of something, across his face. Jill sees it. The force of it makes her continue walking.

'Hey. Wait up. I'll go with you.'

'No,' she snaps, looking at him, then, 'sorry. I have to get the shopping.'

Stoney raises his eyebrows. 'Well, come into Seaview and then The Old Queen can run us up there. She wants to meet you.'

Jill isn't sure when she's become someone to meet, though there is a lethal flattery in the suggestion. 'No. I can't.'

But Stoney isn't listening. His arm is raised in a wave, as a silver-haired lady walks down the steps in front of the house.

'Here she is. Fannie-Annie,' he says, taking Jill's hand. 'Got no choice now.'

His weight pulling on her arm means she can do nothing but follow him across the road; the width of it seems to last forever.

'This is Jill, Mother,' he crows, as the three of them meet at the Seaview gate. 'Jill.' He nods at the lady. 'Annie Brownstone – otherwise known as Fannie-Annie or The Old Queen.'

The woman smiles in a kind way, and some of Jill's fears melt away. Here are the same broad face and high cheekbones, but Annie's sparkle with genuine warmth. And her dress is beautifully cut. Pretty make-up holds the short silvery hair back from harshness.

'Andy has told me all about you,' she says. 'He's never had a girlfriend before. You are lovely.' She drapes an arm around Jill's shoulder and turns her towards the stone steps. 'Come and have a drink.'

It is a plea, and Jill responds. It takes her a moment to remember who Andy is. 'Thank you, I will.'

She swallows down the uncertainty of becoming someone's girlfriend. Is that what she is? Here is an older woman, so unlike her own mother, but showing kindness in the same way. Jill is sure there won't be any harm in allowing Annie Brownstone into her life.

They take the steps together. Towards Seaview House. Crossing the distance between freedom and ownership, Jill thinks, and measured in her own thudding heartbeats. Lucky is straining at his leash again, sniffing at the porch steps and whining quietly.

Annie stops at the front door and turns to her. 'Bring your

dog in, my love,' she says with a smile. 'I'll lock Mac in the kitchen, and he won't know there's an intruder in the house.'

Jill is torn. She has her mum's shopping to do, but Stoney's presence weighs heavily behind her, and his mother's smile radiates warmth.

Lucky is left in the hallway, and Jill is shown into a room at the front of the house. Her first impression is one of blue tranquillity; a sweet water smell, and the ocean. A huge bay window allows sea-light to flood in, a thick, creamy-turquoise carpet completing the illusion. Pushed in front of the window is a heavy navy-blue sofa, and against another wall, a stereo system like nothing Jill has ever seen. Her parents have a wooden radiogram with a lift-up lid and she and Bonnie share a cassette player, but this is something else. Stoney watches her.

'You like Yes?'

He takes a record from the rack and tips it from its cover, holding it carefully so his fingertips touch only the label and the rim. Jill watches his hands.

'I... er... no, haven't heard of them,' she stammers, a kid again. Donny Osmond and The Bay City Rollers are all they ever listen to, though her mum likes Motown.

The record deck is at the top of the high-tech stack; he lifts the lid carefully and puts the circle of red vinyl onto it. Pressing a few buttons sets some green lights flashing. The music starts up. Instrumental, then a high-pitched voice reciting what sounds like poetry. Jill sits down nervously, her hands on her bare knees, and gazes around the room. Paintings, mainly seascapes, hang on each wall, and a white marble fireplace surrounds a silver gas fire. Stoney sits down by her, his thigh brushing hers lightly. Reaching back, she smooths down her ponytail and pulls the ends forward across one shoulder.

'This is a nice room,' she says. 'I like the paintings.'

Stoney turns his eyes on her and shrugs. 'The Old Queen likes her artwork. And here she is.' The door swings open, and

Annie Brownstone comes in, carrying a tray with three tall glasses and a plate of biscuits on it.

'I've put a bowl of water in the hall for your dog,' she says to Jill, 'he'll be fine out there. Mac's been imprisoned.' A small laugh. 'Here you are.' She hands Jill a glass, then passes one to her son. As she sips her own drink, her eyes roam around Jill's face.

'Are you in Andy's year at school?' she asks. 'Fourth form, I mean.'

Jill shakes her head. 'No. Third former.'

Annie looks at her thoughtfully, then turns to her son. 'Take care of her, then,' she tells him, with a wink. It sends a twitch of fear across Jill's shoulder blades. How has she, an ordinary schoolkid, become this other person? There is shopping to get, and her own home to go to. But Annie Brownstone's presence means something, and she doesn't want to be bad mannered.

'Have you got brothers and sisters, my love?' Annie sits down gingerly on the corner of the sofa.

Jill nods. 'I've got Bonnie, she's twelve, then Denny, Moz, and Ray, who aren't at school yet. There's a lot of us.'

She senses Stoney, restless at her side.

Annie peers at her. 'You're the oldest then. Good help to your mum, are you?'

'Mother. Stop pestering.' There is a slight grizzle in Stoney's voice. Unpleasant.

'I'm interested. I always wanted a big family.' She turns back to Jill. 'What's it like?'

'Chaotic sometimes,' she says, tugging at the ragged hems of her shorts, 'but I like it. Wish I had my own space. I have to share with my sister.' A glance around the room. 'I love Seaview, though. This room especially.'

Annie Brownstone beams her approval. 'Well, you're welcome here anytime. There's more than enough space for us

55

all.' She looks at her son. 'Will you stop sulking. I'm only being polite.'

But Stoney isn't listening. He's moved away from the sofa and is kneeling in front of the stereo system, flicking through the vast record collection. Annie turns back to Jill, a wry smile forming on her lips.

Spoilt, she mouths, and they both laugh.

He looks up. 'You can run us up to the Co-op after, can't you, Mumsie? Jill has some shopping to get.'

Jill can't believe what she is hearing. 'No. Don't. Sorry,' she stammers, looking from his mother to him, and back. Why did he have to ask? And why is he saying Mumsie in such a creepy way?

'Course I can, darling.' Annie beams at him. 'Now, I'll leave you two lovebirds alone for a minute, then we'll run up to the shops. Give me a shout when you're ready.'

She takes their empty glasses and carries the tray through to the hallway. Stoney ramps up the music and closes the door behind her. A gentle click. Jill is trapped. Telling herself not to be so stupid, she picks up the green record cover and begins looking at it.

'You like?' Stoney sits down beside her on the squashy sofa.

A hot flush creeps up her neck.

'S'okay,' she murmurs, fixed on the Yes logo. The room smells so clean and unused, nothing like the lounge in her house. She wishes she was there now. And also, she doesn't. Stoney runs his hand along her arm, from wrist to elbow to shoulder, then takes hold of her chin and turns her face to his. Her instinct is to pull away, but he slides his other hand across the back of her head, and she has nowhere to go. When he kisses her this time, his tongue makes its way into her mouth, and she gags in shock for a moment. He releases her and looks into her eyes.

'All right?' he asks softly.

Is she? What is he even asking? 'I'm–'

But he is kissing her again, running his hand across her waist and under the hem of her vest top. She jumps, though the feeling isn't unpleasant, skin on her skin. His hand creeps upwards across her ribs and onto the top of her bra, brushing the side of her breast, and causing her to move away quickly. There are no words. This isn't her. She jumps up.

'I'd better go.'

Stoney grabs at her hand. 'What's up, Jilly?'

What can she say? Don't kiss me? Don't put your hands where they're not wanted? A girlfriend wouldn't behave in that way, she is sure. Lena Clarke certainly wouldn't.

'Nothing. Just need to get my mum's shopping.' She pulls her hand away and smooths down her shorts, looking at her feet. A kid's feet. In kid's shoes.

'Okay,' he sighs. 'I'll get The Old Queen.' But his hand is on her shoulder again, hotter than the sun, and twice as relentless.

Chapter Five

O n the drive home from Seaview, Jill takes tight hold of her thoughts and tries to smooth out her breathing. The air inside the car is clammy, and she runs a hand around the back of her neck as she drives. When she finally pulls into her road, she can't recall a single landmark or manoeuvre. It is no coincidence, the police turning up on her doorstep earlier, asking about the house and its occupants. Nor is the police guard now posted at Seaview's back gate. There will be a simple explanation. There must be. She won't let herself think about it.

There was a time when Seaview had felt like Jill's home. During the long hot summer, when so much in her life changed, the house cast a kind of normality. It stood over her like a parent, enabling and consoling. Now, she knows there was nothing normal about it.

Andrew Brownstone had been an enigma, a riddle for her to solve. They'd shared so much; too much as it turned out. But his love of the landscape, the hands which could be gentle, or be covered in blood, these things marked him out as different, and for Jill, it had been enough. The shopping trip sticks in her mind because of the change it wrought in her. He'd been a boy who hated school, hated convention, and she hadn't known people had those feelings. Yet they'd laughed, talked about families with his mother, looked out at the townscape and discovered they had much in common. And when he'd fished in his pocket for money to buy her an ice cream, she'd wanted to weep. But she'd been fourteen years old, just a girl, still wearing ankle socks and worrying if teachers were looking at her the wrong way.

She tries her front door. Still open. Phil must be in. His presence will be a distraction. He is in the kitchen, tapping away at his laptop. His elbows rest, all bones and rough skin, on the kitchen counter.

'Hi, Mum,' he calls. 'Where'd you go?'

She leans over him and kisses the top of his head: damp hair and citrusy shampoo. 'Uncle Denny needed picking up from the station,' she lies, hoping somehow everything will add up.

'Oh. Is he back?' Phil says absently.

'Yep. Jet-lagged and mardy as ever.' They both laugh.

'I'm going for a shower.' She is aiming for normality. Hoping for it. He nods.

Again, Jill kicks her running shoes into the understairs cupboard. Her shoulders sag. Fatigue hits her. The drag of too much time spent in the past.

Pull yourself together, she thinks. *It's your best subject.*

Later, she will meet with one of her colleagues, a friend. They will share lunch. And everything will be the right way round again. Now, she takes clean towels from the airing cupboard, and locks herself in the bathroom. The floor is slippery, and condensation drips from the mirror. Phil. Never clears up after himself, but the thought makes her smile. She's a mother, a wife, a headteacher. There are elderly parents nearby, to fetch and carry for, and a large extended family. The past can stay where it is, she won't have it coming back to contaminate all she has built, everything she stands for.

She starts to undress: leggings, vest, sports bra and knickers, all go into a pile, then she rummages around in the white cabinet for her shampoo and conditioner.

On the floor of the cubical is a frothy scum. She turns on the shower and lets it run for a moment until the scum swirls away, then she steps under the warm gush of water. Instantly, the sting of grazed flesh hits her. She bites her teeth together and watches the dried blood liquify again and slide down her shins. The pain reminds her she is alive and still the person she was just a few hours ago. But the image of a policeman standing outside Seaview has been burned onto the back of her eyes. It can't be unseen. To survive in life, in her life, she has perfected the ability to wait. Most problems or difficulties, in her opinion, will dissolve when a little time is applied to them. The ointment of time: it heals everything. This will be the same.

Once she feels clean again, she turns the shower dial to the off position, and steps from the cubicle. Towelling her limbs is something she doesn't mind doing. They are the limbs of an athlete. Her age has allowed a layer of padding around her middle, but she feels it as protection. The cuts on her knees aren't as bad as she thought, and patted dry, she decides they won't need dressings, after all. She applies an ample layer of moisturiser to her skin, then creeps into her bedroom and takes her bathrobe down from the hook on the back of the door. She will dress later.

On her dressing table is a tortoise shell comb. While Jill tugs it through her hair, she glances at her face in the mirror. That girl is still there. The one who stopped being a child, at fourteen years old. Something she has never spoken of. It broke her but it made her. People who think she's tough, they have no idea, though none of it matters. She is who she is and would not change her story now.

Phil is calling to her from the kitchen. 'Mum. Mum, come and look at this.'

She stands at the top of the stairs, shivering despite the heat of the day. A creeping horror: she won't like what he is trying to show her. Seaview is on her radar again. Why?

'What, love?' she asks, secretly pleased her voice sounds exactly as it always does. On the stairs, she has a moment of panic. Why is she so nervous? She was the victim, wasn't she?

'It's on Cumbria Police's Facebook site,' Phil says as she walks into the kitchen. 'Look.' He spins his laptop round so she can see the screen. Seaview. The same photo. 'They've found a body. At Seaview House.'

If your life can come crashing down around you, then Jill hears hers splinter. Like a piece of plate glass, dropped from a colossal height. To her son, she is just a mother, standing in her bathrobe, peering at his Facebook. Cumbria Police. Why is Phil even looking at their site?

'Freaky, isn't it?' Phil loves a drama. 'A body. How long's it been there?'

'Does it say anything else?' She doesn't use social media platforms herself. Though half her work life is spent dealing with the damage they cause.

He puts his face very close to the screen. She waits while he reads. 'Just that builders have gone into the area to start demolishing the place. And found human remains.' He scrolls through the story, intent now. 'Asking for help from the public. You lived on the island for a bit, didn't you?'

She sees tiredness in his face.

'You all right, son?'

Leave the subject of Seaview well alone, she thinks.

'Yeah. Why?'

'You look tired. You are taking your meds, aren't you?'

He stretches his face. 'Yes, Mother. Don't start again. Are you taking yours?'

He holds her gaze.

'Well, get out more. Get off that thing.' She gestures towards the laptop. 'Facebook is liquid depression; I've told you before.'

The depression which has plagued her since her late teens, is also preying on her son. It is a bleak and marginalising disease, and she would take every trace from him if she could. As it is, he's home again, while he heals from another bout.

'And I've told you our problem is we can't tolerate idiots. Remove all the idiots from the world, and you and I would be perfectly well.' He lets out a small sad laugh. 'It's what Auntie Bon says, isn't it?'

Bonnie. Here she is again, bright, breezy and always one step ahead of the world. While Jill had struggled with the roots of her life, her sister had scaled the tree, waving. If there was any defending of sisterly loyalty to be done, Bonnie wouldn't shirk her responsibility. Even when Jill didn't deserve it. There had been a girl at school – Lena Clarke – a match for them in years, but smart-mouthed and with a peep-toe already in the world of adults. While Bonnie was a possible candidate for acceptance into her gang, Jill was most definitely not. Her sister never took up that place. Instead, despite the way Jill tried to swat her away as she would a furious bluebottle, Bonnie had been the one to send Lena Clarke scuttling, after a particularly nasty attack. Those things are never forgotten. But Bonnie is like a springer spaniel. And she'll be on the scent of Seaview.

'And Auntie Bon is right, bless her.'

'You're changing the subject, Mother. You did live on the island for a while, didn't you? I'm sure I've heard Nan mention it.'

'Not for very long. I can hardly remember what it was like.'

She hopes Phil can't hear the thunder of her heart or the seawater sloshing around in her brain. Or the serpent on her tongue. To throw him off the scent, she leans in for a kiss.

'Get off, Mother.' A flap of his hand. 'Go. Wherever you're going, go. Please.' But he is beaming, and she winks it back at him. Her clever, insightful son. He knows very little about her past, about the summer of 1976, of continuous heat and endless possibilities. When the end of the school term meant the beginning of something far less wholesome. Her best friend back then, Susie, of the neatly ironed uniforms and pristine white socks, had been wary of Andrew Brownstone. With good reason.

July 1976

On the final day of the summer term, temperatures peak at 100 degrees Fahrenheit in the capital, and a hosepipe ban comes into force. Jill and Susie cling to each other as they watch fifth formers from both schools, stride away for the final time.

Jill rolls her eyes at Susie's obvious glee. 'You said you hated boys.'

'Not all boys.' Susie tilts her head and flashes her dimples. 'Not Ian Postlethwaite, for example.'

But you don't like Stoney, Jill thinks, *so I'm not allowed to, either.*

Does she like him? She hardly knows. But it is good to have a boyfriend, isn't it? Means you are somebody. It rattles Lena Clarke, for sure. She has approached Jill on numerous occasions, and snarled threats through her shiny pink lips. Jill was to *stay away from one guy* or *stay away from another.* As if she's ever heard of these guys, let alone attracted their attention. Which is strange, considering every male Jill has ever seen, only has eyes for Lena's enormous breasts. Including Ian Postlethwaite.

'Jilly.'

She spins round, to find Stoney and two other boys she doesn't know, walking towards them. All long hair and shoulders, their white shirts open at the neck, roll-ups ready between their fingers.

'All right?' Jill catches the faintest scent; nicotine and Stimorol gum. Stoney's freckled face is tinged with hot-pink, and his auburn fringe is plastered across his forehead.

She tells him she is fine, then looks sideways at Susie. Her friend is stepping away.

'What's up with Stuck-Up-Cow?' Stoney lifts his chin.

'Nothing,' she says. 'Going home, like we all are.'

'I'll walk with you then,' he laughs. 'Jilly.'

The group of boys guffaw loudly. 'Stoney's got a hard-on. Stoney's got a hard-on.'

'Fuck off,' he sneers then drapes himself around her. 'Idiots.'

Across her shoulders, Stoney's arm feels heavy and damp, and she wants to shrug it off, but wonders how this will look to his friends; the thought is troubling. But the arm stays where it is.

She calls a goodbye to Susie; they'd talked earlier about the holiday cottage her friend's family took every year, in a place called St Ives. Jill has never heard of it, never mind taking a cottage for three weeks as a holiday. Susie waves her hand feebly, then turns away, joining a group of other girls heading towards the front of the building.

'See you later,' Stoney calls to his friends, then the hot arm guides her away.

When they reach the start of the back path, he takes a cigarette lighter out of his pocket and flicks it at the roll-up in his fingers, inhales deeply, then turns to her.

'So. When'll we go on this walk along the beach? Tomorrow?'

'Can't tomorrow.' A lie.

'When then?'

She shakes her head. 'Dunno. Have to find out what we're doing.'

He backs off. 'Fair enough.'

'Got my grandparents coming tomorrow to stay.' Why had she felt the need to tell him?

'I have my grandparents staying all the time,' he says lightly, 'well, Nana anyway.'

He suddenly seems less dangerous. He has a nana, parents, he is a schoolkid.

'You could come and meet them,' she suggests, against the advice of her fizzing stomach. 'The whole family, I mean. Not just Gran and Grandad.'

He blows out a long plume of smoke, then spits a flake of tobacco from his bottom lip. 'Could do. When? Tomorrow?'

'They won't arrive till late. Sunday?'

He shrugs. 'Sunday then. Tell your Olds you're walking round Walney with me later on, too.'

Telling is something she never does to her parents. Asking works much better, in her opinion. Does Stoney ever ask for anything?

The bus is already at the stop. Stoney takes her hand, and they run to catch it. He leads her up the stairs. She never sits upstairs; it's for smokers, her mum says. Although the small sliding windows have been pulled back, the air on the top deck is as stale as the gym changing rooms on a Friday afternoon. Sweat tickles its way across her neck. More than anything, she wants to lift her hair and feel a blast of sea wind. Stoney walks along the aisle, holding on to the rails as the bus sways away. He takes an empty seat at the front and beckons her to sit next to him. Then begins to roll another cigarette.

'Want one?'

A shake of her head. 'Does your mum know you smoke?' The backs of her legs slide across the seat, and she lifts her nose to the open window.

'The Old Queen. Nah. She wouldn't be bothered anyway; lets me do what I want. The Old Geezer wouldn't like it, but he doesn't like anything, miserable get.'

The bus lurches forward, and they peer out of the front window, watching people and cars fight for home. Groups of fifth formers, grammar and Catholic, jostle for attention, their high spirits and graffitied shirts marking them out as being in charge of the world.

Well, their world anyway, Jill thinks.

'Going lamping with Mick tonight,' Stoney suddenly says.

'What is lamping, exactly?' She knows nothing and wants to know everything.

'It's good fun. Me and Mick go up the fields in the dark. His dog chases rabbits from their burrows, then we shine a torchlight straight at them. They freeze, and we blast them.' He makes a double-clicking noise with his tongue, then blows out a bang.

'It sounds horrible,' she wails. 'Why do you do it?'

He doesn't answer for a moment. Then, 'Mick does it for the farmers. Else the bloody rabbits would wreck their planting. And they'd be out of control if we didn't. He gets a quid for ten bodies. I'll get you a foot, if you like. Supposed to be lucky.'

'Don't bother.' She turns away from him. Cut off a rabbit's foot? Is he joking? Cruelty to animals is something she'll never be able to get her head around.

'Awww! Is Silly Jilly upset?' He begins digging her in the ribs, and in the soft spot just above her collarbone.

'Stop it,' she spits. 'Just stop it.'

But he doesn't. Fingers poke at her, and hands grab her

sides. His hair smells of cigarettes, and she wants to scream. Especially at the sight of his chip-toothed smile.

The clippie comes along to check their bus passes.

'Everything all right, luvvy?' he says. Jill nods, though it's anything but.

By the time they cross the bridge to the island, the heat and cigarette fug at the top of the bus is making Jill feel queasy. She isn't a good traveller and has to stare forward as much as she can, fixing on the horizon. It's her mum's advice, on every journey. But she inevitably vomits, on even the shortest trip; she feels like vomiting now. Stoney is getting up.

'See you Sunday, then,' he says with a smile. 'Jilly.'

He swings past and out into the aisle. Taking the roll-up from his mouth, he reaches for her chin and plants a nicotine-tasting kiss hard on her lips. Then he is gone. She looks down onto the pavement and watches him open the Seaview gate. His swagger unnerves her. Black school trousers, slightly tight; wide shoulders spread with thick auburn hair, and the jut of his chin telling the world to get out of the way.

Her gaze falls across the thin sliver of tide. The sky is white-hot, though it is almost four o'clock, and waves of heat claw upwards from the mudflats. Jill breathes out some of her trapped feelings, her shoulders relaxing downwards. As soon as she's home, she will get down to the beach. Her and Lucky. No boys. No swearing. No cigarette-tainted breath and no grabbing at her face and body.

August 2018

As Jill walks back upstairs, she thinks about Seaview again. And Stoney. Andrew Brownstone: compelling, arrogant, and completely egotistical. It's been years since she's seen him. But his presence permeates her body, as though she had drunk mercury in her teens and it lingers still, causing symptoms and leaking poison. Quicksilver running through her veins, mixing with the blood.

When her grandparents arrived during the summer break, Jill had cried. For her grandad's rakish London clothing, and her gran's stern face, tilted towards the sun. And also for herself. It's a moment which has stayed with her, has affected her handling of every fourteen-year-old girl she's ever worked with. There is a commonality to their story, and one which straddles years and generations like a bridge without end. In the heart of them all is the eternal daughter, grasping at the freedom of childhood with one small hand while reaching away with the other: loving her girlish hairstyle but still hacking at it with sharp, steel scissors.

'Mother.' Phil is calling up the stairs to her.

She stands at the top, looking down at him. 'What?'

'I forgot to say. Uncle Moz phoned. While you were out running.'

'Oh?'

'Yeah. He wanted to talk to you about... erm... Something to do with school, I think. You'll have to ring him back.'

'You're rubbish at taking messages. What about school?'

Phil shrugs up at her. 'I couldn't tell what he meant. But–'

'What?'

'He asked if I'd seen the story about Seaview House.'

Jill waits. Suddenly, everyone's interested. Moz could hardly have any memories of the place. He'd only been a toddler when they'd lived on the island. And he'd never been to Seaview.

'You know what he's like,' Phil is saying. 'Thinks everything going on in the town is his business.'

'Oh, I know what he's like.' Jill exhales loudly. 'I'll phone him.'

The last thing she wants is her family poking around in their collective memory and dragging out snippets of their brief time on the island.

Her youngest brother has built up a successful clothing business in the town centre, which feeds his acquisition of gossip as much as it feeds his family. And if there's some drama to be had from his ever so slight connection with a local news story, he'll be wanting it.

'Hi, sis,' he says almost as soon as she's pressed the dial-up button for his number.

'Hi.'

'Been up to anything good?'

'No. Just running. Enjoying the last days of the holiday. You?'

'I'm in work, actually. And I've got a problem with your school jumpers.'

'Oh?'

'There's almost a hundred on order for the end of the week. And I think they're going to be late.'

Jill runs a hand over her face. There is never a day when work doesn't force its way into her life. But today the distraction is welcome.

'Are they mainly jumpers for the little ones?' she asks.

'Nope. Sorry, sis, but it's all sizes.'

'Okay, well, you do what you can, and I'll send a message out to parents; there'll be no penalty if some kids arrive on the first day without full uniform. Not all our families use you, anyway.'

They talk on for a while about some of the other local uniform suppliers, then he suddenly says, 'By the way. I was talking to Phil about the old house on Walney. Seaview House, wasn't it called? They've found human remains there, haven't they? Bloody strange, isn't it? Creepy, like. We used to live not far from there, didn't we?'

'We did,' she laughs. 'And yet we're all still alive.'

'Funny. Makes you wonder though, doesn't it?'

More than you know, she thinks, and the hairs along her forearms prickle with the knowledge.

July 1976

At her stop, Jill catches sight of Bonnie and Livvy, a tangle of slim brown limbs, heads together and smiling.

'Thanks,' she calls to the clippie, then jumps down into the street.

'Bon, hang on.'

Her sister turns: a wide, white grin. 'Hiya. Holidays! H'ray.'

Jill squeezes in between them and drapes an arm around her sister's shoulder. 'Gran and Gramps tomorrow, too. Can't wait.'

They stroll together up the hill, past stone barns and cottages, kicking at the dusty pavements, with freedom on their heels.

Livvy turns her eyes on Jill. Green cat's eyes. 'You going out with Stoney?' An accusation.

Jill screws up her nose. 'No. Why'd you say that?'

'It's all round the estate,' she shrugs. 'I didn't believe it. He's a nob.'

A shrieking splutter from Bonnie.

'What?' Livvy throws back her head. 'He is. My brother saw him shagging Bev Gunson up against the wall of The Crown.'

Bonnie is bent double, white-blonde hair curtaining her face. She gasps. 'Don't make me laugh anymore. It hurts.'

But Livvy won't be silenced. 'Ask our kid then, if you don't believe me. And they didn't care who was looking.'

'You need to watch your mouth.' A push of anger is coming up from Jill's stomach. Stoney's attention on someone else? Why does it bother her so much? And what exactly has this brother of Livvy's seen? She dares not ask.

'Don't believe me then.' The cat's eyes slide towards Jill. 'But he said you could see bits of their bodies. And everything.'

Her sister has stopped gasping, is now staring, head cocked. 'That's disgusting. What a nob.' She tries out the word.

Jill interrupts. 'Well, nob or not, I'm not going out with him, all right?' Looking at Bonnie, she sees something in her sister's face. Distrust.

'She is.' A whisper to Livvy, just loud enough.

Chapter Six

J ill opens the wardrobe and tries to be bothered about what
to wear for her lunch date. Her husband's wedding shirts
hang, pristine and colourful, alongside her summer
dresses. She pulls one of the shirts forward and holds it to her
face, inhaling the scent of him. If he were here, she wouldn't
be worried. The time in her life when she was about to
crumble, he walked in and gave her a reason to believe
something different about herself. He knows her deepest,
darkest secrets. Except for one.

She chooses a pale green cotton dress, patterned with
apples, then closes the wardrobe door and lays the dress across
the bed. She has slept side-by-side with Stevie for so many
years, and they have discussed every aspect of their lives, yet
she hasn't mentioned Stoney. Ever.

Her husband loves her. He understands her need to be a
good person, a supportive and caring wife, mother and
daughter, a loyal friend. He understands her need, as an
educator of children, for a reputation as clean and solid as
diamond. She needs a medal, he often says. In her head, Jill
calls it *The Imposter's Cross*. Not something she would say to

Stevie. There's safety in being good. Should the worst happen, people won't believe it.

Jill Francis, they would say. The nice lady, the headteacher. The one who always smiles, takes her mum shopping. No, not her.

Stevie was by her side through the long hours of a difficult labour, when she'd screamed at the world and sent midwives, young and old, scurrying away with sky-high eyebrows and pursed lips. He'd stood in the quiet darkness of their bedroom, jiggling the baby on his shoulder while she'd sobbed tears of loving fatigue. At her beloved grandad's funeral, he'd turned off the Frank Sinatra song causing gut-wrenching tears, and filled the awkward silence it left with a supreme effort of conversation and keeping people fed. And when she'd been sucked in by the black hole of depression, he'd wagged his finger at the *what-have-you-got-to-be-depressed-about* brigade and fought her corner. All this. Without Seaview House ever escaping from her lips. The mask has become her real face, can't be taken off now.

She dresses quickly, and slaps on enough make-up for her to feel sharp-faced instead of blurry. Behind the door are her white wedge sandals. She pulls them on, then smooths down her dress. It just about covers her grazed knees. Her feet take the stairs carefully, sideways this time, and in the hallway, she picks up her car keys and handbag, and calls through to Phil.

'I'm going to meet Em now, love. All right?'

'Yep. Have a good time,' comes the reply.

She looks into the kitchen. He is still tapping and peering. 'Lock up if you go out.'

'Will do.'

'And stop searching for tales of dead bodies. Go and find some live ones.'

'Ha ha, Mother.' Phil crinkles his face. 'You look nice, by the way.'

July 1976

Jill wakes to the smell of fried bacon. It drifts up the stairs along with the laughter of her brothers. She kneels up in bed and pushes open the window. The air has a scented warmth to it; garden roses, Ambre Solaire, the sea. Breathing it in sends a pulse of light through her body, and she wants nothing more than to be dressed and outside, under the bleached-blue of the sky.

She chooses shorts and her best cheesecloth shirt, then slips her feet into the now redundant school Jesus-sandals and skips lightly downstairs.

'Come here, Lady Penelope.' Her grandma is sitting at the dining table in a candlewick housecoat. 'Let me braid those rat's tails.'

Jill kisses her cheek, grateful for the gift of time her parents never seem to have, then goes in search of a hairbrush and elastic bands. It isn't long before her hair is tightly braided, plaits reaching down past her shoulders.

'Next,' commands her grandma, as Bonnie comes into the room, and the whole process starts again.

Outside, the morning swells with the promise of wide-open seascapes and glass-topped rock pools. There will be plastic buckets full of sand shrimps and murky water, fish-paste sandwiches, and the milky smell of grown-up coffee. And there will be freedom. She lifts her hand to where the sun is already heating the back of her neck and thinks about taking the plaits out. But there is the car to load up first, or the day will never really get going.

As she gazes along the street, wondering where to start, and hoping someone will come out of the house to help her, she sees Stoney, stomping through the heat haze, hair caught back with a piece of rag and lifting his hand in greeting. He looks like a soldier, in a green T-shirt and shorts with pockets. And there is a small rucksack strapped to his back; he is here for the day.

'Jilly,' he is calling. 'All set?' This is a man. Not a schoolboy.

The way he says Jilly. It feels wrong: too intimate. The name is for her family to use.

'Oh. We're going out for the day. Sorry. I didn't think.'

'What the fuck,' he whispers, coming to a halt in front of her. His fingers pinch at the top of his nose. The moment stretches awkwardly, along with the net curtains in the lounge window, then Bonnie is outside with them.

'Mum. Mum,' she shrieks. 'Jill's boyfriend is here.'

Jill stands, open-mouthed, as her mother and grandparents come out through the front door, shielding their eyes to look at Stoney.

'Hello, Mum. Granny. Grandad,' he beams. 'Jilly's boyfriend is certainly here.'

Her grandad, looking cool in beige chinos and a navy Airtex shirt, steps forward and extends a hand. 'Hello, son. Didn't know our Jill had a boyfriend.' He turns to her mother. 'Did you, Liz?'

Jill looks at her mother's face, expecting, hoping, to see the cold shock of rejection there. Instead, her lips are twitching upwards, almost ready to smile. 'I had heard something,' she says. 'Hello. Jill hasn't told us your name.'

'Andy Brownstone,' he replies, 'but even my ma calls me Stoney.'

A small round of laughter irritates Jill even more than the two lies he has just told. No mention of The Old Queen, is there?

'Well, Stoney,' her gran interrupts. East London. Brash. 'We're all off to West Shore. Are you coming along?'

'Cheers,' he gushes. 'What can I do to help?' He nods

across to where the cool box and windbreak lean up against the front wall of the house. 'Shall I put those in?'

Jill sees a look pass between her mother and her gran. Raised eyebrows and grins better suited to Bonnie.

'Good lad,' chuckles her gran, 'glad of the help. Big strong 'un like you is what we all need.' A wink, then she turns away.

Stoney runs his eyes over her family, the car, everything.

'Looks like we'll be walking,' he says with a wry smile. 'I've stepped into an episode of *The Waltons*.'

'Welcome to my life.' Jill's gran has turned into Lena Clarke. Even the wiggle is there.

Stoney throws back his head and treats her family to a howl of friendly laughter, and a flash of his chipped front tooth. Then Denny lunges at him, grabbing his waist. Jill moves forward to peel her brother away, but Stoney is grinning, hand on Denny's soft brown head.

August 2018

Jill bangs the front door behind her. Em is her friend, though she is fifteen years younger. Her nickname is *Queen Facebook*. Which means there will be the inevitable mention of Seaview House. By now, most of the town will know the icon of the island is coming down. Some, like her son, and possibly her friend, will know a body has been discovered in the vicinity. But none will know what Jill knows; how could they?

Only she knows how it felt to be thrown into the path of Andrew Brownstone, to watch as he charmed even her grandparents. Jill always felt there was an air about him of dishonesty, as though he expected to be liked. And she had liked him; she must have done.

They'd certainly shared a love of the natural world.

Today's Stoney would have been a climate activist, she is sure. The thought brings him back to her for a moment, and a memory hits her enough to bring tears: Stoney and her grandad, sitting on a wall, sharing the heat of cigarettes and a debate on the nuclear arms industry. There had been talk of building nuclear-powered submarines in her town, with opposition as much as support coming from local people.

As far as Jill can remember, Stoney was opposed, and had impressed her grandad with the clarity of his knowledge. His heart had been in the argument, too. She wonders what he would have made of today's town and its ruthless production of high-tech trident submarines, capable of destroying oceans.

But he won't know about it, will he? Because he's not here, hasn't been here for a very long time. Yet he is stomping about in her thoughts so noisily, and with so little care, she can almost believe it was his fault she tripped over earlier. And outside the gates of Seaview, too. She leans against her car and closes her eyes for a moment. And hopes her son doesn't look out of the window.

July 1976

Jill and Stoney step out along the flat belly of brown sand. Lucky runs through the glacier-mint waves at the edge of the tide, as Stoney throws pebbles for him to chase. Jill relaxes a little, time slipping from her shoulders and across the glinting water. The salty wind feels pleasant on her hot skin. Ten minutes takes them from the press of families and holidaymakers, to where the line of pastel sky and turquoise sea stretches out of her sight.

'Oystercatchers,' Stoney is saying. 'Hear the little hooting sound? It's them. But the two with tufts on their heads, they're lapwings.'

Jill watches the birds. Lucky's movements through the water scare a group of them, and they fly upwards, flapping into the heat of the day.

'And look at this,' he calls again, waving a hand at her. 'A moon jellyfish. Could still sting you if you stepped on it now.' He stands over the viscous, silvery puddle, kicking at it with the toe of his boot.

'I don't like them,' she shudders. 'How do you know so much about… creatures?'

'Me and Mick have been hanging around the shore, and the dunes and fields, for as long as I've known him. He's dead clever.'

'What's Mick's proper name?'

Stoney snorts with laughter. 'Not Mick at all, as it happens. He's called Malcom Gibson.'

'How do you get Mick from that?'

'He was good at art. When he was at school, like. Got called Michelangelo.'

Good at art? Jill is confused. And who is Michelangelo?

She frowns. 'Couldn't you just call him Gibbo or something? That'd be much easier.'

Stoney spins away, throwing the stone he has in his hand. Lucky chases it through the waves. 'He's nearly twenty. Gibbo's a name you'd give to your school mates.' Then, facing her again. 'You're good at telling people what's right, aren't you, Jilly?' His lips twist into a sneer, fleetingly, but Jill sees it.

'Why are you being so nasty?'

'Dunno.' He rubs a hand over his face. 'Come on. Let's walk up into the dunes.'

As he marches away, he whistles to Lucky. The dog jumps through the shallow water and follows him. Jill goes after them, though what she wants to do is walk back along the beach and become a granddaughter and sister once more; she doesn't understand why the sight of Stoney's muscled arms in his capped-sleeved T-shirt makes her belly flip over.

The landscape is transformed by the dunes. White sand stretches up high into the blue sky, anchored together only by long reedy grass. Marram grass, Stoney calls it, as he slits pieces open with his nail and pulls out its foamy insides. He shows her sea thrift and sea campion and even the burrow of a sand lizard. Jill watches the backs of his hands as he pulls at a clot of sun-crisped seaweed, to reveal a series of tiny caves, matted with soft grey feathers.

'Sand martin nests,' he tells her, 'but they're long gone now.' He lays the seaweed back carefully, then looks up at her. 'They'll be back next year, but they have to build the nests again. The dunes shift every winter.' He stretches his back. 'The Old Queen reckons by the time she's snuffed it, they'll be gone anyway, washed away by the weather, or something. Let's sit down for a bit. I've got some pop in my rucksack.'

He takes her hand and pulls her down the dune a little, into a shaded area of overhanging grass. Lucky settles himself beside them and begins licking his salt-caked paws. Stoney reaches into his bag and pulls out a plastic bottle full of watery orange liquid. He unscrews the lid and takes a long drink, then pours a little out and passes the bottle over to Jill.

'Don't mind my germs,' he says with a small laugh. 'You're going to get plenty more of them in a minute.'

Jill takes a sip of the drink, and the last drops catch in her throat, making her cough. How is she going to get his germs? Before she has time to think further, the bottle is removed from her hands, and she is being pushed back against the warm sand. Stoney's face looms above hers and her shoulders are pinned.

'Kiss me, Jilly,' he murmurs, and without giving her much choice, his lips are on hers, hot and tasting of orange juice. She responds in a way she thinks she should, trying to kiss him back. He presses his heavy upper body against hers and forces his tongue into her mouth. She tries not to recoil, tries to do the same back to him, but she can hardly breathe. The thought of his saliva mixing with hers makes her shudder. His hand moves from her shoulder, then is on one breast, squeezing and pressing, pulling at the fastenings of her shirt. She yanks his hand away. He lifts his head.

'What's up?'

Her voice won't come. She stretches her cheek towards the clean sand, presses against its powdery softness. But Stoney starts again, kissing, pawing, moving down her neck towards her chest. Strange sensations flood through her, like pulses of electricity. She gives herself up to the feelings. He pulls open her shirt, and while one of his hands holds her fast, the other explores. Her breast is freed from its restraint, and he puts his lips there. Looking down at his large auburn head, she wants to scream, but something about the moment imprisons her as surely as his hand. When it moves over her shorts and fumbles with the button, she is startled into grabbing his wrist and pulling it away.

'No. Stop it,' she whispers. 'Get off me.' With her hands braced against his shoulders, she rolls from under him.

For a moment, Stoney lays on the sand, staring downwards. Then he turns on his side and looks at her. 'What did you do that for?' he says, eyes catching a glint of sunshine.

She can't speak, only shakes her head.

He reaches towards her and tugs lightly on one of her plaits. 'What's wrong with you? I fancy you. You fancy me. Jilly. Answer me.'

'Nothing's wrong,' she says, a flush creeping up from her neck to her cheeks. The talk of fancying is confusing. She is unsure of what it means. 'Can we go back?' She pulls herself away and stands up. Slips heavily down the dune.

He lets out a loud sigh but follows.

'Wait up. Jilly. Wait.'

With Lucky trotting by his side, he catches up with her. Tears begin to roll down her cheeks, stinging her face. What is wrong with her? She can't even do what her boyfriend wants. Is she a bad person? Stoney curls an arm around her shoulder and kisses her on the temple.

'It's all right for you.' His laugh is as jagged as a scallop shell. 'I've got a raging hard-on and can't even do anything about it. Not fair, is it?'

Jill is confused. A wave of nausea creeps from her stomach to her throat. She wants to get back to her grandparents and put as much distance between herself and Stoney as she can.

Chapter Seven

With the car window open and the rush of air blasting at her brain, Jill can almost forget about Seaview House. But one memory persists. It won't be buried like the others. It is pivotal to her life, and lives in glorious technicolour, tagged on to any hot August day since 1976. Stoney taking her childish hand, his clean cotton smell, the auburn hair smothering her face. A sea-blue carpet pressing against her bare back, and the lyrics from *Topographic Oceans* fighting to clean up the corrupt atmosphere of the room.

When he'd pushed into her, he'd mention love, over and over, but all she could focus on was the ladybird crawling across the sleeve of her T-shirt, crumpled in the corner. There had been no force, no unwillingness, just a fourteen-year-old girl, left wondering.

Afterwards, she had asked to use the Seaview bathroom. There were white tiles with a green border, a black toilet seat and pull chain cistern. She won't forget bumping into Reverend Brownstone as she left the room in a daze. He hadn't even acknowledged her, just shuffled by with an armful of brown cardboard files, tied, like Christmas presents, with thin ribbon and red bows.

Annie Brownstone had arrived home from work in her navy-blue uniform and antiseptic perfume, thrilled to have a visitor, fussing around Jill and asking her to stay for tea. Today's Jill would have told her she'd just had sex with her son thank you very much, and what sort of mother was she to have let that happen? But the young Jill had smiled meekly and accepted the offer.

She shakes her head, willing the memory away. Soon, there will be Em and laughter and talk, and she will be herself again. There will be no mention of Stoney. He doesn't exist in the life she leads now. Only she knows that name. But someone has linked them together and passed on this knowledge. And she's sure of who it is.

On the forecourt of the huge sandstone Abbey Hotel, she parks and switches off the ignition. A glance at her wrist tells her she's early – time enough for a stroll in the cool green gardens.

The gravelled paths are lined with ancient cypress trees, and she can't resist standing in the shade and laying her hands on a scaly red-and-brown trunk. There is warmth in the bark, and it is a comfort. A small snort of laughter escapes from her lips. A love of real and natural history has been part of her life for as long as she can remember. It was something she'd shared with Stoney. He has risen from the past and will not be pushed back there, no matter how hard she tries. But he will eventually fade in the face of everything happening in her life now. All she needs to do is wait.

Standing at the front of the hotel, is her friend. Smiling, waving, long blonde hair straightened down her back and a red-and-white summer dress.

'Sorry. Not late, am I?' A beaming smile and the clink of car keys. Jill puts her arms around her, and hugs.

'No. I was early. You look nice.'

Em smiles and slips a hand to the middle of Jill's back. 'Thanks. Shall we go in. Exciting, isn't it.' She giggles just a little. This is the woman who has supported her through some difficult times in the last few years, a woman who finds wonder in every situation. Even a simple lunch on a sunny Saturday.

'How was your holiday?' Jill asks, as they wait at the reception desk.

'Oh. Fab.' The mobile phone is flipped open and Em's holiday photos are soon on show.

'Great. Give me more.' This is the Jill she recognises. Not the one locked away.

A young man, cool in white linen shirt and black trousers, takes them through the bar area and into the hotel's restaurant. Jill tries to look at and appreciate holiday snaps, while negotiating the table and being polite.

The gothic interior of the original hotel building has been transformed with clever painting and modern lights. It feels clean-cut and relaxing, and the restaurant is bright, its white-and-yellow accents alluding to summer, without adding any heat.

While they sit at their table, waiting to be served, Em chatters away, one eye on her phone screen, involving Jill in her scroll through life. She is happy to listen, to nod and frown, but she knows the story of Seaview will rear its head any minute. Nothing is talked about on social media without Em keying into it, one way or another. Mid scroll, she looks up at Jill.

'Did you see the article about the old vicarage on Walney? Seaview House, I think it's called.'

Jill lifts her chin a little.

More scrolling. Em's red fingernails tap against the phone screen then she passes it over. Jill glances. The same photo. The one from *The Gazette*.

'Oh? What about it?' Though she knows well enough.

'A body has been found. Buried in the garden. Police reckon it could have been there for over thirty years.'

Buried?

Jill tries to process this fact, whilst composing her face into a disinterested coolness. She nods. Makes a slight O with her mouth.

'Yep. They found it when the bulldozers moved in to start demolishing the place.' Em scrolls and reads, while Jill stares at the parting in her hair, a dark line of roots showing through the blonde. 'While they were taking down one of the diseased trees. Guess no one's been in the garden for years.'

In truth, the house has been closed up since 1988, Jill knows. There had been a new vicar, housed with his family, in a modern semi, much closer to the church. Seaview had languished on the property market for a few years, and when no sale was forthcoming, had been boarded up and left to crumble.

'Not sure,' she says. 'Don't really know the place, but I've seen it when I'm out running.'

'You,' Em's champagne laughter, 'should get Facebook. Or at least some local news apps. You know how this town works.'

I do, Jill thinks. 'Oh, the news gets to me eventually. It's what I keep you and Phil for, anyway.'

Their drinks arrive before Em can say anything else, and she tucks her phone away in her handbag again, much to Jill's relief.

The afternoon wears on, overlaid by delicious food, sparkling wine and chat about work and family and holidays. Jill focuses on her friend's face and lets her lead their conversation. But as each moment turns into the next, the small squeeze of tension bubbling up in her stomach at the mention of *buried*, becomes a clutching hand tightening its grip around her throat.

July 1976

Mick slides his eyes towards Jill's chest.

'What you brought her for, again?' he growls. 'She's a kid.' Small puffs of rubbery-smelling smoke slip from between his lips, and she watches, fascinated, as he inhales them back up his nose.

Like he's hungry, she thinks.

Stoney puts an arm on her shoulder.

'Fuck off.' A snarl at his friend. 'You're bringing tarts here all the time.'

Mick has set up camp in the field of a local farmer. Hay-time has been left as late as possible this year, Stoney has told her, and he's been recruited to help, now school is finished. Jill doesn't quite understand what hay-timing is, other than an excuse for local lads to move away from home for a few nights and live it up, in the fields near the end of the island. Stoney's face is burned red by the days of shifting hay bales, and the tops of his shoulders are peeling, yet he is as happy as she's ever seen him. But he is right. Mick does bring lots of girls back to the tents, though the way they look and the words they say, classes them as women. Hard-eyed, with breasts falling out of their vest tops, and the scent of three-day-old Charlie, they share cigarettes and swig Strongbow straight from the bottle, leaning into Mick, threading their manicured hands through his hair.

He scares Jill.

There is never a smile from him that isn't a sneer. In his company, Stoney becomes like him, and the conversations invariably turned to sex. Most of what they talk about is out of Jill's realm of understanding, and she often makes excuses to leave. She is about to do this now.

'I'm going home,' she says. 'I'll see you another time.' Stoney grabs at her arm, but she wriggles from his grasp.

'Jilly. Don't,' he whines. 'You've only just got here.'

'See you.' A dip of her head and she is out of the canvas tent, letting the smoky warmth of the evening seep into the tension at the back of her throat. The air inside had been thick with the ripe fug from Mick's cigarettes, mingled with something more human and earthy; she is glad to escape.

The shorn fields shimmer sadly, yellow and broken. Using water for any unauthorised activities is now against the law, along with the endless fun of ice balloons and hosepipe play. Jill's dad comes home teary and exhausted most days, worrying about the desiccated state of the local fells, the scent of burnt vegetation clinging to his clothes and hair.

Rooks, ecstatic and glossy in the fringes of grass, call their surprise as Jill stomps away from the tent. Stoney is hard on her heels. But this is no great clamour for attention: she just wants to go home.

'Wait up,' he calls, matching his stride to hers. 'I thought you were staying till eight?'

She shakes her head and kicks at the cracked stems at her feet. 'I'll see you when hay-time is over.'

He reaches around her shoulder and grabs her ponytail. It is almost blonde, now. As he smooths it down, he lifts her chin to face him.

'If you loved me, you'd stay.'

Jill pulls her head back, out of his grip. 'What are you saying?'

'It's true. Supposed to be my girlfriend. But–'

'But what?' She wrinkles her nose. What is he talking about? Love? She doesn't understand.

'You keep saying no to me. Pushing my hands away. Storming out. Means you don't love me.'

'I'm going home,' she says, with a shrug. She's had enough

of this tiresome talk of love; it feels like blackmail, bribery, something from the world of adult novels.

But Stoney grabs her hair again, this time yanking her head backwards. 'No. You're. Not.'

Instinctively, her hand reaches upwards to her scalp and finds the grasping fist. She tugs at it, using her other elbow to jab at his stomach. 'Get off me,' she yelps. 'It hurts, you idiot.'

Stoney's face registers what he's done. 'God, I am a fucking idiot. You're right.'

Jill feels a burning heat rise from her belly to her face, an urge to escape, a fear of the rabbit hole she is falling down. 'I have to go,' she whispers, more to herself.

'Come back to Seaview with me,' he pleads. 'The Old Queen's got some clean stuff for me, anyways.'

Jill glances at the Timex on her wrist. Still an hour before she has to be in. She wouldn't be breaking any rules, would she? Except her own.

'Go on then,' she says, and he gives her a gap-toothed grin, the one that makes him look like a quirky little brother.

He takes her hand, and together they walk across the quiet fields and follow the shingle path to the beach. A fresh nip of wind cools Jill's forehead and shoulders. The tide is a blade of silver, far away now. Groups of wading birds dig and scratch for shellfish and worms. Even they seem weary of the heat. None call or fly into the quiet evening. There is only the sound of feet, crunching across sand.

'Me and Mick put a long line out last night,' Stoney is saying. 'We're going back at midnight when the tide's out, to see what we've got.'

Jill has to think about this. Midnight. Isn't everyone in bed?

'Does your mum not mind if you're out on the sands so late?' she asks, and he laughs.

'The Old Queen? Nah. Too busy at work to be bothered

about me.' Those last words fire out like bullets from a gun. Jill jumps out of herself.

'What does she do? Your mum? You've never said.'

'Midwife, isn't she. At North Lonsdale. Always wanted me to be a doctor.' He laughs bitterly. 'Fuck that.'

When they reach Seaview, the house is in darkness. Stoney pushes open the front door and Jill follows him inside. Although there is a thin strip of light coming from under the study door, the hallway is silent. Jill's heart thrums. Stoney holds one finger in front of his lips and leads her into the blue room. The door clicks behind them. And then his hands are on her. Stroking at first, then pulling. She watches with a mixture of fear and excitement as he undoes the buckle of his belt and pops open the top button of his jeans.

'I love you, Jilly,' he whispers against her ear as he presses her shoulders. 'Let me.'

And she does. The kissing, the caresses, they feel gentle, like waves lapping against the flat dry sand. Her clothes are lifted away, she is lifted away. There is no connection to this moment for her, and all she wants is to be back with her family, in her bedroom, reading, and arguing with Bonnie, and just be a kid again.

Chapter Eight

AUGUST 2018

'Are you all right, Jill?' Em peers across the table. 'Am I talking too much?' Her hand is spread across her chest.

'No. Sorry. It's the fizz, I think. It never agrees with me.' Jill squeezes the bridge of her nose. Screws up her eyes and waits. But she can't get rid of one image. The garden at the back of Seaview House. What will it look like now?

'Let's get a coffee,' Em is saying. 'Sit in the lounge for a bit.' She waves a distracted hand, and the linen-clad waiter comes over again.

'Can we have two coffees, please?'

He nods. All smooth-skin and superior.

'We'll be in the garden room.'

'No problem, madam,' he replies, then floats away.

'Go and splash some cold water on your face,' Em says. 'I'll meet you in there.'

Jill doesn't argue. She can feel her life unravelling, like a ribbon from a rhythmic gym display. Once it's on view, everyone will clap and laugh and enjoy the spectacle. But someone will be left to wind it up again; her.

She gets up from her seat and teeters for a moment. Then

heads across the restaurant towards the toilets. As she pushes open first one door, then another, and enters the quiet, mirrored room, a memory comes: hiding in the bathroom of the island house, checking to see if her period had come. Willing it to come. Wondering what she would tell her parents. Bonnie had known something was wrong; things could never remain hidden where she was concerned. And through the final suffocating week of summer, when high-humidity made Jill feel her head might explode, her sister learnt to be kind.

Jill smiles as she stands in front of an immaculate porcelain sink and pushes her face towards the mirror. Em is right. Her skin has taken on a greenish pallor. Visible through a light tan and a smattering of make-up. There had been no pregnancy attached to her relationship with Andrew Brownstone. For many years after, she thought about what would have happened if she'd been tied to him in that way. How would she have made sense of a life with his child?

She turns the cold tap on, just slightly, and lets cool water run into her hands. With a scoop, she lifts some to her face, pushes it onto her cheeks and holds her hands there for a moment. She needs to regain control.

When she gets back, Em is lounging on a cane-backed sofa. In front of her is a tray laid out with two silver pots and dark blue coffee cups.

'Better?' A tilt of her head. 'I've poured yours. Wasn't sure if you had milk and sugar, so I've left it.' She pats the space next to her. 'Sit.'

Jill does as she's told. Though she's spent half her life doing the opposite. The sensible, obedient Jill of her childhood and adolescence have been buried for many years. In their briny grave. She shakes away the thought.

'My, you're bossy.' Jill laughs. 'If I didn't know better, I'd say you were a teacher.'

But Em isn't listening. She is on a phone-scroll again.

'Look,' she says, holding it up to Jill's face. 'The police are all over this body thing. You know, the one on Walney. Desperate for help from the public, apparently.' A shudder. 'Funny to think we've all been living our lives, with it just... lying there.'

August 1976

On the last day of August, the weather breaks. Heavy grey skies, full of a week's worry and heat, finally split open and down comes the rain. Jill and Stoney watch the storm from the porch of Seaview House. Forked lightning shimmers at the edge of the tide, and the townscape is swallowed up by a heavy purple darkness. When water overruns the guttering above them, Jill steps back into the tiled hallway, shivering slightly. Home is only ten minutes away, but she can't walk there in the downpour.

'Would you mind if I telephone my dad to come and get me,' she asks, though she knows this will prompt the offer of a lift from Stoney's mother.

He shakes his head. 'Nah. No need. The Old Queen will take you later. Besides, I've got plans.' He lifts a hank of her hair and twirls it around his hand, tugging slightly, and moving her towards him.

She tries to shrug him off; he tightens his grip.

'What's up?' His face looms. 'Not being Chilly Jilly again, are you?'

In truth, she is becoming increasingly unsettled by Stoney's demands. How can she gauge the way the relationship is developing? The thing happening between them – she finds it hard to say the word – leaves her with a hollow feeling in her stomach. Stoney's friendship is compelling but has never been easy. There is no one to confide in, though somewhere in her subconscious a quiet voice is urging her to free herself. But how? She pulls her trapped hair out of his grasp, leaving his bunched fist hanging. His arm falls to his side.

'Mum really wanted me home for tea tonight.' She looks down at her wet plimsolls, hugs her arms around herself.

'Oh. How nice. Mumsie wants me home,' he mimics, shoulders jiggling. 'Well, my Mumsie picked up the new Supertramp album after work tonight and I thought you wanted to listen to it.' He closes the door behind them, then leans against it, swinging his face towards her again. 'Don't go all sulky on me, Jilly.' He sticks out his bottom lip and flutters his eyelashes.

She gives a small laugh; he can always make her laugh. 'Stop being an idiot. I don't sulk. You're the one who sulks.'

He lunges towards her, hands taking hold of her waist, fingers moving against her ribs.

'Sulky, am I?' he grins. The fingers dig deeper.

Jill shrieks with laughter as he pushes her into the blue room and down onto the sofa.

She thumps her fists against his chest. 'Get off, you pig. Get off.'

'You think I'm a pig. Okay.' He begins to make snorting noises against her bare stomach, holding her shoulders so she can't escape his heaviness. The snorts move up her body, until his lips are on hers, insistent as always.

She pushes at his shoulders. 'I don't want to,' she whispers, but her words are swallowed up. She tries again. 'No. Stop it. I want to go home.'

His head jerks back, and he looks down at her with cool green eyes. 'But I don't want you to.'

Jill rolls from under him and lands in a heap on the floor.

'Can't always get what you want.' Those words come out before she can stop them, and their effect is toxic.

93

'Well fuck off home then.'

She picks herself up and moves quickly towards the hallway, springing for the front door. Stoney is behind her in an instant, his hand over hers, dragging it away.

'Sorry. Sorry. I didn't mean it. Please, just stay.'

Jill's eyes smart. The sound of the rain, pelting against the front door, makes her want to run outside, to let it wash over her face and hair. She wants her mum. And dad. Her family. But she can't open the door.

'Jilly. Jilly.' Stoney takes her face in his hands. Angry tears spill from her eyes. 'Come on. Let's get a drink. The Old Queen is in her study. She'll make us something to eat.' His large thumbs smudge the tears across her cheeks. Jill stares past him and into the scented gloom of the hallway. Is it possible to love a place, yet feel trapped by it, she wonders?

But it's just a house, it can't hurt you, can it?

She shivers, and lets herself be kissed and soothed, enjoying the attention.

August 2018

Jill kisses Em on both cheeks. Fluffs up her blonde hair. There is a freshness to the woman. Jill hasn't felt fresh since she was fourteen years old, when she would look in the mirror and see a grown-up staring back, a knowing expression, head tilted to hide her neck from family and friends. They would have been fascinated and horrified in equal measure if they'd been able to zoom in on the blue room at Seaview House. Her best friend at the time, Susie Craig, had never been sold on Andrew Brownstone.

That parental influence could loom large enough in your life to dictate your friendships, was something which came between her and Susie, in the end. Now, she has nothing but respect for those parents; they risk their relationships with their children to keep them safe. It's what she does herself. Her son hasn't been allowed the same freedoms she'd had. But the threat isn't over; she must stay vigilant.

'One more week, then back to it,' she says, rolling her eyes. Em matches the look, and giggles. Professional people with years of experience, and they are schoolgirls again. She watches as her friend climbs into her car and opens the window.

'See you soon,' she calls, blowing a kiss from her beautifully manicured hand.

Jill does the same, then turns back to her own life. A dual life in reality, and now another word has been added to the layer of internal deceit; *buried.*

With her keys in the ignition, Jill suddenly stops, looks across at the tall sandstone building and the taller sky. The heat of the afternoon washes white, but there are shadows too. And from a high gable comes the sarcastic screeching of a crow. A pair actually and stirring up the starlings roosting along the roofline. They scatter. One or two head for the treetops but most cling together, a fluid cloud of darting black, safety in numbers.

She decides then: there will be no more of this toxic deceit. When questions are asked of her, she must now be truthful. Truth has two aspects according to her mother; it can be liberating but will always find a way to be told.

The traffic waits as she pulls out from the hotel gates, and Jill joins the easy flow into the town centre. Stevie will still be at work, oblivious to her dilemma. His understanding of her dark moods and need to feel free, has helped her reshape the person she thought she was. But he knows nothing of Seaview House, except its well-loved position in the town's timeline. Soon, he will know everything, she is sure. Perhaps she should confess, tell him the truth about her life before, but how would the story begin? She clicks open the car window, allowing the fast wind to filter in.

Tell Stevie everything? she asks herself. *I can't. I just can't.*

***

August 1976

Later, with the rain still pouring and an early darkness spreading, Annie Brownstone drives Jill home. Despite Stoney's protests for her to stay, his mother had read the situation and responded firmly. He had gone into his bedroom, pleading a headache, leaving Jill embarrassed at accepting the offer of a lift.

Outside Jill's house, they sit together for a moment in the car, watching as the wipers fight bravely against torrents of water.

Annie takes her hand and rubs the back of it gently. 'Don't let our Andy bully you, love,' she says with a whisper. 'He's a big baby really. Used to getting what he wants.'

Jill sees adoration in her eyes. She thinks of her brothers. Of Denny and Ray and little Moz. No excuses are ever made for their bad behaviour. She nods and thanks Annie for the food and the lift, then makes a dash up the garden path, through the splash of puddles, to the front door of her house. There, she turns to wave, Annie now just a silver-and-black blur behind a windscreen of running water.

Her parents are sitting together in the lounge. Bonnie, at her mother's feet, is allowing her sun-bleached hair to be combed through. She is wearing her pyjamas.

'Hi,' Jill calls, smiling at her dad. 'Bet you're glad it's raining, finally.'

He doesn't return the smile. She senses tension. Her mother's eyes stay fixed on Bonnie.

'Where have you been, Jill?' he asks.

'At Stoney's. You knew where I was.' She frowns. Something doesn't feel right.

'We wanted to talk to you. All of you, but we've told the others now.' He rubs both hands across his face and sighs. 'I'm taking a promotion, to assistant chief fire officer. A house comes with it. Over in town.'

Jill stares at him. 'But we've only been here a few months. We haven't even unpacked all the boxes.' She looks at her mother. 'Mum?'

'It means I won't have to work,' she says. 'It was all too much, with the boys and everything.'

Jill's breath catches in her throat. 'But I like it here. I thought you liked it. Right by the beach and everything. I'm not moving.'

She spins round and storms into the kitchen. Lucky is lying on a blanket by the back door. She throws herself down beside him and puts her arms around his neck, allowing herself to weep into his black-and-white fur. Her mother appears at the door.

'Stop it, now,' she says angrily. 'You don't get to rule this family. We cannot afford this house. It's as simple as that. But your dad and I will be glad to get you away from Stoney as well. We are not happy about you living in each other's pockets.'

Jill looks into her mother's face. What is she saying? There has been no mention of Stoney before; they seem to like him. 'Is he the real reason we are moving? That's horrible. You're horrible.'

'Get to your room, madam,' roars her mother. 'Now! I knew the lad was a bad influence on you.' When Jill doesn't move, she continues her rant. 'I said, up to your room. And you can forget about seeing him again. He isn't in charge of you; we are.'

The rise in her mother's voice; Jill recognises it. She responds, getting up and pushing past her into the lounge.

No eye contact from her dad.

'You can't stop me seeing Stoney, wherever we live. We'll bump into each other outside school, anyway,' she hisses, then, slamming the door behind her, stamps up the stairs to her bedroom and throws herself down on her bed. The tears flow, she can do nothing to stop them, but they are not for Stoney. They are for the loss of her parents' trust.

When Bonnie creeps into her bed, much later, Jill is still sitting at the window of the bedroom, watching the rain.

'You all right, sis?' she whispers into the darkness. The bed creaks.

Jill wants to answer, wants to say, yes, she is all right, and thank her for asking. But the words burn her throat, threatening to come out as gasping sobs, so she says nothing. There is a fear in her which words can't define. She feels it deep in her belly and around the base of her neck. Rubbing these areas won't make it go away, so she lies down, fully clothed, and closes her eyes on the world.

Chapter Nine

AUGUST 2018

Along the main road, Jill catches sight of a young couple, hand-in-hand and laughing. She wonders what their story is. They can only be teenagers; he is all legs and hair shaved high up the back of his head; she bounces along in trainers, showing him something on her phone. This is how they discover themselves, and the world. But Jill has mopped up enough young women, in her job, to know how fine the line is between discovery, and something much more dangerous.

By the end of the summer, Andrew Brownstone was already changed in ways beyond anything her fourteen-year-old self could imagine. He'd been missing for the last week of the holidays, away on a trawler with Malcom Gibson. He came back jaded, and with a permanent sneer across his lips: the guy had introduced him to a world full of temptations for boys-becoming-men, and Jill had been the collateral damage. No child could be expected to deal with the emotional instability in Stoney's character, but she became its physical outlet.

In the final few weeks of their relationship, his sexual suggestions became more and more graphic, and her refusal became more and more inflammatory. She understands this, now. Her younger self only wondered why her sense of revulsion far outweighed what she knew would be the result of her constant refusal. These are only words and images. Her character would perhaps be unchanged, had she never met Stoney; there is no way of knowing. But it was not the end of their story.

As she turns into the neat housing estate where she lives, Jill forces herself back into her preferred role, and lets the images of her past dissolve quietly away, leaving an eerily empty place in her racing mind. Phil is standing on the drive, his bicycle upside down, an oily cloth in his hand. He looks up as she pulls in, gives a small wave, then continues rubbing away at one wheel.

Thunk. The car door closes, and she moves in to kiss her son.

'Mother. Don't. I'm all oily.' But he is grinning. He doesn't have a girlfriend. Or boyfriend. If he did, she would be welcoming and grateful, but she would also be vigilant. One whiff of mistreatment and she would be on it. He knows this, has always known her need for fair and respectful treatment.

She smiles at him. 'Still love you, oily or not,' she says with a laugh. 'I'm going to start your tea. Dad will be here soon.'

'What are we having?' he asks, without looking up.

She has to think about this. 'Ham, egg and chips? I've eaten already, so it might as well be yours and Dad's favourite.'

'Nice one,' comes the reply. 'Oh. Forgot to say. Someone came to the door earlier. Looking for you.'

'Who?' A squeeze of her heart.

'Dunno. An old guy.'

'From school? A teacher? Who?'

Phil lifts one shoulder. Drops it again. 'Never gave me his name. Just asked for Jill Holland.'

Who knows her as Jill Holland? An echo. Little Jill Holland.

'Well.' She presses her temples. 'What did he look like?'

'Old. Grey hair. Sort of leathery skin. Sunken face.' He sucks in his cheeks. 'Forgot your name used to be Holland before you married Dad. Told the guy you didn't live here. Sorry.'

Relief.

'Do you think he believed you?'

'Mother. What is this?' Phil stretches his eyes. 'He went off again. Okay?'

'Yeah. Sorry.' But Jill is rattled. Only a few days ago, Seaview was still in its strongbox. And now it is being held in front of her face, in all its forms. Why? Someone has escaped from the box is why.

Stepping inside the house causes a surge of emotion. The clean fabric conditioner smell, the soft-white brightness of the place; it envelopes her as much as a physical hug would. She hates dirt and clutter and darkness. Her home has no dingy corners or hidden dust motes, unlike her life. Seeking them out has been a kind of therapy. Her mother might call her house-proud; Jill knows better.

By the time she has finished cooking, Stevie walks in. She hears the front door close, and the familiar rattle of keys and cameras.

'How was it?' A question she always asks, but this time it is accompanied by her arms around his waist and her head against his chest, inhaling the cedar smell of him.

'It was great. And so is this welcome home.' He leans down and kisses the top of her head. 'Everything all right?'

She steps back and meets his gaze. 'Yep. Nice lunch with Em, but I missed you. She did, too.'

One eyebrow lifts. 'Next time, hey?'

She nods. 'Tea's ready. Your favourite.'

They begin the familiar ritual of a family meal. Trays on their knees, and Jill grabbing chips from Stevie's plate while she listens to stories from his working day. The bride bossed. The groom cried. The registrar was one he hadn't met before, a bit uppity. This is her normal, and she wants to lock it up in a place where the past can't touch it or taint it. Phil bolts his food, as always, and drops the tray noisily onto the kitchen counter.

'Did you tell Dad about the old house. Seaview. Finding the body?' He calls through to them, then she hears a heavy thudding on the stairs followed by the slam of his bedroom door.

Stevie looks up at her. 'What's he talking about?'

She stretches her arms backwards, rolling her shoulders. 'Oh, I don't know. Something he's seen on Facebook. You know what he's like. Reckons the police have dug up a body in the grounds of the old house on the prom.'

Stevie says nothing, and she likes his disinterest. Takes it and runs with it.

'Shall we walk down to The Ruin, after tea?' she asks. 'It's always cool down there. No rush though.'

'Okay.' He fiddles with the television remote control box, attention marching away with the rugby game he has found.

In the kitchen, Jill starts to wash up and tidy. Two uniformed police officers have stood in this kitchen today, shiny with youth, and clutching certificates in *how to be polite*. But neither her son nor her husband knows this. And when Stevie carries through his tray and kisses her again, this time on the bare patch between the neck of her dress and her hair, she closes her eyes, wishing herself away.

'I'll just go and start downloading, and get changed, then we'll go,' he says, and she is glad. Even if she feels the residue of Seaview rising, laying against her skin, he doesn't seem to sense it. It will seep back down eventually.

'No probs.' There is something she needs to do, and it must be now. She marches upstairs.

Phil is lying on his bed, scrolling through his phone.

'Can you help me with something?' she asks. He doesn't look up.

'What?'

'I want to install Facebook. It's about time.'

'Mother. You're so anti. Well, I thought you were.'

She will have to tell another lie. A small one to prevent a bigger one. 'I just want to keep up with the news.'

He swings himself to an upright position. 'Give us your phone,' he holds out his hand. 'I'll need your email address.'

She tells him, then waits.

'And a password. One you won't forget. I know what you're like.'

'Just use my name,' she says. 'And the house number.'

'Very secure,' he laughs. 'I hope it's not what you use for your work accounts.'

It isn't. But she just wants Facebook up and running, so she can find out if Malcom Gibson has a presence. She's tried other platforms and hit a wall. If he is the one who has linked her to Seaview and Stoney, she wants to know about it.

Phil is handing the phone back to her. 'My mother. Queen of Facebook.'

'You're referring to Em,' she laughs, 'not me. See you in a bit.'

Downstairs, she checks her husband is in his office then opens Facebook and types in Malcom Gibson's name. A list appears. None of which seems to be who she is looking for, though she probably wouldn't recognise him now.

'You ready, darling?' Stevie has heard her moving about.

'Whenever you are.' Malcom Gibson will have to wait.

Later, walking in the cool green shade of the great Abbey of Furness, Jill relaxes a little. There is a tranquillity to the place, a sense of lives lived out so only their stories endure. Who will care about what happened to her? These huge slabs of crumbling sandstone will still be standing when her tale has become a small part of the history of this town. Seaview will be gone, and unborn people will weave new stories for their time. But she knows the police will be back.

September 1976

'You've been really quiet this morning.' Susie slips her arm through Jill's as they walk through the gates of the school and out onto the wide street. At least this friendship hasn't changed. Six weeks apart, and they're straight back into their usual ebb and flow.

'I'm starving. Hard to get used to not eating every five minutes like you do when you're off.' A lame excuse, Jill thinks, but Susie laughs.

'I know. We had an ice cream every morning at ten o'clock, when we were in St Ives. But I'm paying for it now. Had to get a skirt with a bigger waist size this time.' She tugs at the side zip of her school skirt. 'But you. You've gone slimmer and altogether more – *Lena Clarke*!'

'Have not.' But the thought brings a slosh of acid to Jill's stomach. 'And I hope it was meant to be a compliment.'

'It was.' Susie gives a playful wiggle. 'I can be like her too. Now, where are we heading?'

Jill chews at her lip, considering the options. The town centre is too far away, and the Co-op at the end of the back path is likely to be crowded out by boys from their school and the Catholic one.

'How about Green's?' she suggests. 'The pies are nice from there. So are the cream buns.'

Susie puts her hand on her stomach. 'Okay. Just this once. But my mum says pies clog your arteries, whatever that means.'

Green's bakery is about half a mile from school, across the main road. The air is damp, the skies heavy with ominous grey cloud. Jill wishes she could take her blazer off. A layer of sticky sweat is forming across her shoulders in the place where thick black fabric meets the collar of her blouse. Susie's hand on her arm is only making her feel hotter.

A large crowd is already gathered outside when they arrive, and no one is queueing. A loud group of grammar boys push and jostle, sending up clouds of cigarette smoke, and some fifth-form girls Jill recognises are leaning nonchalantly against the bakery wall, munching on packets of crisps and swigging from cans of Cresta.

'Jilly,' comes the cry, and Stoney emerges from the middle of the group. He swaggers over, nodding slightly at Susie. She lets Jill's arm drop away and steps back. Stoney slips his hand around the back of Jill's neck and pulls her head towards his, planting a kiss on her forehead.

'Missed ya,' he whispers into her hair.

Blood rushes to her face as the other boys cheer and clap.

'Stoney? Is this your cute little shag?' one calls out. The fifth-form girls stop munching, interested now. They blink at Jill, cocking their heads slightly, waiting to be entertained. With an arm slung casually around Jill's shoulders, Stoney pushes her towards his gang.

'I'm here with my friend,' she says coldly, shrugging him off, but when she turns back to Susie, Jill can't see her. She peers along the street, both ways, but there is no sign.

From the ranks of the fifth-formers, a round-faced girl with long, white-blonde hair shouts out to her.

'I was Stoney's first. Good, in't he.' Some of the other girls almost spit out their crisps.

'Fuck off, Bev,' Stoney retaliates, sending her a dirty look. 'I must have been blind that night.'

Jill is out of her depth. And she wants Susie. But Stoney is pawing at her again. With a force that comes as a surprise, she elbows him in the stomach.

'Don't be awkward,' he mutters, sliding a hand around her waist. 'I haven't seen you for ages.' A wink, over her shoulder at his friends. One steps forward, gangly and dark-haired. He grabs at the top of Stoney's arm.

'Leave her alone,' he snarls, face ugly with rage. 'You're such a fucking pothead, look at you.' Lips twisting, he gives Stoney's arm a hard tug, yanking him away.

'Gonna make me?' Stoney sticks out his chin, then his chest.

'Someone needs to.' An arc of spittle.

'You're a pathetic little wanker, Tillo.' Stoney runs his eyes down to the other boy's feet. Then back up to his face, with a push against the top of his shoulder. 'I wouldn't waste my piss on you.'

The dark-haired boy steps away. 'One of these days, someone's gonna get the better of you. *Stoney.*' The name slides out through the pout of his lips and into the inverted commas of his fingers. Stoney clicks his tongue. The sound makes her shudder.

'Not if I get them first.' A flick of auburn hair and he turns away.

Confusion fills Jill's mind, and she has the urge to run away. But she is Stoney's girlfriend. Isn't she?

A blink at the open door of the bakery shows her Susie, a collection of paper bags in her hands. She locks eyes with Jill and points down the road; her meaning understood in an instant. Leaving Stoney snarling at the other boy, she hurries away with her friend.

'Jilly. Come to Seaview tonight.' His call is followed by more tumbling guffaws and cheers.

I don't think so.

Jill runs to catch up with her friend, and they scramble

quite a way along the road before Susie stops and begins rummaging through the paper bags.

'Please tell me you're not going out with that idiot,' she says. 'I got you cheese and onion. I know you're not keen on meat.' She peers at Jill. 'Well?'

'Thanks. I like cheese and onion.'

'No. I mean him. You're not, are you?'

Jill is lost for words. Seeing Stoney again hasn't made her feel good. His expression has a new hardness: he looks older, tired. There is something unkempt about his appearance too: his collar is up, and the grammar school tie is missing. But how can she walk away from their relationship? His presence looms large in her thoughts and he's there whenever she manages to escape from the girls' school building.

'I kind of am,' she finally says, 'but it's nothing serious.'

Susie frowns. 'I hope it isn't. He's a nutter, as I've told you before.' She bites into her pie, and an oily juice runs down her chin. 'My mum would kill me if she could see me at this moment,' she says with a laugh.

And mine, Jill thinks.

August 2018

Jill stretches out her legs and places both bare feet on her husband's lap. The glorious heat of the day has drained away, leaving behind sharper air, fragranced with lavender and dog rose. It drifts in through the open door. Leaning back against the sofa, she watches as he flicks through the television channels, in search of sporting highlights. They have been the sort of parents who stay at home so their child can fly free, safe in the knowledge there is a secure base where predictability lies. Giving up freedom to become good parents is something she has never found difficult, though she knows it isn't the case for everyone. Her own parents have always been there, and she's tried to copy their example.

'How do you think Phil is, today?' Stevie asks suddenly, swapping the television controller for her feet.

'Okay. Why?'

Stevie shakes his head. 'No reason. Just checking.'

'You've hardly seen him today. Don't start fussing around him again. He's embarrassed enough as it is.'

She understands only too well how the depressed mind can misread concern, twisting it into scorn, or worse.

'I'm not fussing,' Stevie says. 'I care, that's all. He's my lad too, you know.'

'I know.'

He hears her tone and turns. 'What?' he asks, lifting one eyebrow.

Jill smiles at him. 'Nothing. You're trying to be *good-Dad* at the moment, are you?'

A long-standing joke between them – they are, and have always been, either *good-Dad* and *bad-Dad*, or *good-Mum* and *bad-Mum*, depending on the mood Phil is in.

'Yep. So, you must be bad-Mum.'

It is the last thing Jill wants to be. If she's done anything worthwhile with her life, it has been her parenting. Criticism of it always resulted in an explosion of her anger, rarely seen, warning the critic to leave well alone. How they will enjoy it when her long-buried secrets come out. There cannot be police at the door and strangers asking after her, without someone noticing.

She thinks of Stevie coming face-to-face with PC Rose Atherton, picking at the scabs of her past, and her stomach heaves as though she's fallen from a great height.

She jumps up from the sofa.

'Let's have an early night.' Her voice is trembling. She

coughs, as cover. When Stevie grins furtively, she adds, 'I've got the new Belinda Bauer waiting for me.'

'Shame you haven't got a new husband waiting for you, too.'

'Ha.' But as she turns away, he takes hold of her arm. Pulls her towards him.

'Something's wrong, isn't it? I know you.'

She shakes her head, leaning into him for a moment. 'I'm fine,' she breathes. How can she tell him he doesn't know her at all? 'Always sad at the end of the holidays, aren't I?'

He rests his chin on the top of her head, and she soaks up his warmth.

'It's more than that. If it's about school, just let me know, and I won't push anymore.' This is what he always says when she's preoccupied with her job. Though she often uses him as a sounding board.

'*Honestly*, there's nothing wrong. But give me a few days of being back at work, then there will be plenty.'

She hates herself for using the word; there is nothing honest about her. For one terrifying second, her brain starts to form some sentences, to tell Stevie what he wants to know. Then her mouth bites down on them. And they scurry away, back into their grey, jelly-like strongbox.

'Okay. Well, if you're sure. Let's go up.'

He turns away, and her thoughts tumble again. Back to a silvery-blue sea and white-hot sky. She and Stevie move around each other, pulling out plugs and locking doors. But the house won't settle.

'You go up,' Jill murmurs. 'I'm just going to stand on the doorstep for a minute. I need some air.'

Stevie frowns, knows better than to keep chewing over his concerns. 'See you in a bit,' he says, then takes himself upstairs.

There is a simple Yale lock on the front door. It clicks

quietly behind her as she lets herself out. The air has a soft quality: it has won the fight with the heat of the day and is kicking back, relaxing. She walks down the drive, squeezing herself past Stevie's Land Rover. The sky is cast with evening-summer blue and there is only the thinnest hint of a moon. Everywhere is quiet. The neighbouring houses are in darkness. Not one yellow window. Not one flare of violet television light.

But someone is standing on the opposite pavement. Just in front of her neighbour's thick beech hedge. Jill's heart squeezes, forcing her body into high alert. She squints into the darkness. It's hard to tell if this is a man or woman, young or old. It's just a dark shape. And it's moving away. She watches, wondering whether to call Stevie. What would she say? Someone's been standing opposite our house, but they've gone now. He'd really be on her case then. The figure fades into the shadowy area between street lamps. Jill waits. Then a pool of weak silver light shows her a man. And he is hurrying away.

She darts back down the drive and stops on her porch. The man has gone. Her heart is thudding against her ribs. What is happening? This isn't the life she normally lives, standing in the street, jumping at shadows. But her reality suddenly feels fragile. A house built on sand, as her mother would say.

And who the hell is trying to topple it?

Lying in bed, much later, she listens to her husband's delicate snores and the creaking of her son's wooden bed, and she wonders if they will have to learn to cope without her. Then there is Malcom Gibson; he has no digital presence as far as she can tell. Perhaps he still lives quietly over on Walney Island. She needs to know, needs to find him. But what would she ask?

How do you even remember me?
Did you tell the police I knew Andrew Brownstone?
Why would you?

Mick drags himself up from her memory, hard-eyed and

aware. He'd want to know why she was asking. And the thought terrifies her.

September 1976

Jill stares across the water as she walks. Though the houses on the other side are wrapped in a grey twilight, the sky is still holding the last fading promise of summer. The salt breeze has a playful bite to it, forcing her out of lightweight clothing and into an anorak. Taking it out of the cupboard feels like the end of something. This is the first time she's been allowed to visit Seaview, since returning to school, and it will be one of her last island walks. The thought has been creeping its way around her brain, leaving a darkness in its wake she can't shake off. It frightens her; she isn't sleeping well. With a shiver, she pulls her zip up as high as it will go. It catches the stray ends of her hair.

At the gates of Seaview, she stands for a moment, looking up at the garden. Annie's garden. Yellow hands of horse chestnut leaves are spread across the lawn, and clumps of black-eyed rudbeckia blaze in the borders. Nobody would ever guess what the gardens are like at the back. It's the confusion of the place, and thinking about it makes Jill's stomach coil in on itself. Avoiding Stoney at school is also confusing. She hardly knows him anymore, so why is she even here? There are no answers, but her legs tremble at the thought of being turned away.

On the porch, she runs her hands over the stone gargoyles, and reaches out for the black door knocker. There is still time to go home, to walk back down those steps and away from a relationship which is at best deceitful, and at worst, dangerous.

As it turns out, there is no need for worry. Annie answers

the door and throws her arms around Jill, holding on to her more than her son has ever done.

'Jill,' she breathes into her hair, 'you are so welcome. There is bad news, sadly.' She steps back, keeping hold of Jill's shoulders. Annie's face is raw and shiny. Behind her stands Stoney's father, eyes narrowed to the ground.

'Nan has died,' he says simply. Jill has hardly ever heard his voice. Now, it sounds flat and hard. 'It might not be the best time for you to be here.'

'Oh. I'm sorry,' she stammers, and steps back onto the porch.

'She was very elderly, my dear, no need to be sorry.' Annie reaches for her arm. 'Ignore Mr Brownstone.' A gentle tug brings Jill back into the hallway again. Her head is spinning. Is she wanted, or not?

Stoney's father holds his ground, muttering something Jill can't quite hear. Something about a purse.

Annie turns to face him, pushing Jill behind her. 'Don't start again, Richard. Not now.' And he is brushed aside, while Annie leads the way to the back of the house, opening the door to the kitchen and ushering her in. Stoney is sitting in the fireside chair, his grandma's favourite; Mac is at his feet, growling and staring in the direction of her footsteps. As she walks towards him, Stoney twists his lips into a sneer.

'You've remembered who I am then?' he snarls, his expression wretched. 'Thought I'd been dumped.'

Jill steps towards him, reaching out a hand. 'Sorry about your nan.' It is all she can think of to say.

He snorts lightly. Slaps her hand away. 'Have you told her, Mumsie dear?' And to Jill, 'I'm supposed to have pinched money from Nana's purse.' A flick of his head. 'Then she dies.'

Annie rounds on him. 'Don't be like that, son,' she wheedles. 'Nobody's blaming you.'

'What the fuck are you talking about, Mother? *He's*

blaming me.' A nod towards the open doorway where Reverend Brownstone waits, rubbing his hands together, a stiff smile on his lips.

'This is a family matter, Andrew,' he says. 'And we have guests, in case you hadn't noticed.'

Annie takes her chance. 'Well, I've noticed. Shall I make us all a cup of tea? Jill?'

Stoney interrupts, getting up from the chair. 'Nah. No tea for us.' He grabs Jill's hand. 'We've got business to attend to.' Though she pulls back, his hold is strong, dragging her past both adults and out of the room.

'Get off me,' she cries, trying to free herself.

'Andy.' Annie shouts after her son, but he slams the door of the blue room behind him.

Jill is pushed onto the navy-blue sofa, her senses jarring at the lemon freshness of the room.

'Where have you been?' Stoney glowers down at her. 'I've been waiting all week.'

Jill takes some deep breaths. 'Waiting for me,' she growls, 'or waiting for sex?'

'What are you saying? Who've you been talking to?' He falls to his knees in front of her. 'I love you, Jilly.' He winds a hand through her hair.

'Don't.' A whisper.

'Don't what? Don't kiss you?' Then his lips are on hers. She tries to move her head away.

He bites down. 'You know you want to.'

And in a way, she does. It gives her a sense of control, a sense of being wanted and needed by another human being. She accepts the rough kisses and gives him the handfuls of her body he is already grabbing. When her skirt is raised and her knickers removed, she doesn't try to stop him, and as always, when it is over, and *love* is mentioned again, she looks at his lips, and wonders.

A knock on the door startles them both. Annie.

'I've brought tea,' comes the muffled call.

Stoney jumps up and rearranges his clothing. 'Hold up, Mother,' he calls. Jill gets dressed quickly and smooths down her hair. She catches a glimpse of Annie's face as he takes the tray from her hands, though the door is slammed back at her immediately.

'Stupid cow,' he mutters.

Jill frowns. 'Don't be so nasty. She's trying to be kind.'

'Oh, here we go again. Jilly's telling everyone what to do. I can't stand the old bat.' He puts the tray down on the hearth. 'You gonna have a go about the purse, too?'

'I don't know anything about it, so I can't, can I?'

But Jill wants to know. So, she waits.

Suddenly, Stoney kicks the mugs from the tray and sends them flying against the wall at the side of the fireplace. Steaming brown tea begins dripping onto the carpet.

'I borrowed a tenner. Out of Nan's purse. But The Old Geezer caught me. Took a swing at me.' His eyes glitter. 'Nana witnessed it all. Fucking crying and everything, she was.'

'Could you not have asked your mum. If you wanted money, I mean?' Jill has no idea what she is saying. She just wants to get away. Something about him seems different. Like all his edges have become jagged.

'I was going to ask. But no one gave me the chance. You believe me, don't you. Jilly?'

A shrug of her shoulders is all it takes. Three steps bring him across the room, and he hits her across the side of her temple. For a moment, Jill can do nothing. Small pinpricks of light spin in front of her, glinting in the blue-grey darkness, and she thinks she might vomit. When she can stand up, she moves towards the door, but Stoney is quicker, blocking and grabbing at her.

'Sorry. I'm sorry. Jilly. Sorry.' He begins to sob. Clinging to her waist, he falls to his knees and lays his head against her stomach, nuzzling and panting. She feels sick.

'Let go of me. I want to go home,' she says coldly. He doesn't move. 'I'll call your mum if you don't.' No matter how hard she pushes him back, she can gain no ground.

He lifts his face to look at her. 'Don't. Please don't. I won't do it again. I'm not right at the moment.'

Jill's thoughts are racing. She's been given a crack across the side of the head. This can't be right, can it? But his nana has just died. Is it a good excuse? The thing between them, like gorging on a favourite meal only to find it makes you ill, is crumbling her insides. And who can she tell? Deciding she is on her own with this, she tries again to get free.

'I am going home.' Pushing against his shoulders causes him to lose his balance and he falls away from her and the door. Her hand is on the handle when he speaks again, a chill in his tone.

'I'll kill myself if you go. I will.'

A moment's hesitation, then she spins round to face him. 'What are you talking about?' Fingers on her temples. 'It's pathetic.'

'I will. Watch.' With a snatching grasp, he lifts the big brass carriage clock from the mantel above the fire and begins to smash it against his own head. Hearing the first sickening thud, makes Jill react instantly. Dragging the clock from his hands, she throws it onto a fireside chair and grabs his wrists with all the force she can muster. If Annie Brownstone hears anything, she certainly doesn't arrive. For a moment, the room is silent. The door stays closed. Stoney begins to cry again, and above all her fear and frustration, Jill feels a wave of sympathy.

She leads him back to the sofa and slumps down with him, letting him cry into her shoulder. This room, this house, has somehow become her captor. If there is a way out of the situation without hurting anyone, she would take it gladly, but the weight of Stoney's angst and fear weigh heavily. She allows her own tears to flow then, wishing someone strong and safe would come along and take the situation out of her hands.

Stoney recovers very quickly. Within ten minutes, the sobs have ceased, and his hand is running up her bare leg, under her skirt.

This can't happen again.

She darts up and away from him, opening the blue room door and making as much noise as she can. Annie Brownstone is out of the kitchen in an instant, moving towards Jill in the darkness. She hears a click, then harsh white light smashes across the tension.

'I'm off home now, Mrs Brownstone.' An anxious smile stretches her lips. 'Sorry again about your mum.'

Annie darts a look over Jill's shoulder, towards her son. 'I hope you're going to walk her home.' She moves forward, holding her arms out. 'You take care of yourself, love,' she whispers, snatching Jill into an embrace, 'and I'll see you soon.'

Outside, the early gold of evening has drained away, leaving the surface of the tide black and spattered with trapped light. The air tastes of seaweed and woodsmoke, and a sadness wells up in Jill. This is her place, and she wants to stay. With Stoney? She isn't so sure.

Together, they make their way through Seaview's garden, and out onto the promenade.

'I'm going to see Mick, once you've got home,' Stoney is saying. 'He's got some… stuff… for me.' The tone of his voice jars, like the last hour hadn't happened.

'Oh?' Jill yawns herself into showing an interest. 'Does he live near me, then?'

He nods. 'Yep. He has his own place. Liness Barn.'

'How does that work?'

'His folks are dead, I think. Something happened to them a couple of years ago. It was their place but it's his now. He does what he likes. Wish I could. I'm sick of living with The fucking Olds.'

Jill huddles down in her anorak and turns away from him. She will never be sick of living with her family. They mean everything; Stoney seems to be constantly complaining about his.

'I like your mum,' she says, more to herself, 'and your place is beautiful. So's the island. I'll miss it.'

He throws an arm round her shoulder and pulls her to him.

'And I'll miss you when you go,' he says softly.

Chapter Ten

SEPTEMBER 2018

There is a darkness in the sky, and the first heavy raindrops after the spell of mellow weather, send a chalky sadness up from the ground.

Jill has a day of admin and personnel issues to deal with, and a *he-said-she-said* between two of her staff, even before the children have set foot in school for the new term. Any distraction feels welcome.

The drive to work is unhurried. Rush hour is over and the roads are quiet. By Wednesday, she will be joining the eight o'clock gang, heading to the local factories and to the aeronautical firm where thousands of the townsfolk work. Buses will be crammed with school children, shouldering their way into adulthood, simmering with confidence in their superior knowledge. Had she been the same? But she won't think about it now. Another issue presses down on her. She should go to the police station, tell them everything she knows about Andrew Brownstone. But dare she? How will her own story end if she does?

At the entrance to her school, she hesitates for a moment, then zooms past. She will visit Seaview, needs to visit Seaview;

the place is trickling out its story and she has to know what she's dealing with.

There is the secret way in. The one created by Stoney when he had been thrust from the house. Then she will see. See the truth in these stories of buried bodies and the like. But the core of her says there was no burial; there was something different.

The bridge draws her in, as it always does, and then she is on the island again. The grey of the sky obscures everything, widening the horizon and tilting her perspective. Rain saturates her windscreen, even with the wipers pelting across. A lone pedestrian, a woman, stands at the traffic lights as Jill stops. There is the hunch of yellow raincoat and wellies, and a hand lifted in thanks.

A memory flashes up: a day of torrential rain and running, of swishing tyres and soaking feet.

This time, Jill doesn't swing the car onto the promenade, continuing instead up the wide hill leading to the west shore, though it isn't where she intends to go. When she can park, she pulls in and switches off the engine. There is nothing illegal about what she is doing, but the sense of it sits on her shoulder, whispering a warning. Down some steps and across the small public park is a patch of woodland. It backs directly onto the overgrown rear garden of Seaview House.

October 1976

The trust is back. There were no fireworks, no blazing in like a comet, but each small action created a spark: good grades in her homework; taking Ray, Denny and Moz to play in the fields behind the new house; shrugging off questions about

Stoney, and eventually the fire has caught. And now Jill is being allowed to stay home while the family go on a day trip.

'Good girl. Take Lucky for a walk in between studying, won't you.' A grin from her dad. 'I've left a couple of quid by the telephone if you want to get yourself some chips later.'

She watches, waving until the car disappears around the corner at the end of the street.

October has been full of cold, brilliant sunshine, perfect for exploring the area and carving out some new places for her and Lucky to walk. But nothing feels the same.

She lets her thoughts drift. To the island, to Seaview. There is no easy way of visiting now. Bus pass cards don't count during weekends and walking both ways can take more than an hour. On the day she sneaked across after school, she'd felt like an outsider, watching the local folk with their sailing craft and fishing rods, all windswept hair and hard eyes focused on her. And Stoney had been distracted anyway. He'd muttered about his father and exams, then turned on Annie with an explosive force, in response to some small thing.

Lucky follows Jill back into the house, sitting by her feet while she empties her school bag onto the kitchen table. He nudges at her legs, whining and making small wet sneezes. Even a walk doesn't calm him, and in the end, she sends him to his basket in the dining room, closing the door to keep him there.

With everyone gone, an uncomfortable silence creeps through the house. It eventually finds its way into Jill's head. Thoughts of Stoney come to fill the emptiness. Is he at home, waiting for her? Though he is just as likely to be out with Mick. Either way, without the distraction of her family, the image won't allow itself to be buried.

Her mother's bicycle is in the shed. She could be at Seaview within twenty minutes. An hour with him, a short cycle back, she tells herself, then she can finish her work. Her mother will never know.

She looks at herself in the hall mirror. Saturday clothes and damply flat hair from her walk with Lucky. A cycle ride in the rain won't add anything. The island doesn't care what she looks like. Maybe she won't even go to Seaview, just splash along the prom and pretend.

She locks the front and back doors, then zips the keys into her jeans pocket. The bike is the easy part. She can do that.

September 2018

With her anorak on, and the hood zipped tightly, Jill locks the car and hurries through the park and into the woods. The rain continues to fall, drops splattering against the overhead foliage.

The place is deserted. There is not even a hardened dog-walker. Her trainers slip on the sun-baked mud, now slimy with water. She follows a path lined with broad dock leaves and twisted arcs of brambles. Up ahead she can see the tall wooden garden fence of Seaview. It is green with algae and the rot of years. But still impenetrable. There used to be a place where the planking came loose. It is almost thirty years since she first knew this fact, something may have changed.

Not a sound comes from the other side of the fence. Surely there would be voices if police were investigating somewhere nearby. She finds the plank is still moveable. It has been nailed at some point, but she can lift it backwards enough to peer into the garden.

Her heart leaps in her throat.

A white gazebo has been thrown up in the middle of a jungle of lawn. Police tape surrounds it, giving a two-metre clearance. A figure, dressed from head-to-toe in high-vis waterproofs is standing just shy of the tent itself. Jill jumps backwards, letting the plank fall back into its place. Somebody has found something of significance buried in the garden of Seaview.

She leans back against the fence and steadies herself with a breathing drill. Is there a logical explanation for what she is seeing? Could it just be a coincidence? She wipes the rain from her face. Nothing makes sense. Adrenaline is creating a creeping numbness in her brain. She can't think straight; it's making her want to run.

She does run.

Back through the dense shadows of the woodland, out across the park and along the tarmac to her car. Panting gasps of breath shoot from her mouth, and her heart is trying to escape from her chest. She doesn't believe in coincidence.

October 1976

Traffic crawls along the wet roads, and the town centre is full of people in brightly coloured rain macs, heads down and hurrying; twice Jill must pull hard on her brakes so as not to run into anyone. By the time she reaches the bridge, the rain has pushed its way through her hood, cold and sharp and clinging to her neck. She bumps the bike onto the walkway and stops to look at the view.

Heavy grey clouds obscure most of the estuary, the tide high and a dirty green. But the smell speaks to her, of freedom and herself. With her chin on her wet hands, she watches a pair of black-headed gulls playing chase. Stoney and the island. They are bound tightly together in her heart. But which one does she really want? Perhaps she should just go home again, be the one who walks away, though it feels too cruel.

A car horn sounds behind her: headlights, and a white Wartburg. Annie Brownstone, spikey-silver hair and dark lipstick, her husband next to her at the wheel, faceless as ever.

'Our Andy's at home, Jill, love,' she calls. 'He's been missing you.' A khaki-clad arm flashes through the window, then the traffic lights change, and the car moves away with a swish of wet tyres. Decision made. But she will push the bike along the promenade for a few more minutes, allow herself to be an island girl again, and then she'll go to Seaview.

When she reaches the gates of the house, Jill lifts the bike and tucks it away behind a laurel hedge running the length of the front wall. Seaview is in darkness; perhaps Stoney isn't in after all. Forcing herself forward, she takes the stone steps two at a time. They are slippery, covered in a mush of decaying leaves and water droplets. She pulls down her hood and tries to tidy the wet strands of hair sticking to her face. On the porch, she turns. Her favourite view, dark silver now, against the glitter of the townscape. There is still time to walk away. Back down those steps for good. But she doesn't. She pulls on the black doorknocker and she waits. Finally, the door opens, and Seaview's cinnamon-sweet smell filters out.

'Oh. Jilly.' Stoney. Peering at her. The door is pulled back, the hallway dark. 'Come in.' He wears a pair of denim shorts and a Led Zeppelin T-shirt. His feet are bare.

She steps in, but he disappears into the gloom, then the backdoor latch clicks shut. Rain drips from the bottom of her anorak, and she isn't quite sure what to do next. Puddles of water are forming around her feet, soaking the floor tiles. She tries to thin them out with the toe of her plimsoll, but they just expand. She unzips, then reaches for the front door again, intending to lay the anorak on the porch to drip. Stoney emerges from the kitchen.

'Where you going?' He glowers down the hallway, thin voice echoing.

'Just putting my jacket outside. It's dripping all over your floor.'

He steps towards her and takes it from her hands. 'Sorry. I'm being an idiot. I'll hang it in the kitchen to dry.'

Something feels wrong. Why is he sitting in the dark? She thinks about Annie Brownstone's words. *He's been missing you.* It doesn't seem likely.

It isn't long before Stoney re-emerges from the kitchen, but to Jill, those moments stretch out forever.

'Come through here.' His voice trails off as he opens the door to the blue room. Jill follows, her hand searching for the light switch.

'No,' he shouts, then quieter, 'don't switch it on. I've got a migraine, thanks to The Old Queen.'

He presses some buttons on the stereo system, while Jill stands awkwardly.

'Sit down, for Christ's sake,' he mutters, grabbing her arm and pulling her onto the sofa with him.

Electronic orchestral music starts up, clanging, repetitively drilling. Stoney lets out a long sigh. Jill can hardly see his face in the grey light of the room, and she moves away from the sweet woody scent of his breath.

'Yeah. Fucking Old Queen. Wants me to apply for a trade in the shipyard, instead of staying on in sixth form. Says I'm not working hard enough.'

'Are you? Revising and stuff?'

'Whether I am or I'm not,' he snaps, 'there's no chance of me going into the yard as a grunt. It'd be boring as hell. And I'm not going to help build fucking nuclear subs, am I?' He snatches at Jill's hand and kisses the palm. 'But I'm glad you're here now.' A pause. 'Jilly.'

She looks down at the outline of his head, tries to resist the usual pawing and grabbing; they need to talk. But his lips are travelling up her arm, leaving a tingling sensation in their wake. He's asked her nothing about herself. She is wet, she is cold, but nothing. She scouts around for easy topics of conversation.

'It's pouring out there. I've just seen your parents on the bridge. Are they okay? With your nan dying and everything?'

'Fuck's sake,' Stoney mutters, rubbing his temples. 'Yes. They're okay. But I'm not.'

'Why don't you tell me about it?' she murmurs, reaching out to touch the side of his face.

'I don't want to talk.' Her hand is slapped away. 'And anyway, I'm sick of you refusing all the time.'

'Refusing? You've hardly seen me.' Jill shakes her head. 'I've just cycled through the rain. Aren't you bothered?' She leans backwards, off her knees, and tries to stand up. Then he is pulling her back down on the sofa and snaking his hand up her jumper. Something flickers across her consciousness, and she almost gives in. But there is an anger in her too.

'Stop it. I don't want to,' she whispers into the confusing darkness of the room. 'Can't we just talk?'

He does move away, and Jill relaxes for a second, sliding herself into a sitting position next to him. Then she feels his arm swing across her body, and he punches backwards, hitting her hard in the stomach.

She hears him say, 'Fuck off. I don't wanna talk,' then he flings himself onto the floor in front of the stereo. The blow has been enough to knock the wind from her, but she jumps up and dives for the door. And this time, she isn't being cajoled back.

She yanks open the front door and runs out into the rain. Stoney is behind her instantly.

'Jilly. Jilly, don't be like that. Come back inside.'

Like she is a child who needs to be soothed.

I don't think so.

She is down the steps in seconds. Stoney charges after her,

feet bare and shouting. With one glance back, she jumps on the bike and cycles as hard as she can away from him. He calls her name. Cries out. Begs. She looks over her shoulder again. There he is. Running through the rain, bare feet slapping against the pavement, features melting with the distance. But she cycles away.

On the bridge, Jill thinks about home. Lucky will be there, waiting. She's left her coat behind, but she has her keys, and her self-respect. There will be fallout, but as the rain streams down her face, freedom flashes through her, and she smiles.

She pedals hard; Stoney isn't following, but she dare not relax. There is still pain in her stomach where he punched her, but it spurs her on. Her jumper is saturated, and spray from the road has forced its way into her plimsolls.

Finally, she reaches the end of her road, and the new house comes into view. Abandoning the bike on the driveway, she lets herself in, then turns the key again for safety. Water drips from her hair, her clothes, her feet. Lucky is whining, trapped in the dining room. Set free, he barks joyfully and jumps at her, putting his paws against her thighs. Jill begins to cry then. Huge, gasping sobs. She sits down with him on the kitchen floor and buries her face in the warm fur on the back of his neck. He nuzzles softly at her hands.

'I've done it,' she weeps. The dog licks her face, and she hugs him even harder.

September 2018

The memory of that day at Seaview – the rain, the creeping darkness, the stomach punch – has stayed, vivid and jangling, in Jill's memory. It has never been spoken, but throughout her career, she has fought against physical and coercive control. It hasn't always won her friends, but it has been a necessity. A silent pact with herself; an atonement.

She starts up the car and tries to align her breathing with the swipe of the windscreen wipers. It is ridiculous, the way she can't stop herself from digging around in the past.

She thinks about Malcom Gibson again. Maybe she should telephone PC Rose Atherton and tell her everything she knows. But what does she know? The only certainty is the *punch* didn't signal the end of her relationship with Andrew Brownstone.

Jill closes her office door and rests her forehead against its glass panel. Coming back to work, after what she has just seen in Seaview's garden, has taken some doing. What she really wants is to go back home and lock herself out of sight. Then take a knife and strip away all she knows. But she won't do this. She will carry on in her role of wife and mother and headteacher. Roles hard-won and nothing whatsoever to do with Jill Holland.

Jill has never been much of a gardener. She's always hated the feel of soil beneath her fingernails, but she never did understand why Annie Brownstone hadn't given the back garden at Seaview the same attention as the front. This one had been groomed and clipped, with striped lawns and artful froths of sea holly and corncockles. Nothing like the wasteland at the back.

Annie herself had been full of contradictions: a good mother with a rebelling son, kind but incredibly short-sighted when it came to what was going on behind the closed doors of her own house.

How had Annie Brownstone never noticed her son was having sex just a few feet away? She remembers liking the woman, admiring her, in fact. Now, she realises how damaging the glorification of her son had been.

On Jill's desk is a swathe of Post-it notes and a neat pile of letters. Each one will demand something from Jill Francis. None will be interested in the level of anxiety she is feeling, right now; they will only want their demands met. And that feels comforting. It feels like a fresh breeze on a hot day, sharp seawater on swollen feet.

There is a knock on the door. It opens, and in walks her head of history, Joe Lewis, with his curly blond hair and shiny face.

'Have you got a minute? Now, I mean?'

A tilt of his head tells Jill he's trying to look tame and reasonable. She's heard different.

'Course. I asked you to come, remember.'

He steps into the room and pushes the door closed, leaning himself against it.

'Sit down. Please.' Jill points to the chair on the other side of her desk. Can't quite believe she's the one in charge.

Joe shuffles across the carpet and sits himself down, dimpling his cheeks at her. She's not convinced.

'Have you had a good holiday?' he says. 'Go anywhere nice?'

'It was just good to be at home. Especially after the summer term.' There had been an OFSTED inspection, and not one they wanted to relive, other than to smile wanly and say they'd passed. 'What did you get up to?'

He flinches, then realises she's referring to the holidays. 'Oh. I went to Dubrovnik, actually. It was beautiful.'

'Sounds good.' She pauses. 'Did you want to wait until Kieran gets here? Before we formalise things? I could make you a coffee or something.'

'No. It's fine. I'm not really sure what Kieran's problem is, actually. We've always got on so well.'

He says this in a tone which tells Jill exactly what she wants to know. Jealousy is at the root of this issue. And lies. Joe believes in preserving dignity and peace by keeping things hidden. Kieran likes to know where he stands, always. These feelings have infiltrated their work to such an extent, they've stopped speaking to each other. And now Jill must help them find a way through. Ironic, she thinks. Because while she can sympathise with both points of view, she understands exactly what Joe is doing.

'From what I can gather, Kieran felt left out when everyone else knew why you had those few days off at the end of term. Except him.'

There is a long exhale from Joe, then he lays his hands flat in front of him, on the desk. 'I didn't want him to worry. If other people found out,' he shrugs, 'what could I do about it?'

Jill must choose the right words. 'So, you didn't tell him because you care about him?'

Joe's face burns red. The shine is exaggerated. 'Guess so.'

'Have you told him this?'

'No. I couldn't.' His hand moves to the top of his chest. 'No.'

'Then you'll just have to keep lying to him. But lies burn you up in the end, don't they?' *Listen to the expert*, she thinks. 'The fact he's bothered about your lie should tell you something, Joe.'

'Like what?'

'I'd say he cares about you, too.'

A snort. 'He called me sneaky, in front of the whole department. I wouldn't say that was caring, Jill. Would you?'

How old are these people? Jill thinks. But she knows exactly how old they are. They are mature adults, trying to grapple with unpredictable feelings, and they can't get it right. What hope did she have, at the age of fourteen? She tries to shake away the thought. Andrew Brownstone is well and truly out of his box now and painting a salty layer over aspects of her life.

The door opens again, and another man walks in.

'Well,' she whispers to Joe. 'If you don't tell him, I will.'

They both watch as Kieran saunters across the room, wearing trousers which emphasise how slim he is, and a neatly trimmed beard.

'Hi, all.' He tilts his hips towards Joe. 'Okay?'

'Thought you weren't coming.' A glower from Joe, better suited to one of his pupils.

'I've been having a coffee in the staffroom. Chatting. I do have other friends, you know.'

Jill clears her throat and shifts on her chair. 'Let's not,' she says, but Kieran is leaning across the desk towards her in a way that says she's about to be dragged into a conspiracy.

'I must tell you,' he says, one hand hiding his mouth.

Joe growls loudly, but Kieran won't be silenced.

'I guess you've been following the story. You know. About the old vicarage on Walney, and the body? It's breaking Facebook, as they say.'

This isn't what Jill wants to hear. That the story is being dragged around the town and picked over is bad enough, never mind her staff gnawing on its bones.

Joe is listening now. 'Gruesome, isn't it,' he says. 'Why? What else has happened?'

'Well.' Kieran takes a dramatic breath. 'It's a guy, apparently. The body is a guy.'

Jill steadies herself with some deep breathing. Of course the body is male. Had she expected anything different?

'Jill?' Kieran is peering at her, head tilted, eyebrows meeting. 'Are you okay?'

She gives him a small nod of her head. But she is far from okay. And what she's wondering is exactly where the body will be now.

Part II

Chapter Eleven

SEPTEMBER 2018

J ill once loved the island. Though she often runs along its wide promenade, shoulder-to-shoulder with Seaview House, she hasn't walked its beaches for many years. Especially not the pink-and-blue shingle beach she had thought of as her own. There's something about shifting sand that puts her on high alert; she needs solid surfaces in her life.

Today, she is heading to her workplace again. Stevie is taking a young couple for a pre-wedding shoot. This is all the rage, now. Show the world how happy you are, via a clutch of photographs in an iconic place. But photographs can be deceiving.

The first four years of her teaching career were spent, day after long day, on the island, at a comprehensive school still standing on the West Shore. It has been rebranded since then, but Jill's memories haven't. She remembers her friend Susie Craig's mammoth efforts to get her enrolled onto the school's teaching programme, and then her own need to prove herself, resulting in a fast-track up the management ladder and a headship shortly afterwards.

She was off the island again by 1988, and it felt like such a relief. It was the year she visited Seaview for what she thought would be the last time. But she won't think about it now; images from then should stay buried, or she won't cope. Shaking her head, as though the memory can somehow be dissolved by one small action, she drives towards her school, her sanctuary.

The site manager's van is in the car park, along with a few other vehicles. The lights are on, the windows are open. She parks her car and steps out into the morning sunshine. There are bags to carry in, but they can wait. More important to get herself seen, let her staff know she is around and available.

It is eerily quiet as Jill walks towards the building. She strains to hear the sound of hoovers or banter, but there is nothing. It must be coffee time, she thinks, so perhaps she will get half an hour to herself. At the front door, she pauses and turns to look across the beguiling expanse of the playing fields. Someone is standing next to a distant gate. One used by the children, one which should be locked.

From this far away, it's difficult to tell on which side of the gate the person is standing. Perhaps they're on the pavement and simply waiting for someone, scrolling through their phone, even. But she'll need to go and check. There's a path leading up to the gate. She glances at her shoes, then decides to take them off. Walking so far will hurt otherwise.

In truth, she could easily let the site manager go down and check: there are no children on the premises today, so no one is at risk. With her shoes in one hand, she steps carefully along the path, enjoying the feeling of clean tarmac under her feet.

It isn't long before the figure starts to come into focus, and she can see he's on the other side of the gate. It's a man. He's dressed in blue: jeans and some kind of anorak. She can't tell if he's looking at her, but suddenly, he moves away again, hurrying away down the road in front of the school. He has the same loping walk as the man she saw outside her house just a few days ago. The tiny flash of action in the stillness of the morning sets her heart jumping, then she chides herself for being so stupid. This is an urban area, of course there will be people going about their business. She needs to get control. Her staff are waiting.

Once she's back at the front doors of the building, she slips on her shoes again, takes a few deep breaths then pushes her way inside. From the reception area, a wide staircase leads up to her office and the staff common rooms. There is the faint aroma of coffee, and she smiles; how well she knows the way her people work.

As she stands behind the closed staffroom door for a moment, she listens. There is laughter, low voices, she can put faces to all of it.

'Hello,' she beams, pushing open the door. 'Happy new term, if I haven't seen you already.'

She is instantly bombarded with questions.

'Good holiday?'

'Did you hear about Vic and Mary Lyons?'

'When are the painters coming?'

The site manager steps in. 'Leave her alone,' she says, a gravelly voice from years of cigarette smoking. 'Sorry, Mrs Francis.'

Jill smiles. There is always the formality. 'Don't worry about it, Sandra,' she says lightly, 'just lead me to the coffee.' Together, they catch up on the happenings since their last meeting, plotting how the year will pan out.

One of the senior staff, a tall wiry lady named Carol, hands Jill a cup of coffee. She accepts it gratefully, then casts across the two low tables at the side of the room, searching for biscuits. A copy of *The Gazette* lies there, unopened, by the smooth look of it. Carol follows her gaze.

'Got some shortbread in the cupboard, if you'd like one,'

she says, picking up the newspaper. 'Bad business. Did you see?'

Jill feels her pulse in her throat. Why is she so jittery, today? 'The story about Seaview House? Yes, I did see.'

Carol shakes out the paper. 'This is the guy, they reckon, the one who's buried there.'

She folds the paper, presenting the front-page photograph. The last thing Jill wants to see. She knows already it will be Stoney. Andrew Brownstone. And there he is, peering out at her. It is an old photograph. His hair is long still, but he has the hacked-off fringe. She wonders who would have given out the photo: school or college perhaps. There were no relatives – or friends – as far as she can remember.

'He looks a right hard case, doesn't he,' continues Carol, waving the paper around, 'though they don't say it's definitely him. Just want to contact him. Urgent like.'

Jill stretches the expression on her face; she needs to look surprised but not engaged. 'Oh. It all happens in Barrow, doesn't it,' she says. What she wants is to grab the paper from Carol and scan the text for anything to set her mind at rest. Or scroll through her phone, though she thinks it's rude, tells her pupils the same. How long does it take to identify a body? What would be left of it after more than thirty years? But who knows about that length of time, apart from her? Or did she read it somewhere? She changes the subject decisively, knowing what will distract the assembled group.

'Did I hear Mary Lyons is having a fling with the guy who does the gardens?' She twists up the side of her lip a little. 'Not true, is it?'

Everyone is staring at her now. 'It is? Oh, my.' Her hands fly to her cheeks.

It seems her chair of governors, a woman of similar age to Jill, has attracted the attention of the jaunty young maintenance apprentice. Not only have they been sleeping together, but she's moved him into her house. Vic, her husband is still living there.

'Talk about *having it all*,' shrieks Carol. 'How's she going to show her face here now? I mean—'

There is laughter and some spluttering of coffee, and Andrew Brownstone is forgotten. Jill listens distractedly, wondering how it would be if they found out the truth about their boss. Would there be a ring of people picking over the bones of her story while they sipped coffee and ate shortbread? She shudders. Over the years of her teaching career, she's tried to make sure her other life is featureless, giving no texture for passing predators to grab on to or hide within. How would it be if the hidden poked through?

'And on that note,' she says, when she can finally walk towards the door. 'I'll see you all later.'

She needs time to think, to get herself into the mode she's lived in for more than thirty years; she isn't given any. Her telephone rings loudly in her handbag. She has it set to the old-fashioned tone, the one Phil hates. The phone is in her bag, tangled with keys and tissues. There is an unknown number on the screen. She accepts the call.

'Hello. Jill Francis speaking.' Her school voice.

It is Rose Atherton. Police Constable Rose Atherton. She asks Jill to make an appointment at the station, at her own convenience, because there are some questions she might be able to help them answer, in connection with Andrew Brownstone.

In her office, Jill sits down and gazes through the window across the faded green of the playing fields. There is a hollow feeling under her ribs. Has Rose Atherton somehow got her hands on extra information? What more is there to know?

Malcom Gibson niggles away, like a tiny piece of grit in the toe of a shoe. Has he been feeding information to the police? Waiting outside her house? Hanging around at her school?

What could he possibly have to say to her? He could still live in the decaying Liness Barn, on the island. Does she dare go and have a look? What would it achieve? She chews at her fingernail. Half an hour there and back? Nobody would even miss her.

The traffic on the promenade is heavy, the tide high and full. Seaview is somewhere to her left, shrouded in thick green leaves. She takes one quick look, then the traffic creeps forward. A salty-hot breeze reaches her nostrils and carries her back to 1976: she and Andrew Brownstone, sitting on a bench in the early morning, discussing the simplicity of fishing and the complexities of life. How Rose Atherton would enjoy access to Jill's memories.

Finally, the traffic thins again. Jill is able to pull away and drive her car up the gentle slope to North Scale village. And here, she can see Bonnie and Livvy, arm-in-arm again, and laughing at the world. She wants to turn the car around, wants to pull away from the past, but she has to know who has linked it with her present.

She stops at the top of the slope. It is the main road, so she parks the car half-on and half-off the pavement. Down a short tarmac path, she remembers, is Liness Barn. *Was* Liness Barn. It may not even be here anymore. But she has to find out.

At the bottom of the path lies the answer. A beautiful barn conversion, with a creamy, plastered exterior, broken up by expertly placed slabs of perfect pink sandstone. Jill thinks it is probably three barns, knocked together. To the side of a half-glazed door is an iron-black plaque. *Liness Barns* stands out in white letters, circled with painted bluebells and cockleshells, and at the back of the house is the sea. She cannot imagine

Malcom Gibson living here. Mick, with his dark looks and rabbit's-foot necklace.

She hears a sound, just behind. Coming down the slope is a baby's buggy. It is shaded from the summer's day by a white lacy canopy. A young woman grips the two handles.

'Hello,' she calls, all bobbing ponytail and Lycra. 'Coming down is easier than going up.' She gasps as she comes to a stop.

'Rather you than me,' laughs Jill, though she's well aware of what it's like to run in the heat.

'Did you want something? Sorry. That sounds rude. It's just, you're staring at my house.' The woman starts to open a low wooden gate. Jill steps forwards to help her.

'No. Just admiring the place. I remember when it was a set of old barns.'

'Thanks.' The gate closes between them. 'We've only had the place for ten years. It was partly converted then. We finished it. Me and my husband.'

'You've done a fabulous job.' Jill tilts her head towards the building. 'With the outside, I mean. I love it.'

'Thank you. Well. I'd better get on.' The woman walks away, one hand on the buggy, the other running over the back of her neck.

So, Malcom Gibson doesn't live here anymore. Jill pictures him in a penthouse retirement flat, somewhere warm. With a fox terrier, and a mobile phone full of news apps he can interrogate. But it doesn't tell her anything about who is reporting to Rose Atherton. She needs to think, to remember, to find any holes in the story she is going to build for this astute policewoman.

No more than half a minute from here is the beach where she first met Andrew Brownstone. Without thinking too much, she steps around the corner of the barn conversion, towards the open skyline and the sea. Though the water is stippled with sunlight, the salt wind light and fragrant, she notices the plastic bottles caught between rocks, and the ugly concrete reinforcements holding up what used to be, she remembers, Chapel Field.

Jill would come to this beach when she wanted to clear her head; she hasn't been here since her family left the island all those years ago. Standing here now, watching the gulls drift, she realises her relationship with Stoney wasn't all bad.

October 1979

Grey-and-white geese flew in a noisy dart above Jill's head. Two were out of line with the rest and falling behind. She wondered how it would feel to be heading south, keeping the fade of the summer in your sight. Chasing it.

She had nothing to chase, on this autumn afternoon. There was only her tired shoulders and a soft late heat that felt vaguely sad. In the trees above her, conker shells weighed heavily, and the pavement was littered with brown shiny fruits, waiting to be collected by kids from the Catholic school standing alongside her college.

The workload in her A-level year felt almost impossible, every teacher loading up past papers like they were something vital to life. She was looking forward to the weekend, if only to walk Lucky, and enjoy some time away from the pressures of written science and maths. And there was Saturday night. Her friend Jay's birthday, and the chance to blot out her unreliable memories of Stoney. The mess and colour of autumn reminded her of him, of the last visit to Seaview. Almost three years had passed, yet the shadow of his presence was always there. It pushed hard against her well-being, so she spent a lot of energy trying to fill up the hollows in her stomach and behind her eyes. And when he'd turned up at college at the start of the year, she wanted to leave.

She'd been talked out of it by her mother, who assumed Jill was struggling with herself. The final year at the grammar school had been spent, head down, avoiding social contact, creating worry for her parents and a creeping misery for herself.

Seeing Susie with other friends only added to the feeling. When she'd bumped into Stoney in the town centre one afternoon, hand-in-hand with a tiny smiling girl, Jill had cried for the rest of the day, without being able to say why.

And now he was at her college. She'd seen him once or twice across the coffee lounge, a blur of auburn hair and tight jaw, and a circle of interested students.

Watch out, she'd wanted to scream, *starlight is infinitely cold.*

She had a new group of friends now, though. None like Susie, who'd shunned A-levels in favour of secretarial college, but they were warm and friendly and made her feel part of something.

With a sigh, she hitched her heavy bag so it wasn't biting into her shoulder and turned her face towards home.

Jay's expression had a smudged quality by the time Jill went to give her a birthday hug. She was standing at the bar of the pub, looking glamorous in a full-length Indian-print dress, blonde hair hanging to her shoulders.

'How much have you had, Jay?' she asked, elbowing away the hordes of males plying her with drinks and staring down the front of her dress.

'Not enough.' A slurred reply. 'And he's... he's getting me more.' Jay's arm waved unsteadily.

Jill grabbed her hand. 'You don't have to drink the world

dry on your first night of being an adult you know. Come and sit with us.'

Jay let herself be led into a corner booth where Leanne, Sal and Riah were sitting, half-pint glasses in front of them. Music blared from the juke box, and a layer of cigarette smoke hung above them, scattering the light.

'Here she is.' Jill pushed Jay forward into Sal's hands. 'Sit her down, for God's sake.'

Jay began kissing and hugging them. All droopy arms and nodding. 'Wanna go into town,' she pouted. 'Never been on a pub crawl before.'

Jill was glad when Riah shook her head. 'You've asked all these people, darling,' she pointed towards the gathered crowds. 'We can't just go. Besides, you're already too drunk.'

Jay's chin dropped to her chest. 'You're no fun, you lot.' She paused. 'What if I stop drinking for a bit? Can we go then?'

'Stay on lemonade for the next hour,' Jill told her, 'and we might get the bus down.'

I sound like a teacher, she thought, but she had to admit there was something quite exciting about a trawl around the town centre pubs, the freedom of adulthood but with the support of her friends. The sort of friends who'd never have let her fall prey to Andrew Brownstone.

Jay's head rolled sideways onto Sal's shoulder, and she tutted loudly. 'I wasn't like this on my eighteenth,' she huffed.

'No. You were worse.' Leanne had a point.

Jill slid herself in beside them all. People came over to wish Jay happy birthday, and she raised her hand in thanks, without looking up.

The night wore on, the crowds thinned out and Jay perked up a little, insisting they call for a taxi to take them into town. Leanne knew the bus timetable by heart and soon the five of them were sitting on the back seat of a single decker, high spirits keeping them laughing and joking as much as their alcohol consumption.

'Where're we going first?' asked Jay, as the bus pulled into the town centre. 'I wanna go to all the dives, not the wine bars – you know what types will be in there.'

Jill shook her head. 'What types do you think will be in your so-called dives?' she laughed. 'Bikers and druggies? Is that who you want to mix with?'

Jay stopped in front of her, pushing a finger into the padding of her quilted jacket. 'Your trouble is, you're a baby. Everything worries you. Always worried about your reputation, aren't you. Who cares? I *like* bikers and druggies.' She stuck out her bottom lip. 'It's my birthday. I get to choose.'

They laughed then. Hanging on to each other in the unfamiliar light of the evening town. Jill knew it well enough in the daylight, with its tall Victorian buildings and friendly smiles, but this was something different. Flat slabs of darkness and glowing windows, neon and curry. They hurried towards the first pub they could see. Its frontage stood straight up from the street, flat and white and advertising itself as The King's Arms.

'Here,' squealed Jay, pointing.

'Here?' cried Jill, with a shake of her head. Jay couldn't have made a worse choice. The place was well-known across the town, and not for its bar meals and cheap wine. But it was too late. Her friend had pushed open the black-painted doors, and was walking in.

The air inside the pub smelled thickly of cigarettes and earth. It scratched at Jill's memory, as she followed her friends into the half-lit interior. The place was packed out. Groups of men in leather jackets slouched at the bar, lifting pints of dark beer. Hard-faced women, their breasts hanging out of tight velour tops, smoked suggestively, suspicion in their eyes. In the dark recesses and shadowy corners, people huddled together in a way that reminded Jill of schoolboys at the bike sheds.

One of the bar staff roughed out a welcome, and Jay jumped in, ordering rum and Cokes for them all.

'I'll just have a lemonade,' whispered Jill, leaning her chin down onto her friend's shoulder, so that she reached up and stroked her face.

'Sorry, doll, ordered for you now,' Jay replied, her gaze on the myriad of optics behind the bar, 'and this is just for starters. Go grab us a table.'

Jill cast around for a place to sit. There was another room, well-lit, where two older men were intent on a game of pool. Behind them were some empty tables. She led the way, beckoning the others to follow.

'All right, darlin',' called one of the men as they scrambled past.

Jill nodded, wondering what she was doing in a place like this. But at least the locals were friendly. She gave a small laugh, just for herself, and probably at herself. Here she was again, judging everyone and everything.

Once they were seated and waiting for Jay to bring their drinks, Jill took a deep breath and let her shoulders relax a little.

'Nice place,' snickered Riah, shifting about on her chair, 'and I can smell pot. Let Jay have her head, and then we'll get moving.'

Sal patted down her dark hair. 'First choice, a drug den. Typical.'

Leanne laughed nervously, looking across the table. 'Hope it doesn't get raided.'

'Stop being so daft.' Riah grinned at them all. 'It's a pub. People smoke dope in pubs. Get over it.'

'Listen to her,' sneered Sal. She turned her gaze on Riah. 'When did you get all hippy-dippy?' It set them off laughing, until they were interrupted by Jay, who carried their drinks on a tin tray, a packet of crisps between her teeth. She put everything on the table and began passing a small glass to each of them.

'What's so funny?' she asked, pushing in between Jill and Riah, 'and who's been on the wacky-baccy?' She sniffed loudly and set them off again. The crisps were split open and placed between them. 'Cheers, everyone.'

Jill smiled to herself. These were her friends. Through the first year of sixth form, they'd given her humour, honesty, and a set of solid shoulders to lean on, everything she'd needed to create a new Jill Holland. One which didn't feel so grubby and lost. She sniffed at the drink. An earthy warmth filled her nostrils, but alcohol was something she'd chosen to avoid; loss of control was her biggest fear. Another legacy from the early years of her teens.

'I'm just going to the bar,' she told them, getting up. 'I need something to water it down with.' She pointed to her glass. 'Or you could drink it for me. See you in a min.'

As she pushed her way back through the crowd, Jill felt a thrill of excitement run across her shoulders. Little Jill Holland, ordering a drink from a bar. In an actual pub. Even if it was only lemonade. With elbows resting in between the pools of spilt beer, she waited to be served.

'Jilly.' A sudden pressure on her shoulder. She glanced sideways. A pale, freckled hand. Stoney. Cool green eyes regarding hers.

'How you doing?'

'Fine,' she nodded. Aloof. Though her heart thudded, and her middle fizzed with heat. 'You?' A lift of her shoulder shrugged his hand away.

A frown flickered across his brow. 'Been trying to talk to you at college. You avoiding me?'

'Yep.' No point lying.

A blonde lady, puffy faced and heavily draped in gold jewellery, nodded at him from behind the bar. 'Love?'

'Southern Comfort and lemonade please, Yvonne.' Why was he shouting? 'And—' his gaze turned on Jill, 'she'll have—'

Jill shook her head. 'It's fine, I'll get my own.' Then looking at Yvonne, she added, 'Just a lemonade please.'

Stoney mumbled something and reached into his pocket. He pulled out a handful of change, then cupped it in his palm before passing coins across to Yvonne.

'I said I'd get my own.' Jill tried to wish him away from the clean chill of her personal space, and from her sight.

'Can we talk for just five minutes?' This wasn't like Stoney. Pleading. Begging, almost. But then she remembered the last time. Barefoot, on the steps of Seaview.

'Go for it,' she said, and he smiled.

The years slipped away to the first day she'd met him on the beach, fading evening sunshine and gulls screeching across the flats. He sipped at his drink.

'The Old Queen had a stroke, you know,' he said, wiping his damp lips with one finger. 'She's had to give up work.'

More staring. Waiting. 'Oh no,' she gasped. 'Is she all right?'

He rubbed his hand across the fine gingery-blond stubble on his chin. 'Nah. Far from it. The Old Geezer's going to retire and care for her, full-time like. She's staying at Seaview, though; she'd love to see you.' He sipped again. Still looking at her.

I can't, thought Jill. *I just can't.* But she nodded. 'I can try and get over. How come you're at sixth form? Aren't you nearly twenty?'

'Fucked up my O-levels, then found a job I wanted, but I needed maths and English, so I'm having to re-sit.'

'Oh?' This surprised her. 'What job was it?'

'Warden at the nature reserve at the end of the island. Why the fuck I need maths and English, I don't know.' He laughed bitterly. 'Setting a few traps and ringing a few gulls. I've already been doing it on a temping basis. What about you? Going to *university*, I guess?'

The force of the word made Jill start. It hung in the air between them, like it was waiting for a fight. 'What's wrong with going to university?' she said, trying to make it sound like something infinitely light and amusing.

'Thatcher's new system, that's what it is. Rise of the Capitalists. She wants watching.'

'What are you talking about? Not a fan of women, are you?' Jill could feel her anger rising. If the country had a woman as its leader, why would it make any difference? Stoney's objections would be more to do with authority figures, anyway. 'Are you going to leave the country now she's in?'

'If only, Jilly,' he said. 'If only.' And here was the chip-toothed grin again. She had to laugh with him.

'Idiot.'

'That's me. Your friendly neighbourhood idiot.' He thought for a moment, then held out his hands. 'But there's plenty around who could join me.'

'You don't have a very high opinion of people, do you?'

'Nah.' A twist of his lips. Those green eyes meeting hers. 'Still like the beach, though.'

'D'you still live at Seaview?' She couldn't resist asking.

He snorted. 'On and off. Been dossing down with Mick some of the time. Giving The Old Queen a bit of peace.'

Her eyes raked over his clothes.

Not at home at the moment, then.

A wave of emotion washed over her, buoyed up by the grubby collar of his shirt. In a moment of total clarity, Jill realised she was bonded to Stoney in a way which was tender yet brittle, and as chilling as the sea on a winter's day.

'I've missed you, Jilly,' he whispered, reaching up to touch her hair. She let him look at her. Didn't move a muscle. When his hand came down again, she turned away, with the pretence of sipping her drink.

'You hardly knew me.' The words surprised her. There was a power to them.

'You're dead right,' he whispered. 'But I'd like another chance to try.'

Jill shuddered. Had he forgotten the things he'd forced a fourteen-year-old girl to do?

'I don't think so,' she said coldly, lifting her drink and meeting his intensity. He raised his eyebrows, tilting his head slightly.

'Where the fuck do you get off,' he snarled, 'talking like that?'

But Riah had come up behind him, and it made Jill bold.

'And where the fuck have *you* learnt to talk to women like that?' A lurch of her heart. Was it her speaking? Really?

'Jill. Where've you been?' Riah called. 'We're ready for the off. Drink up.'

She reached around Stoney's side and took Jill by the hand, pulling her away. Over her shoulder, Jill took one last look at him, at the orange glittery drink, and his hand lifting it to his lips.

They left the pub, Riah's arm linked through Jill's in a huddle against the chill of the autumn evening. The others followed.

'What you talking to him for?' Riah asked as soon as they were out of earshot. 'Stoney's a good name for him. Off his head most of the time.'

Jill looked at her, confused. 'Do you know him?'

Riah shook her head sharply. 'As if,' she sneered, 'but my brother does. He was at The Tec with him. Spent most of his time smoking dope and abusing the teachers, he said. But you clearly know him. Spill.'

There was no way Jill was going to *spill* anything. 'I used to live near him on the island. Was just asking after his mum and dad.'

'Well, don't ask, darling,' Riah laughed. A dark laugh. 'He put the window of his house through, when his mother wouldn't give him money to buy pot, apparently. Don't quote me though.' She held up her hands.

A sick feeling twisted itself through Jill's stomach, fizzing and bubbling with the lemonade she had drunk. She thought of Annie Brownstone, cowering in Seaview, wondering what her son would do next. But what Stoney wanted, he took.

She looked at Riah. 'Poor woman. I really liked her.'

'Shame she has a dickhead for a son, then.' Riah pulled her mouth into a grim smile. 'Come on. Let's catch the others.'

'I'm going now, Mum,' Jill called from the front door. 'I'll pick up the meat on the way back.'

Silence.

'Mum?'

A lemony tang wafted through the hallway. Saturday was *chores* day, and it was in full swing. Denny sat on the stairs, twisting away at his Rubik's Cube.

'She's polishing,' he said. 'Up there.' One finger jabbed skywards. There was a shuffle of slippers on the landing, then their mother appeared.

'Get a pound out of my purse,' she called, peering over the banister. 'Do you need bus fare as well?'

Jill shook her head. 'I'm going to walk into town. Lucky hates the bus anyway. I'll be back by teatime.'

'Okay, love. I'll see you later.'

The morning was bright and clear. Jill inhaled deeply as she stepped outside: woodsmoke and the scent of summer's decline. Lucky strained against his leash, and she wrapped the cracked leather around her hand to rein him in.

She tugged at the zip of her anorak and tucked her hair in at the collar. It would be windy on the island, and she was heading here, despite what she'd said to her mother. If Annie Brownstone was lying ill and needing female company, why should Stoney be allowed to stand between them. The woman had been kind; Jill hadn't forgotten the way she'd been welcomed into Seaview. Better to remember her kindness than dwell on the fact that Annie must have realised what was happening under her own roof, yet done nothing. And Jill could hardly bring it up now. She's certain of one thing, though: if she ever has children, she will make it her business to get to the heart of them and stay there.

A shortcut took her across the fields of her old school. At the gates, she stopped for a moment and glanced up at the red-brick buildings, vivid in the October sunshine. The entrance door of the nearest one was newly painted in glossy black, but the carved lintel still proclaimed it to be for *girls*. The system was so dated. She hoped all schools would be mixed gender before she became a teacher.

If she ever did. Nobody in her family had been to university; why should she be any different? Jill Holland, a teacher? *Don't make me laugh*. A little voice drilled away constantly in her head. But she was determined to keep trying. And if Stoney thought universities were full of people to despise, what did she care? They were worlds apart, now.

The pavements in this part of town were lined with tall sycamore and beech trees, their fruits scattered and rotting. Jill kicked at the debris with the toe of her boot. It had been more than three years since she'd walked this way with Stoney, hand-in-hand, wearing school uniform. How must that girl have looked to the outside world? There would have been a smile, she's sure, but no one would have noticed she was being dragged along.

As she walked, Jill kept her thoughts firmly fixed on what she would say to Annie Brownstone. Would the woman even be able to speak? She'd heard of people suffering a stroke, but quite what it looked like, she couldn't imagine. And there was no one to ask.

When she got close to the island, Jill felt its pull: the open skies and clean air. Though there had been no visits since the horrible rainy afternoon, and she'd tried hard to forget the place, it was in her blood. As she approached the wide stretch of water, reflecting the fading blue of the autumn sky, there was a certainty in her footsteps, a need to lay her feelings at the gates of Seaview and come to a compromise with them. She didn't intend to fight against Stoney her whole life.

Halfway across the road-bridge, she stopped. Black Combe was sharp in the distance and the estuary stretched itself away towards the open sea and sky. With the screech of gulls, and a flash of briny wind against her cheeks, she saw herself at fourteen years old, enjoying the same scene. If she could go back, she would take her younger self by the hand and show her how to be confident, give her a voice. As if sensing her unsettled feelings, Lucky sat himself down on her feet and lay his head against her knee. Jangling his leash made him jump up, and he began pulling again, forcing Jill to take the next steps towards the end of the bridge and her visit to Seaview House.

At the gates, she stopped. This was her final chance to step away from the Brownstones. She let her gaze travel up the stone steps, to the front door.

Everything looked the same. The garden was a little overgrown, but the red front door with its black knocker, and the fish gargoyles on the pillars of the porch, they were exactly as she remembered. The curtains of the blue room were closed, overlapping in an untidy way, and the windows had a drab salty sheen. Using the adrenaline zipping through her body, Jill took the steps two at a time and knocked on the door before reason stopped her.

Reverend Brownstone answered her knock. Not a face she was used to seeing, wisps of white hair and his age settled around his stomach.

'Hello, my dear. Can I help you?' he said, rubbing his chin. 'Ah. Jill. Of course. Andrew said you might visit.' He stepped back from the door, holding it open. 'Come in.'

'Is it okay if I bring Lucky?' she asked. 'Will it upset Mac?'

Reverend Brownstone smiled; she could see Stoney in his smile. 'Mac will not mind,' he said. 'He is watching from heaven.'

Jill hesitated. 'Oh. I'm sorry. Are you sure it's okay?' A flush spread across her cheeks. She knelt to stroke her dog. Reverend Brownstone faded into the gloom of the hall.

'Bring him in,' he called, 'and I shall take him to the kitchen, give him a drink. You go in and see Annie.' He pointed at the door of the blue room and reached out to take Lucky's leash from her trembling hand. The dog went willingly, and she was left on her own, not knowing whether she should knock.

She stepped inside, blinking in surprise. The room was cool, and as clean as she remembered, nothing like the hospital ward she had been imagining. The navy sofa was gone and in its place was a kind of day bed, where Annie Brownstone reclined, a fine-knit blanket around her shoulders. She was fully dressed, book in hand and gold-rimmed glasses perched on her nose.

She smiled a welcome. 'My dear, it's so good to see you.' She dropped the book into her lap and held out the same hand; the other hung limply against the blanket.

'Hello, Annie.' Jill leaned forward to kiss her cheek, then

sat down on the edge of the bed, the older lady still clinging to her hand. 'How are you doing?'

A weak smile. 'Oh, I'm all right, I guess. But still struggling to use my right side, which is annoying.' The short silver hair lay flat, and there was no trace of her favourite chocolate-coloured lipstick.

'Can you walk at all?' Jill wondered if she should mention Stoney. He was their mutual interest, after all.

'Not much at the moment, I'm afraid, but I've been referred for physio, if it ever happens.' She wriggled her back a little, and Jill reached forwards to straighten the cushion behind her. 'Thanks, love. You're looking very beautiful, you know. Healthy. Young.' She ran the back of her good hand over Jill's cheek.

'I'll be eighteen in a couple of months,' Jill said with a laugh, 'so not young.'

Annie stared at her, then said, 'Eighteen. What I wouldn't give to be that age again.'

The door opened a little and Reverend Brownstone peered into the room. 'Can I get you anything? A cup of tea perhaps? Annie?'

His wife nodded. 'Thank you. Yes. Would you like some tea, Jill?'

'I would, thanks,' she replied, knowing this would extend her stay for another half an hour. Though she was enjoying talking to Annie again, she wanted to be away before Stoney appeared. Unless he was here already. Annie read her thoughts.

'Andy didn't come home last night. He often stays at Malcom Gibson's.' She gave the smallest of shudders, but it was enough.

'That's Mick, isn't it?' Jill asked. 'Still friends with him then?'

'Yes. Still friends with him.' Her lips pressed into a hard

line, and she looked away. 'I suppose you know they smoke cannabis.'

'I didn't,' she said, 'but I had heard a few things.'

She left the comment in the air and waited for Annie's response.

'I don't understand him, Jill. He's had everything he wanted. Never had to fight for anything. Not like other kids. And he's clever. But he gets involved with drugs. Why?'

Jill took a deep breath. There was nothing she could offer. 'Don't know,' she murmured.

'I was really upset when he told me he'd broken up with you,' Annie continued. 'It was a shame when you moved off the island.'

So that was the story. How much of the truth did this woman know?

'He did seem to be getting really moody,' Jill ventured, and Annie tilted her head quizzically.

'You think he was… dabbling… even then?'

Dabbling? Jill hadn't thought about his cannabis use when she was fourteen, but she had known he and Mick looked through pornographic magazines to get ideas. Perhaps the two things went together.

'Maybe,' she said. 'He messed up his exams, too, didn't he? How badly?'

Annie sighed. 'Oh, my love. What are we letting ourselves get bogged down with my errant son for? I wish so much I'd had more children. A daughter, like you, perhaps. We've no other family to speak of.' The door opened. 'Have we, darling?' Reverend Brownstone came into the room balancing two mugs and a plate of fruit cake on a tray.

'What's that, my dear?'

'I was telling Jill we are the last of our families, apart from Andy. Sad really. Perhaps he'll marry and have children though.' She winked, but her husband's face remained expressionless. He laid the tray down on a small table by Annie's bedside, then exited the room awkwardly, mumbling something about letters he had to write.

When the door latch clicked, Annie turned to her again. 'He's had to retire, to look after me, you know, and he's hating it. Living in Seaview and not being the vicar. I'd love to move to a bungalow, but we don't have the money.'

Jill passed her the tea and helped her to lift it to her lips. She was beginning to feel out of her depth with all this family talk, in a family that wasn't hers.

'You are so good, my dear.' Annie touched her hand. 'Thank you for coming to see me.' There was a sincerity to her words. Jill relaxed.

They spent a pleasant fifteen minutes enjoying their tea, while Jill asked about the artwork on the walls of the room. It turned out Annie was a collector and lover of seascapes, especially those by local artists, and Jill was captivated by her stories of people who had dedicated themselves to their love of the island.

'Perhaps you'll come and live back here when you're older,' Annie said with a grin. 'I think you feel the love, too.'

'You're right,' laughed Jill, 'and so does Lucky. But I must go and retrieve him from your kitchen. He'll have settled himself in Mac's basket.' The older lady's face was drooping, a small string of saliva running from the corner of her mouth. Tears pressed against the back of Jill's eyes. If this was her mother, she'd never leave her side. There would be no putrid little backstories, everything would be sparkling and fresh.

'I'll let you get some rest,' she whispered, kissing Annie's cheek, 'and I will come back and see you again. Promise.'

She pulled the woollen blanket across Annie's chest, and retrieved the mugs and plate from the table, trying not to clink anything together.

In the hallway, she could see the study door was firmly

closed; hardwood and silence. Her intention was to collect Lucky, then let herself out without disturbing anyone. As she opened the kitchen door, the tang of burning tobacco filtered out. The room was in darkness. Stoney was sitting in the old fireside chair, flicking ash into an empty fireplace. His free hand stroked Lucky's head.

'Jilly.'

His use of her nickname caused a catch in her throat. She put down the tray.

'Sorry. I was just going to get my dog and go home.' She reached across to take Lucky by the collar, but Stoney's hand was on hers.

'Don't. Don't go yet, Jilly. Stay. Please.'

She could only shake her head. There was something about him that unsettled her, disturbed her to the core. Yet here she was.

'Your poor mum.'

Stoney huffed and turned towards the fireplace, shoving Lucky with his foot. The dog yelped. Jill knelt and put her arms around his furry neck, scanning the room for his lead.

'Leave my dog alone. You bully.' She glowered at his back. 'You can't even look at me, can you?'

He threw the last of his cigarette away, then spun his head towards her. 'Why are you always such a bitch? Pretending to be so good. Why are you even bothered about The Old Queen? What about me?'

He jumped up from the chair and crashed towards her. 'Me, Jilly.' Fist pounding against his chest. 'What about me.'

Jill stood up, keeping a hand on Lucky's collar. 'Don't be so pathetic,' she snarled. 'Your mum's ill in there, and all you can think about is—'

He cut her off. 'What, Jilly? What preachy thing are you going to accuse me of now?'

She shook her head. What was the point of trying to talk to him? There was only one person in his world.

His eyes were on her again. 'Just get out. Go on. Get out.' A thumb towards the door.

Jill could see Lucky's leash. She made a grab for it and clicked it onto his collar. In a flash, Stoney was there, blocking her path. A small growl rose in the dog's throat. Jill tried to push her way out, but Stoney's hand grabbed onto her chin and held it tightly, while he smashed his lips into hers. She kept very still, didn't respond, and he pulled back slightly.

'I don't think so,' she whispered, then slid out of his grasp, dragging Lucky with her.

Reverend Brownstone was standing in the hall, his face shadowed.

'It was nice to see you, my dear,' he said as Jill moved towards the front door with Lucky. 'Shall you visit again?'

She wanted to tell him *yes*, wanted to pretend the situation was completely normal, when all she wished was to be out of the house, and away. Then Stoney appeared in the hallway.

'What the—' He lurched towards them and planted himself in front of Jill.

'Stay where you are,' he snarled, then to his father, 'keep out of my business. I've said this to you before.'

'Now, Andrew—' Reverend Brownstone began to speak, but Stoney lunged at him.

'I'll decide when she goes home, not you.' He grabbed at his father's sweater, clasping two handfuls at the neckline. 'Now, lay off.'

Jill pushed her arm between the two men.

'Get off him,' she shrieked, then fell away as Stoney's elbow jabbed her stomach. She could only watch in horror as he slid one hand up from his father's chest and pressed against his throat.

Jill's eyes flashed to the door of the blue room. Annie was in there. And she'd be able to hear everything. Lucky was whining softly, and tucking him behind her, she reached for Stoney once again, yanking his wrist away from Reverend Brownstone's neck.

'Stoney. Stoney, please. I'll do anything you say. Just leave him. Stoney.'

Fear clutched at her insides. A flux of acid welled up in her throat; it tasted of tea and fruit cake. But Stoney was stepping away.

'Do you know what, Jilly?' Ice-cold. 'You can fuck off home, after all. There's nothing you could do to interest me.' Then he stormed down the hallway and slammed into the kitchen.

Jill stared after him for a moment, then turned to Reverend Brownstone. He was trying to tidy his bunched-up clerical shirt.

'I'm so sorry,' she whispered, shaking her head. 'I'll go now.' And with Lucky held in tight control, she stepped onto the porch of Seaview House. This had to be the last time she visited. It had to be.

Chapter Twelve

Dirty yellow brickwork, and empty-eyed windows. Jill peered up at the student hostel and tried to swallow down the tightness in her throat. This was her new home, a new start, but it felt like the worst kind of torture.

After the clarity and freshness of northern air, London had a peculiar smell. Disinfectant and something metallic, like the lumps of lead from her chemistry lab at the grammar school. A combined sciences degree in the capital might not have been the best choice, but here she was. Standing in front of Platts now, misery washing over her like the waves from West Shore, she realised it had been a mistake. When her predicted exam grades had been high, she'd been offered a place at King's. The accolade and back-patting from her parents and friends had carried her through to this point, but the reality was sharp enough to slice her heart in two.

She shook open the map in her hand. The zoology department was somewhere in Herne Hill, but she had no landmarks to focus on, only a black circle along a thread of red road.

At breakfast, the other students from her block had stared,

scanning their eyes across her clothes and hair. She'd smiled and tried not to get in their way as they shrieked and wailed in high-pitched southern accents, full of enthusiasm for their new life of freedom in London. Many were from the suburbs. They'd come down in their cars and had parents nearby. One or two were from further afield, but none made a move to include Jill in anything, and social skills had never been her strong point. None were heading to zoology either; she was on her own.

It was a beautiful morning, clear and crisp. It made Jill think of late autumn days on the island, of tramping across open fields in her walking boots with Lucky running ahead through decaying thistles and bracken. Her jaw tightened. Now wasn't the time for memories; this was her new life, and she was desperate to find her place in it.

Jill took a deep breath and began to walk. Red-brick houses lined the road, each one set back behind ornate gates and dense green hedges. Traffic crawled slowly by. She tried to make eye contact with her fellow pedestrians, but most didn't bother, or showed surprise when she nodded a greeting. At Half-Moon Lane she could see a large park looming up to her left. A place to stroll at lunchtime, perhaps. The zoology department was along this road somewhere: number sixty-eight, according to her student welcome pack.

She found it at the end of a long driveway. It looked like a grand mansion, with a wide roof made from glass, and hundreds of windows at three levels. Jill noticed a smaller building to one side, a Victorian villa with a well-tended area of grassland and garden, laid out with many glasshouses and wooden slatted structures. A lot like Seaview, but without the sea.

A few people were hanging around at the entrance to the main building, wearing the same red, white and blue scarf Jill had looped around her neck. She relaxed a little and tried again to gain acceptance with a smile.

Relief flooded through her, as a girl with long red hair and a heart-shaped face, returned the smile.

'Hello,' she said. A southern accent. 'We're waiting for one of the older students to show us in.'

Jill nodded. 'Good. Wasn't sure if this was the place.' She looked across at the others, standing nearby. 'Are you waiting for the first zoology practical?'

'Yes. I'm Jebbie, by the way.' And when Jill cocked her head slightly, she continued. 'Genevieve really. But it's rather difficult to spell.' A silvery laugh.

'I'm Jill.' She held out her hand.

The other girl took her fingertips and shook them gently. There was a jangle of coloured bracelets.

'Pleased to meet you.'

Before anything else could be said, two people came out through the glass doors at the front of the building and began to usher them all inside. Jill stepped back to allow Jebbie in. Other students had taken her attention, and she was tossing her red hair from side to side as she laughed and chatted and gestured with her hands.

Everything was taking so much effort. How did you make conversation when you had no common ground? Jill had watched Bonnie do it, and succeed with ease, so why couldn't she?

Once inside the building, there was the familiar smell of science labs and coffee. She followed the group as they were led up a wide marble staircase and into a long corridor lined with fire safety doors. Footsteps clattered and echoed, and Jill tried to swallow down her anxiety.

As they were taken into a bright room, full of benches and glassware, the other students clumped together. Jill thought of the flock of plovers she had once seen, settled safely, shoulder-to-shoulder, against a bitter sea wind. If she tried to break into the ring, would they accept her or simply scatter and settle elsewhere? And how on earth did she go about breaking in?

She took her lab coat from her bag and slipped it on, then sat down on a stool and waited. The familiarity of the scene was a comfort: she could measure out ethanol and handle a scalpel, and the tutor had a kind face. Excitement bubbled across the room when the lab technician began to hand out small glass jars with stoppered lids, and wads of cotton wool. The tutor followed behind, placing a white mesh cage at the end of each bench. Jill gasped. Behind the mesh were four or five tiny frogs, bodies pulsating, eyes half closed.

'Calm down, children,' he was saying as he moved between the edgy students, 'the little blighters are already half-stoned. You'll just have to finish the job with your ethanol. Then–' He dragged two fingers across his throat and made a choking noise.

Screeches of laughter filled the room. Jill gulped down a bubble of nausea. How was she going to anaesthetise a living creature, then hack it to pieces? It wasn't her, no matter how she loved the subject. There had been nothing like this during her A-levels.

Stoney had killed rabbits and birds, she remembered. And she'd been revolted. Now she was expected to do the same. She wasn't sure if she could. Less than a month ago she had been at home, living through the summer with her friends, and trying to avoid him. What would he make of all this, she wondered?

Get a grip, she told herself. If she was ever going to become a science teacher, there would be lab work exactly like this. Would she always baulk when something living was involved?

'Don't look so worried. This is exciting, isn't it?' Jebbie had moved to stand beside her. 'Though a little cruel, I think.' She giggled. 'The guys who are helping today told us there wouldn't be too much of the *in vivo* work. I suppose we should be glad of that.'

Jill lifted her chin and grimaced, but Jebbie's attention was on one of the other students. With a curl of her hand, she beckoned him over.

'This is Simon,' she said as he approached.

'And this is—'

'Jill,' said Jebbie. 'I was just telling her not to worry about the *in vivo* work.'

'Yeah,' agreed Simon, moving his gaze away. 'I could do with a smoke. When's coffee time?' He peered at the wall clock hanging just above the door. 'God, it's ages yet.'

Jebbie began to giggle again and patted at Simon's arm.

'Heavy night, hey?'

'Oh, yes.'

He wandered away and Jill was on her own, once again.

Later, head resting against the bus window, she thought about Stoney. Was this lack of belonging what he'd felt? Is that why he'd experimented with drugs? Her family, and the life she'd led, had sheltered her so much; now her emotions felt as raw as those he'd sometimes shown.

The bus crawled towards the city centre. The sparkling sunshine of the afternoon was draining away behind the buildings of Borough High Street, and she hoped she'd left enough time. Finally, on Waterloo Road, she decided to jump off and walk. More than anything, she wanted to get to Waterloo Bridge and experience the famous sunset. There had been photographs of it in one of the London brochures her grandad had sent her when she'd accepted her place at King's. She was prepared to do anything to lift herself out of the black pit she was slipping into. It was a long bus ride from Platt's, but she had nothing else to do; no particular place to be; no one waiting for her.

The sun had almost gone. A thin line of pale orange lit up the iconic skyline. Jill looked across the water, wrapping her scarf more tightly against the creeping chill of the autumn evening. There was a beauty to be found in the silhouetted history of the city, but she felt nothing except the profound need to be back in her hometown, to stand on the shore and watch the same sun sinking over the western horizon and into the Irish Sea.

January 1984

Jill woke to the sound of music blasting out somewhere on her landing. One of the newer students had a serious radio habit and hadn't responded to her pleas for a noise curfew.

She looked at her wristwatch. Bonnie would be on the train by now, heading her way for a visit. She'd promised to meet her at King's Cross, though the timings had been a little vague. That was her sister, never worrying about the troubles of everyday life. She would be there by lunchtime, she'd told Jill during their brief telephone conversation, and would find her somehow. There had been no explanation about the visit other than Bonnie was missing her.

Jill glanced around the room and wondered where Bonnie was going to sleep. There wasn't a sofa in the tiny student bedsit. It would have to be top-to-tail on Jill's bed, as they'd done when they were children. She hoped her sister was bringing a sleeping bag. With only a small and flaky radiator for heating, Jill had taken to wearing a sweater over her nightdress and using her coat as a bedspread.

The room had no curtains, just a grey slatted blind that

hardly held back daylight. It cast drab shadows across the wall above Jill's bed. With a sigh, she slid from beneath her sheets and blankets and wondered if she would have enough energy to make it through another day. On her desk was a calendar. It had been given to her as a Christmas gift. Each month was printed over a famous seascape. Already, Jill had circled the date in May that she would be leaving London for the last time. And on every day since the start of January she had put a black cross. She knew exactly how many were left.

She washed in the grubby basin and put on her usual outfit of jeans, sweatshirt, and suede boots, then knotted a patterned silk scarf around her neck. She parted her hair and braided it loosely in two plaits. Breakfast would have to wait until she met up with Bonnie.

Outside, the sky was flat and white, the cold taking a swipe at the bare patches of skin behind Jill's ears. She would never get used to London, with its gritty air and faint smell of Jeyes Fluid. And even in the brightest part of summer, when she'd walk the parks and heaths and stood by the Thames at Dartford, the place never felt like home.

Jill tucked her braids into the collar of her anorak and pulled the zip as high as it would go. There was a bus stop outside Platts. From here, she would be able to get to the city centre, then there was another wait for a bus to King's Cross. That Bonnie would be at the end of the journey was the only reason Jill could bring herself to do it.

Course work and studying for exams might be causing the fatigue she was experiencing, but in her heart, she knew there was something more. Behind her eyes was the constant pressure of tears and she would fantasise about going to sleep and never waking up.

From the window of the bus, she watched the London landscape flash by in a blur of angular buildings and soot-covered trees. In half-finished conversations with her colleagues and tutors, Jill had tried mentioning her worries, but there was never enough time. She felt like the piece of dying pondweed in her zoology department aquarium, surrounded by bright and darting fishes who would, on occasion, take a small bite.

As it turned out, the journey took Jill less than two hours. Inside the station, she searched until she found a timetable for the Leeds-King's Cross trains. One was due to arrive at noon. Waiting for an hour on the platform was the last thing she wanted. There was something about watching trains come and go that made her sad. As though all the energy of saying goodbye had clumped together, with its particular scent of diesel and copper coins, and was waiting to be inhaled by unsuspecting travellers. As far as she was concerned, when May finally arrived and she could take the train home for the last time, she was never going to use one again.

Jill crossed the road in front of the station and found somewhere by the railings to wait. From here, she had a view of the place, with its huge glass windows and central clock tower. Like a surprised face, she thought. Taxis flew past, black and orange and bumper-to-bumper, spewing out fumes and occasionally loud warnings.

She'd been to visit Bonnie once in her whole time at Leeds University, and the city centre was nothing like this. With her hands in her anorak pockets, gaze fixed firmly on the glass entrance porch of the station, she waited.

Suddenly, she was aware of someone standing beside her. An arm pressing against hers. A face she didn't recognise. An older man wearing a pale-blue flecked suit.

'Business,' he muttered, eyes to the ground.

Jill froze. What was he talking about?

'Business, ma'am,' he said again.

For a moment, Jill was unable to connect his words with anything she could make sense of. Only that they had the tone of a question. Then she realised what was being asked of her.

'No,' she spat, horrified. The man scuttled away. How could he have been mistaken? Here she was, wearing a zip-up anorak, hair braided like a schoolgirl and not a scrap of make-up in sight, and she was being mistaken for–. She wouldn't put a name to it, only blamed herself for loitering outside a railway station. Her eyes stung with tears; she hated this place. Was it any wonder she felt like she had been living under a permanently wintry sky for the last three years?

Bonnie arrived just as Jill was about to leave for the bus stop. She watched as her sister stepped onto the pavement, grinning widely and wearing a heavily embroidered coat that reached to the ground.

'Bon.' Jill waved her arms from her place on the other side of the road. 'Bon, I'm here.'

Within seconds, she was caught up in a floral-scented embrace while passers-by huffed and stepped around them.

'Look at you,' laughed Bonnie, stepping away, hands still clinging to Jill's shoulders. 'Proper student. Not like me.'

'Ordinary, you mean,' Jill said. 'And I love your hair.' She reached up to touch Bonnie's shaggy blonde mane. 'Have you had it permed?'

'I have. It cost me most of this term's grant.'

'Well, it looks great,' laughed Jill. 'Very *Jennifer Grey*. Your coat is fabulous, too.'

Bonnie tugged her shoulder bag up higher and linked her arm through Jill's.

'Can we find a café or something,' she said. 'I need coffee and I have some news.'

'What news?' Jill let herself be led along the pavement. 'Bonnie. What news?'

'Shush. Coffee first.'

As they walked together, Jill thought about the time in her life when having a sister like Bonnie made her feel jealous. At school, friends had fallen at her feet, and had been so carelessly discarded. Bonnie had been like a fickle princess in the presence of her servants. Adored and admired and mourned sadly when she moved on. People hardly ever noticed Jill, the quiet, mousy-haired older sister. But when she had bothered to dig deeper into Bonnie's personality, kindness and a love of people sprang to the surface. In their late teens, they'd found each other, though they had been together for all their lives.

And now they were standing in front of a tatty building with greasy windows and a pale-blue frontage, and Bonnie was peering at the sign above the door.

'*The Last Resort*,' she spluttered. 'Perfect name. Let's go in here, shall we?'

Jill followed as her sister marched in. A bell tinkled somewhere. Tables were pushed up against each wall, leaving an aisle down the middle leading up to a smeary glass counter.

'Grab a table,' whispered Bonnie, 'and I'll go and see if there's anything safe to eat and drink.' She pinched at her nose. 'Stinks though, doesn't it.'

Jill could only smell the acrid burn of cigarettes. She chose a table well away from where a group of women were smoking heavily, heads together and laughing. She watched as Bonnie chatted to the rosy-faced man who was serving. Her sister seemed to handle life in a way that said she'd been practising forever. Though she was only twenty-one years old. At twenty-two, Jill felt as naïve and gauche as if she were still fourteen and trying to negotiate her way around some of the dangerous grammar school girls. And boys.

'He's going to bring our toast over in a minute.' Bonnie brought two white mugs to the table. Each was filled with a sticky mess of frothed milk. 'It is coffee, he assured me.' She slid one of the mugs towards Jill. 'Load it up with sugar. It'll be fine.'

'Never mind the coffee,' Jill hissed. 'What's this news of yours? Bon, come on. What have you done?'

Bonnie sat down and reached across the table for Jill's hand.

'It's not about me, sis. Mum wanted me to tell you in person, to be here with you, that's all. Lucky died. Last week, it was. Mum found him dead in his basket. She knew you'd be upset and didn't want you told without one of us being there. Here.' Her voice quivered a little. 'Sorry.'

Jill wasn't sure how to respond. When she'd last been home, Lucky had been well. The thought of not seeing him again sent a rush of sickly shock through her body.

'Where is he now?' she gasped, making Bonnie stretch her eyes.

'The vet took him.'

'Where?'

Bonnie sucked in a deep breath. 'Jill. Why does it matter? He's gone, okay. He was old, in dog years. It happens.'

'It matters,' Jill cried. 'It matters. It—'

And out poured every tear, every held-back emotion and every regret Jill ever had. Each took the form of a wet, breathy sob. Bonnie moved to sit beside her, one hand on her shoulder and passing her folded paper napkins from a glass on the table.

'Wow. Mum was right to send me with the news,' she said when Jill finally calmed enough to blow her nose. 'That was a bit of an overreaction. Is everything okay?'

'No.'

'Want to tell me?'

'Yes. No. I don't know,' Jill stammered. 'I feel stupid. Telling my little sister about my problems.'

'Fair point,' laughed Bonnie. 'You've always hated telling me anything. But it might help. Talking, I mean.'

Jill wanted to hug her. They'd shared a childhood without it being a sisterhood. There was closeness and the ties that bind a family, but Jill had always struck out on her own. Bonnie had been the loud to her quiet, the sunshine to her shadow. And yet here she was, offering Jill the thing she was missing the most. A taste of home.

'I don't think I'm well,' she ventured, dabbing at her eyes. 'Everything feels *black*.'

'Tell me more,' said Bonnie, taking a sip of her coffee. 'Urgh. Cold.'

Jill covered her face with her hands and sighed.

'I feel so sad all the time.'

'Your dog's just died. You're allowed to feel sad.'

'It's like that. But all the time,' Jill continued. 'I can hardly get out of bed, some mornings. I don't want to do anything or go anywhere. All I can think of is how to stop feeling like it.'

Bonnie paused for a moment and raked her fingers through her hair. 'It's depression,' she said. 'One of the girls in my dance class is having the same feelings. The doctor told her it's depression. There's treatment, you know. Have you even been to see a doctor?'

Jill shook her head.

'Well, you should. Janie – that's the girl – is much better now she's got pills.'

'Pills? There aren't pills for feeling sad.'

'There are.' Bonnie held up her hand as the ruddy-faced man walked towards them with two plates of toast. 'Can you give us a minute?' He backed away.

'They're called anti-depressants, apparently. You might need them, Jill.'

'I just need to get away from London, I think.' Jill couldn't see herself telling a doctor she felt sad and asking for medicine. She'd heard of people needing tranquillisers for those kinds of problems. Hadn't she always used the power of nature as a cure for her worries? When had things changed?

'Do you remember that other time when you felt low?' Bonnie was asking.

'When?'

'I think it was when we moved off Walney Island. You had to leave your boyfriend behind, I think. Something like that. Andy Brownstone, he was called, wasn't he?'

'Oh, him.' Jill would rather not remember.

'Yeah, him.' Bonnie had become the little sister again. 'You cried for weeks after we left, didn't you? Not sure if it was for the island, or for that guy. But it went on for ages. You might have had depression then.'

'Might have,' Jill agreed. It had been a time of regret and sadness; she remembers that much. 'But I got over it, didn't I? Without doctors or pills.'

Bonnie slid herself away from the table and stood up.

'You must have done,' she said, picking up the half-empty mugs. 'I'm going to get a top-up. And our toast. Then we can talk about it a bit more.'

As she watched her sister glide up the aisle of the café, Jill wondered how much Bonnie knew about what happened with Stoney. Would anything be gained from telling her now? She didn't think so. But all this crying over a lost dog has exposed a truth Jill hadn't ever acknowledged: Andrew Brownstone had a lot to answer for.

Chapter Thirteen

MAY 1984

The train finally pulled into Lancaster station, the brightness of the day sharpening Jill's black mood. A glance through the window gave her some relief. There was an openness to the platform, a comfort in the warm limestone brickwork and relaxed faces, so unlike the steel girders and glossy bodies of the Euston platform she had left, five hours earlier. A final wave of homesickness threatened to overwhelm her. Lucky then, that she was going home.

She laid her head against her rucksack and inhaled deeply. For the best part of three years, she had existed without any feelings, keeping them buried so she might get through her degree and become what she was meant to be. But what she wanted to be was happy. How did that stack up in the story of her life? Did everyone struggle with university, or was it just her?

Leanne and Sal had gone off to art college together, and hardly came home. Riah had married at eighteen, and as for Jay – she never heard from her. Edinburgh had been too much of a pull. There had been summer meet-ups in the first year of being away, but these had dwindled to nothing. None of them knew Lucky had died. His loss felt as heavy as the rucksack Jill was dragging home. Her dream of being a teacher had sunk along with what Bonnie called the dipping happy chemicals in her brain. She'd been right in her diagnosis of depression, and Jill was taking medication, though she was yet to feel any effects. Only the thought that one day soon she would be out walking again in her beloved landscape, kept her alive.

She shifted her position on the lumpy velour seat and reached into her shoulder bag. There was a packet of Polo mints somewhere. The passengers who had shared her booth were gone, the last two getting off here in Lancaster. Now she could eat sweets without having to share them round. She was never sure of social protocols and terrible at small talk. London students had struggled with her. While they responded to the energy of the city with beaming faces and open minds, hers had been clotted with misery. In another hour she would be home.

Her parents had been understanding when she'd tried to tell them how she was feeling, but Bonnie had settled well into her college, and they were focused completely on the boys. Denny hadn't had the best start at the comprehensive school. Jill was their adult daughter, who could look after herself. Her mother sounded happy she was coming home, if only for the extra pair of hands – at least she would be needed again.

Ten minutes later, the train began its tired chug out of the station and on towards Barrow. Jill allowed her breathing to tune into the rhythm of the ancient carriage and the Lancashire countryside. The beauty of the May afternoon rolled past, vast blue skies above thick green woodland and granite-grey escarpments.

Crossing the Kent viaduct was almost too much, the wide estuary and silvery-soft strip of tide forcing her to blink away her tears. Flocks of wading birds beat upwards, disturbed by the train, soaring above the sea on a briny wind. She watched their glide and swoop with envy. Her summer was going to be spent walking by the shore. Alone, but she didn't care.

When the train pulled into the grand Victorian station at Grange-Over-Sands, Jill noticed a lone figure on the platform. Green combat jacket, a small duffle bag on his back, setting her heart pounding. Long auburn hair in a low ponytail and a glowering expression – Stoney. And he was climbing into her carriage. She lowered her head and waited.

A shuffle of footsteps near her seat. Then his voice.

'Jilly? Jilly. It is you.' He sounded older, weary.

A tilt of her head. 'Hello, Stoney.'

He pulled himself into the seat opposite and swung his bag onto the table between them.

'Haven't seen you for ages. You been okay?'

'Yep. Have you?' She wanted to scream that she hadn't been okay, that it was partly his fault.

'The Old Queen died. It's not been great.'

Annie Brownstone dead? A wave of sickness hit Jill, leaving her speechless. She looked into his eyes, so similar to his mother's, and hers filled with tears, running in salty trails down her cheeks. Stoney reached for her hands.

'Shite, isn't it. The Old Geezer's in pieces.'

Jill looked into his face. Something was different, more than just three years of ageing. The pale skin was taut across his cheekbones, dark around his eyes.

'It's so sad, Stoney. I'm sorry,' she whispered. 'When was this?'

'February,' he replied, 'a second stroke got her in the end.'

February. When she had been drowning in her own misery, back in London. Thinking life had nothing to offer, completely mired in self-pity.

'Sorry. I didn't know. I've been away. College.'

He nodded. 'Yeah. I heard you'd gone. Any good?'

'I've finished, actually,' she told him. 'I wasn't keen. You'll laugh, but I couldn't do the animal dissection. Going home now, though, and looking forward to it. What about you?'

He did laugh, but not in an unkind way.

'This pigging war's a bastard,' he said. 'I had a job lined up in the Falklands. New Island. On a nature reserve. Can't go now.' A shrug.

'That's a shame.'

'Both stuck back at home then, hey?' He laughed bitterly.

'I can't wait,' she told him, and it was the truth. 'I guess it's just you and your dad at Seaview now?'

'I don't want to talk about it, Jilly. If you don't mind.'

'Oh. Sorry.' She slid her hands across her knees.

'Not your fault. But there's no happy families at Seaview. The fucking opposite, actually.'

He leaned out into the aisle, nodded at a man in the next booth from them. Then settled himself back against his seat again.

As the train pulled away from Grange, Jill wondered what he was thinking. Did he remember the last time they met? When he'd called her a bitch, and she'd regarded him with such loathing. Did it even matter now?

The train rounded the tip of the Low Furness coast and tidal flats of Morecambe Bay, the water just a sparkle in the distance. A flock of long-billed birds took flight.

'Curlews,' he said, staring upwards into the sunlight. 'I've just taken an injured one to the sanctuary in Kent's Bank.'

'What? On the train?'

He smiled. 'Yep, on the train. I had it wrapped in a towel and then inside my bag.'

Here was a side of Stoney she hadn't seen before. He could shoot rabbits for sport, treat human beings with complete disregard, but would travel twenty miles by train to save a seabird. He didn't match up. For seven years, she had blamed him for every one of her losses. She had been his experiment, and to that, she hadn't given consent. She had never considered him as a person too, with feelings and complications to his life.

'Was it badly injured?'

'I think its wing will have to come off. Looked like it had been chewed by a rat. They probably won't release it, but I couldn't just leave it there.'

'Where did you find it?'

'It was stuck on the mudflats just opposite Seaview. Wasn't moving with the tide like the others. It just looked at me. Probably would have drowned.'

She was holding her breath. 'Could it not fly?'

'Nope.'

'Poor thing.'

He scratched at the gingery stubble on his chin. 'Let's take that walk. Around the tip of the island. The one we never had, and I'll show you a huge colony of them.'

His offer was tempting. Walking by the sea was exactly what she intended to do with her time? And if he wanted more? She could handle it.

'Why not,' she shrugged, enjoying the eagerness in his face. 'It'd be good.'

They watched as the landscape changed again, leaving behind the tidal waters of the Leven Estuary, and flattening into the low fells of the Furness peninsular. At this time of year, beacons of bright gorse were dotted across the vivid green bracken, and small flocks of Herdwicks munched on the short, thick grass. Rocky outcrops of sandstone appeared on the slopes, the final sign she would soon be home. She wanted to cry out. Even the graffitied walls of the railway arches at the centre of her town sent a warmth through her body. She was back in her place, finally.

Once the train pulled into the station, the weight of her rucksack made her unsteady, and she stumbled onto the platform. Stoney followed, taking a roll-up from his Old Holborn pouch, and flicking his lighter aggressively at its tip.

'Bloody stupid idea, this non-smoking carriages on trains. Be banning it in pubs next.' He inhaled deeply, desperately. 'Wanna drag?'

She shook her head. 'I'm going to the bus stop. I'll catch up with you at some point.'

'Okay. Well, I'm going to walk over to the island now. I'll see if The Old Geezer will lend me his car and I'll come over for you, sometime?'

The weariness of the journey, and of the last three years, suddenly caught up with Jill. Home was calling.

'Yep,' she yawned, 'still live in the same place. Give me some time to find my feet again first though, eh?'

Stoney stepped towards her, putting his hands lightly on her shoulders. Then brushed her forehead with his lips.

'I've missed you, Jilly.'

Had she missed him? It was hard to tell.

'Bye,' she said quietly. Then watched him walk away.

In the darkness of her bedroom, Jill allowed herself to cry. But it was not the stiff-jawed, trickly tears she'd been doing a lot of lately. It was choking sobs over which she had no control. For Annie Brownstone. For Lucky. For Moz's reaction when he'd seen her come through the front door. His dive had nearly knocked her off her feet. Denny and Ray had smiled and allowed her to kiss the tops of their heads. Then she'd fallen into her mother's open arms.

'You've got thin,' she'd said into Jill's hair. 'That university didn't feed you properly. What's a girl doing going to university? Well, you're home now.'

And she was. Layers of angst peeled back and dissolved,

until her shoulders unclenched as much as the knots in her stomach. There had been talk of another family dog, though her mother had given a slight shake of her head when the boys couldn't see and distracted them with talk of a camping holiday at the end of July.

Jill looked around her room, at the shelves of books and the soft toys piled high on Bonnie's bed. What would happen in her life now? She was twenty-two years old, with a science degree and a driving licence. And nothing much else.

Tomorrow, she would have to think about finding some part-time work, but it would have to be local. Her nerves were too raw, too exposed, to move away from home again. For now, anyway. Meeting up with Stoney would have to wait. But their shared history had a pull to it, like the ebbing tide. And no matter how many times she threw him into its depths, he would appear again, bobbing in the shallows.

Chapter Fourteen

JUNE 1984

Jill waved as Moz skipped across the playground, soft hair blowing upwards from the crown of his head. Walking him to school had been a way of helping with the Denny problem. She was causing quite a stir, with her long ponytail and her Greenpeace T-shirts, not quite old enough to be his mother, but far too old to be a sibling.

Moz's friends thought she was cool. Their big sisters weren't grown up, and they certainly didn't wear T-shirts adorned with fake blood and swear words. They raced over to him now, and she watched the routine of chest-bumping and jostling. Hands pushed into the pockets of her jeans, she waited. Children of all ages charged around the playground, caught up in their games and their worlds. A dark-haired woman, wearing a floral pinafore and white blouse, wove her way through their play, chatting to parents and smothering them in smiles.

'I'll see you later, Mozzy-boy,' Jill called as her brother zoomed by, arms stretched out, face alight with joy. 'Your teacher's just come out.'

I wish I was her, Jill thought.

Moz dazzled with his smile. 'Bye, Jill.' Still a baby's voice.

The June morning had a clarity to it, and there was promising warmth in the sun. Jill had been home for three weeks, and already her spirits were lifting. Her days had mostly been spent walking across fields and along the winding pathways of her favourite local beauty spot.

The great Abbey of Furness was a tumble of ruined walls and sprouting grasses, mainly ignored by the people of her town. But for Jill, the place took her away from herself and into the stories and energies of another era. It was possible to climb the surrounding slopes, to look down on its sandstone and lichen façade and be transported back to the time of the Tudors.

She would sit for hours, the sun on her back, gazing across the wooded valley which was its home, watching ravens and red kites fight for the highest roosting positions. They raked at the air, calling out their superiority in a swoop of chestnut-and-black gloss, and she would laugh her thoughts up to them. But she missed human company, missed the warmth of an arm slung around her shoulders, and joke shared closely at the expense of the world.

As she neared home, Jill could see Stoney's white car parked across the drive of her house. He was standing on the doorstep, talking to her mother. Auburn hair and a red T-shirt, and his gestures pointing across in the direction of the school. Her stomach did a cartwheel, though she would have struggled to explain why. Stoney waved as she approached.

'Jilly. Was just talking about you.' All chipped tooth and brashness.

'Well, I'm here now, so no need to.' Jill lifted her chin and nodded at him, trying to ignore the strange feeling at her core.

'I've come to whisk you away.' His laugh grabbed at her shoulders.

'Go on, love,' her mother said, with the tiniest of smiles. 'I think I can manage without you.'

Stoney was walking back towards the Wartburg, nodding at her to follow.

'Let me at least change my shoes and get a sweater,' she told him.

Inside the house, she picked up a navy sweatshirt and her trainers from the bedroom. She tugged her hands through her hair and bunched it into an elastic band. She would have to do. It was hardly a date; her relationship with Stoney had zoomed past the date stage within weeks of them first meeting. But suddenly, it mattered. Company, the island wind, it would be a change. She hadn't felt able to walk there since Lucky died, so perhaps things would be different after this.

'I'll park up at West Shore, and we can walk to the North End from there.' Stoney pushed something into the glove compartment as she climbed into the car. 'That okay?'

She nodded. The warm cotton smell of him, his large hands on the steering wheel, so familiar. Though he was thinner than she remembered.

'Haven't been to the beach for ages,' she sighed. 'Stupid really, when I like it so much.'

'You not got your dog anymore?'

'Nope.'

'Nothing stays the same,' he said with a grim smile. 'Have to be grown up about it, don't we?'

'It just makes me feel sad. Everything does.'

'Never mind.' He licked at his lips. 'I've bought a flask of coffee and a packet of mint Yoyos. They were your favourite, weren't they?'

'Great,' she laughed, 'very domesticated.'

A moment passed. 'Been looking after myself since I was fifteen. Used to it now.'

'Don't say that. You had a brilliant mum.'

'Yeah, right.'

'You did. Annie was lovely. To me, especially. I won't forget it.'

Stoney kept his focus on the road. Jill waited. He must have something to say about Annie. Surely? The silence felt dense, murky somehow. She watched the landscape flash by in a blur of red-brick and simplicity. Her hometown. He was part of it. So, what was the tiny jarring at the back of her consciousness?

As they drove across the bridge, a hot gritty wind filtered in through the car windows. Jill looked towards Seaview House. It stared back at her from cool, green shadows. Stoney was silent, gazing at the wide stretch of turquoise sea, and blowing his hair away from his face. Was he remembering, as she was?

A meandering lane led to the shore car park. Families were already walking, beach gear in hand, towards a day on the sands. She thought of the summer of 1976. Heat hazes and the shattering of water with stones. She smiled at the thought of her grandad, cigarette between his fingers even on the beach, teaching the boys how to play cricket.

'Do you remember, Stoney, the day you came down here with my family?'

He turned his face to her. 'I do. Your grandad gave me a fag. He was a good geezer. I liked him,' Stoney frowned. 'Grandparents still around, are they?'

'Oh yes. I saw them a bit when I was in London. They asked about you.'

He pulled onto the beach car park and swung to face the width of the Irish Sea.

'And what did you tell them?'

'Just that I hadn't seen you for a while,' she stared across the greenish-blue expanse, 'and I thought you were doing okay.'

'When you clearly weren't. Did you tell them you were struggling?'

'I couldn't spoil things for them. They loved showing people their granddaughter. The student. Like I was a trophy, or something.' That wasn't fair. It was the place's fault, not theirs. But Stoney was opening his door and stepping away.

'Nothing like being here though, is there?' he crooned. 'London can go to hell!'

A slam of her door, and she was there. The smell of open water and seaweed. Warm and inviting. She breathed in the radiant energy of the place.

'You not getting out much?' Stoney asked, with a shot of laughter. He lifted his rucksack from the back seat, holding out his hand. 'Come on, beach-bum,' he grinned.

Within minutes, they were on the gritty brown sand, balancing, removing their shoes. She watched as Stoney rolled up his jeans and tucked his boots under one arm. The tide was close by, rolling gently, enticing. She ran into the shallow water. Jolts of icy energy ran up her legs, making her weave in and out, up and down, towards Stoney and away from him. The sun burned the back of her neck. Reaching into the water, she cupped a handful, splashed it under her hair and squealed. Stoney watched. Crouched on the sand for a while. Then began to move again.

'Let's go up into the dunes for a bit if you're getting too hot.' He lifted his shoulders and rolled them backwards. 'There's always a good breeze up there.'

'Why not?' She couldn't help herself. The open space and stretch of sky were freeing her, once again.

This is what she needed. Exactly what she needed.

They climbed the dune together, close but not touching. She told him about Denny's problems at school, about Bonnie's college success. And about her own wish to become a teacher. He shook his head, laughed a little. In a snarky way, she thought.

'What's wrong with being a teacher?'

'You. Jilly.'

'What about me?'

'Soz. I didn't mean it in a bad way. Just—' A flare of something in his face. 'You're not exactly Miss Confident, are you?'

She turned away, scrunched her toes in the sand. But what could she say in her own defence? That she did have confidence. Or that it wasn't needed. Neither of those things were true.

Stoney stopped suddenly, put his fingers to his lips. Then he came up behind her, hands on her shoulders, mouth to her ear.

'Look. There. Skylark.' He pointed into the low grass of the dune just in front of them. She shivered at the sudden contact.

'You can hardly see it. The camouflage is superb. Keep still and we'll hear it in a minute.'

He was right. The small tawny-and-white bird took flight, shattering the soft heat with its joyous call.

'How do you know all this stuff?' she whispered. 'How did you even see it?'

He patted the side of his nose with a heavy finger. 'Misspent youth,' he laughed. 'Come on. Friends again.' A wink and a click of his tongue.

The sand on the dunes was dry and almost white, a hot powder of sunshine and glinting rock. Jill found a shaded spot and sat down on her sweatshirt, offering half to Stoney. He wriggled in beside her and opened his rucksack, passing her the thermos then taking out his tobacco pouch.

'Gasping,' he said, holding it up. 'You pour the coffee. Hope you like sugar. Get the biscuits out too.'

Jill poured while he rolled and lit a cigarette, dragging its smoke in deeply, blowing out long plumes.

'So quiet,' he said with a sigh. 'Just how I like it. Surprised you chose London. Thought you were into peace and nature and stuff, too?'

'I realise it was a mistake now.' She munched her biscuit and nodded. 'But the course was exactly what I thought I wanted.'

'Should've asked me. I'd have told you London would be no good.' He turned his face to the sun.

'At eighteen, I just wanted to get away, I guess.' She shielded her eyes with a trembling hand. 'Try somewhere new.'

He peered up at her. 'Yeah, but London. That was a bit drastic.'

'I was born there. I was looking for my roots.'

'Roots? What the hell do you mean?' His laughter cut across her thinking.

The conversation was getting away from her. There were things she wanted to ask him. Sizeable things, bubbling away in her stomach, weighed down by their own gravity. But what would they look like laid out on the clean white cloth of this summer's afternoon?

'I just needed something *big* to happen in my life.' She was going to save the recriminations for another time. What was the point today? 'It didn't quite work out.'

'London is certainly big,' he nodded. 'I'll give you that. Place to lose yourself if it's what you want. Freaks me out.'

'And me, as it turns out. I certainly lost myself there. But I'm slowly remembering who I am.'

He took another puff of his cigarette.

'People change, Jilly, they really do.' He leaned his head on her shoulder. 'I wish—'

'What?'

'Oh, nothing.'

He moved away, and Jill felt something like regret. What was wrong with her? Was she confusing her own loneliness with something more earthy and crude? Either way, just being here with Stoney was like coming home.

She sat listening to the reedy whistle of dune grass and the soft lap of water. Maybe there was something to be made from her relationship with Stoney, after all, something solid and real. Not based on what she was craving right now.

'Come on.' He sat up. Raked at his scalp. 'Finish your drink. I want to get to the North Shore before the tide comes right in.'

They swilled down lukewarm coffee, and packed up, ready to begin the trek across the dunes, and onto the flat salt marshes at the end of the island.

From where she stood, Jill could see across the estuary to Black Combe and the Coniston Mountains. Electric blue skies provided a perfect backlight, showing up the dark hollows and faded green slopes as though they were simply yards away, not miles. The glittering tide lapped at the very edge of the marsh, and small groups of birds bobbed happily, unaware of the scrutiny from Stoney's binoculars.

'Redshanks.' He passed the glasses over to her. 'There's hundreds of them nesting here this year.'

She scanned across the waterline, taking in the beauty of the place. She could see the small towns of Millom and Haverigg, so close it felt possible to step across the sands and be in someone's back garden.

Stoney took the binoculars from her hands. 'Here. Let me look a minute,' he said with a laugh. 'Yep. An egret. Lookster.'

Wading, white and lonely, was a prehistoric-looking bird with a dagger of a beak and thin black legs. Jill watched as it plunged its head into the shallows again and again, fishing desperately.

'They're hungry this time of year,' he told her. 'It'll be wanting to nest.'

She smiled up at him.

'What?' he asked.

'You,' she grinned.

He lifted his shoulders in answer, then tramped away across the spongy grassland. She followed. The incoming tide was dragging in a hot breeze, and she could feel her forearms and the bridge of her nose burning. But the allure of the marsh was a distraction, and she lost her sense of time and place. Stoney picked out for her delicate flowers hidden by marsh grass and knelt to unearth burrows and nests completely camouflaged to the untrained eye.

By mid-afternoon they were walking back along a concrete track laid for trucks and four-wheel drives with business at the north end of the island. Stoney was sunburned, though to Jill, he still looked fresh. She, however, was wilting. But glowing with the joy of spending a fascinating day doing exactly what she loved.

When they arrived back at the car, she slumped into the passenger seat. The air inside was boiling.

'Tired?' quizzed Stoney, swinging into the driver's seat. 'I know the perfect place to get a cup of tea. Seaview?'

A clot of fear formed in her belly. The place would be full of ghosts. Losses.

'I don't want to disturb your dad,' she hedged, but Stoney was shaking his head.

'Doesn't show himself much, these days.' He turned on the ignition. 'The Old Geezer won't bother us.'

This was exactly what she didn't want to hear. Her recollection of the house was ocean-blue and sea-salt fresh, and part of her longed to see it again. Another part just wanted to escape.

'Okay. Well, just a quick drink then, and I'll get off home. Don't want to take up all your time.' She watched the stroke of his hands on the steering wheel.

'It's been a good day,' he said. 'Haven't been up the dunes for yonks.'

'It has.' She slid her arm across his shoulder and laid her head there, just for the briefest moment. He turned slightly and grinned.

As he drove, Jill let her eyes rest on the hawthorn hedgerows and shorn yellow fields. Reminders of another era. Another version of herself. Stoney seemed different, too. More appreciative. Less hungry. He pulled the car alongside the kerb at the bottom of Seaview's steps, opened Jill's door and led her up to the porch, arm around her shoulders. She almost jumped away. Being at Seaview, with its blue tranquillity and lurking shadows, was only adding to her confusion.

The hallway was cold, despite the heat of the day, and it tasted of dust. Jill cleared her throat. Stoney pulled her towards the kitchen.

'Hope The Old Geezer has left some milk,' he muttered. 'It's the only way I know he's living here, sometimes. The milk going down.'

Jill stared around the kitchen. It was different now, reminding her of the one in Platts with its piled-up stained plates and smell of rotting grease. And Mac's bed was missing. Along with the old armchair where she'd first seen Stoney's gran.

'Don't worry about it. Water will be fine.' Jill scanned around the room for any sign of crockery or glasses, but Stoney was rummaging around in a cupboard she remembered as the pantry.

'Got some Long Life here,' he called. 'You put the kettle on.' A chink of cups.

She lifted the grimy kettle and filled it from one of the brass taps over the sink. Stoney was moving about behind her, slamming cupboard doors, sending motes of dust dancing through a slant of sunlight from the window. Suddenly, his fingers were on the back of her neck.

'You're very red, Jilly.' He stepped away again. 'I've got some Ponds, somewhere. It was The Old Queen's.'

'Oh.' A lurch of her heart. 'It'll be fine. I can't feel it at the moment.' But her hand touched the place, and it burned.

She stared at the two cups, side by side on the countertop, each with a beige corner of teabag pointing upwards, waiting to be blanched. Stoney splattered the carton of Long Life down beside them, then patted his pocket.

'I'm going out the back. To light up. Do the business, would you.' He nodded towards the kettle.

Annie Brownstone would never have let the place get so seedy. Jill thought about offering to clean up a little. But that would leave a judgement. She shook away the thought. Best make the tea and step outside. Leave loaded judgements for another day.

Stoney was sitting on a step, in front of French windows, cigarette between his lips and face towards the sun. The garden was in no better shape than when Jill had first seen it. More a mesh of interwoven and arcing branches and brambles than a garden. With no end to it, and no escape.

She passed Stoney a cup, then sat down on the step above his.

'Ta.' He took a sip. 'Piss poor with sterilised milk, but better than nothing.'

'Cheeky.' Jill wanted to elevate herself to his level of banter. But she felt younger than she ever had in his presence. 'I did my best.'

She gazed across the green light of the garden. Wondered why Annie Brownstone had never tended this part of Seaview. Wished she were here now, neutralising the charged air.

Stoney threw the dying end of his cigarette onto a spread

of grey paving stones, then ground it in with the toe of his boot. He laid his head on Jill's arm and looked up at her.

'Funny how things turn out.' He tucked some strands of hair behind his ear. 'Us, sitting here, I mean.'

'Why *funny*?'

'Like it was meant to be, I suppose.' He shifted his head. 'You and me.'

'There is no you and me, Stoney.'

His hand slid up her arm. 'There could be.'

His touch. Enough to make her feel important but not threatened. Wanted but not smothered. She said nothing. Waited. He lifted the cup from her hands and placed it, with his, at the side of the steps, then knelt in front of her and brushed his lips over the knuckles of both her hands.

'Like I said,' he whispered. 'You and me, Jilly.'

She rummaged amongst the feelings of gratitude and loneliness trying to force their way out through her stomach. Below the unexpected pulse of desire, she could find no love, no future. Only the soft and pliable wish to comply, to make someone else happy. And her smile was the only encouragement he needed.

'Let's go inside,' he said, lifting her upwards. 'Who knows what might happen.'

He pulled open one of the French windows and led Jill into a small sitting room she hadn't seen before. Sunlight pooled on the wooden floor, and a rocking chair full of cushions was tucked away behind an overloaded bookshelf.

'This was The Old Queen's room,' Stoney told her as he tugged at her hand. She wanted to linger. To take in the titles of Annie's books and pore over the two paintings on the wall. But it all passed by in a blur of sea spray and faded turquoise, then they were in the hallway and at the foot of the stairs.

'You never saw my room, did you?' He grinned. 'First time for everything.'

He clicked his tongue against the inside of his cheek, and Jill's desire dropped like a stone, smashing against the pale blue swirls of the stair carpet. How could she go through with this? She and Stoney weren't even in the same book, never mind on the same page. But she followed him. Into the coiled tension of his bedroom, sweat-tinged and with dark curtains pulled across the window, a bed demanding satisfaction. Watched as he removed his boots and jeans, then slid away his Y-fronts. Let herself be guided towards him and kissed. Lifted her own T-shirt off and pinged her bra away.

'You owe me, Jilly,' he gasped, pressing his hardness against her stomach, and guiding her hand there.

She tried to match caress for caress; why did she feel so hollowed-out? Then she was on the bed, his lips to her throat and a knee between her legs. Stoney fumbled with the button of her jeans, and a bolt of fear shot through her. Balancing on the edge of a knife was exactly what she was doing, and as he slid a hand under the fabric of her knickers, she suddenly realised pretending was going to cause her to fall. With a jerk of her body, she tried to roll away, but she was trapped.

'I can't,' she cried. Any energy she had left went into that cry.

'Fuck's sake, Jilly.' Stoney's face blurred above her. His clean-cotton smell replaced by something salty and corrupt.

She locked eyes with him. A jolt of ice. He nuzzled at her face, but she turned her head away.

'I said no.'

He groaned into the pillow. She waited.

'Finish me off, at least.' He rolled onto his back. And Jill could see what he wanted.

Afterwards, he reached across the bed and grabbed a crumple of navy fabric – a T-shirt, she thought – and shoved it towards her.

'Wipe your hands,' he muttered, arm behind his head again and blatant.

'Can you take me home?' Jill fought down a burn of acid that was grabbing at the back of her throat. She clutched at her own shirt, turning her back and then sliding it over her head.

'Course,' he said. 'But can I have a fag first?'

Chapter Fifteen

JUNE 1984

Jill stretched her legs towards the muted sky and pulled hard on the chains of her swing. Then let herself go and enjoyed the rush of sun-soft air. Stoney sat on the swing next to her, feet on the ground and blowing circles of grey smoke into the afternoon. After her bedroom experience at Seaview, she'd promised herself she wouldn't see him again. Yet, here she was. When he'd turned up after a few days, a plea for an afternoon's company on his lips, she found it difficult to refuse. Wanted to refuse. But the flare of his intelligence tempted her in, as it always did.

'I don't think those little ankle-biters are happy,' he called as she zoomed by, 'us being on their swings and stuff.' He stuck his cigarette between his lips and stood up. Then bowed at the two young women who clutched the hands of three small children.

'All yours, ladies.'

They turned and walked away.

'There's gratitude,' he laughed, taking a skip towards the back of Jill's swing, and catching at the seat. She slid forward and came to a stop.

'Hey. I was enjoying that.' Her feet hit the floor and she hopped away. 'Have you come over all man-of-the-people?'

'Doubt it.' He flicked the end of the cigarette. 'Just fancy a bit of a walk.' He tilted his head towards the pebbly beach. 'Tide's in. We can chuck some stones.'

'Can't spend our lives chucking stones though, can we?'

'Meaning?'

Jill pushed her hands into the pockets of her jeans. Peered down at her sandalled feet. *Meaning we can't be free spirits forever.* 'I need to look for work. So do you,' she said.

Stoney picked up a piece of flat granite, then pulled back his arm and spun it across the flat surface of the tide. 'I'll never be a wage-slave. Saw what it did to The Old Queen.'

Jill frowned. What was he saying about Annie Brownstone? 'Your mother was dedicated to her job. She was nobody's slave.'

Except yours.

'Yeah, well.' Another stone-skim. 'I'll never work for The Establishment. But, be my guest, Miss Holland.' He extended his arm towards her. She caught a flash of soft inner-elbow.

Jill looked out at the sea, a cool jade-green on this washed-out summer's day. More than anything, she wanted to belong. To be part of something more important than herself. And if it meant joining a part of society creating such scathing disregard, then she would.

'Better get going,' she said. 'I promised I'd be home for tea.' She glanced at him. 'If that's not too conformist.'

Stoney snorted. 'Well, here's something even more edgy. Would you mind if I drop in on Mick, first?' He tapped the side of his nose. 'He's got something of mine.'

She did mind. But said nothing. Just lifted her head in agreement. They crunched back up the beach, stepping carefully. Something had shifted, and Jill wanted to free herself.

Stoney pulled the car away from the west shore and along a

sea road linked with the island's secondary school. Jill stared out at the 1970s flat roofed building, so different from the place where she'd made the transition from child to young adult. A group of girls, with navy-blue shorts and rounders bats swinging, moved across the wide fields. A woman was coming out of the front gate, young and immaculately dressed, a leather portfolio tucked under her arm. Something about her gait cut across Jill's memory, and she sat forward in her seat, peering through the open car window.

'Can you pull over for a minute, Stoney?' She tilted her head. 'Please?'

He slowed at the kerb, glancing sideways as Jill opened the door. 'I'll just be a minute,' she said. As she climbed out, the young woman trotted by. Then stopped to stare.

'Jill?' she gasped. 'Jill Holland?' There was the sunny smile. Jill's heart jumped.

'Susie.' She held out her arms, and they embraced. Jill caught the smell of expensive perfume, and quickly stepped away again, looking down at her own jeans and faded T-shirt.

But her friend was grinning. 'You're beautiful. A proper student.'

Jill shook her head. 'I was one. Finished now though.'

'Oh. So, did you become a teacher then? I know it's what you wanted to do.'

'No. I did my degree, but it didn't work out, in the end.'

Susie eyed the car. 'Is that Andy Brownstone? You still with him?' She gave a small wave.

'I was never with him.' Jill shuffled her feet. 'And I'm not with him now. We're just friends.'

Susie peered at her. 'Oh. What happened to the teaching?'

Jill shrugged. 'Not sure. I don't want to go back to college. I didn't enjoy it. But hey, what about you? Do you work here?' She pointed towards the school building.

'I do. I'm one of the secretaries. How about that?'

They hugged again. 'You certainly look the part,' Jill said, stepping back to admire her friend's wide-shouldered cream blouse and pencil skirt. 'And those shoes.'

Susie paused, patting her hand over the melting make-up line across her forehead.

'Are you okay?' Jill asked. 'It's hot, isn't it?'

'I was just thinking. You should get in touch with the headteacher here,' Susie replied. 'He's running a new scheme – it's a trial really – where you train to be a teacher on the job and get your Cert-Ed from Charlotte Mason. That college up in The Lakes.'

'Really?' Jill wanted to ask more questions, but she was conscious of Stoney, waiting for her in the stifling car. 'Can we meet up and talk about it a bit more?' She took Susie's hands in hers, hopeful now.

'Course we can,' came the reply. 'I finish at two every day. Come over and we can have lunch in the canteen. They won't mind. Tomorrow? Or Thursday?'

Jill's thoughts were racing. There was something in Susie's idea, she was sure, and she'd heard of the teacher training college in the Lake District. Never considered it for herself, though. What college would be interested in someone like her? Susie came from a different world, where opportunities were always to hand. One of Annie Brownstone's paintings sprung up in Jill's memory. A pastel sky and seascape with a sailboat far away on the line of the horizon. The same boat was in the foreground, too. Jill had often gazed at it and wondered why it was so affecting.

'I'll be outside at two tomorrow, if that's okay,' she said to her friend. 'You won't get into trouble, will you?'

Susie giggled. 'I'm a school secretary. We virtually run the place.' Jill was in awe. Quiet little Susie, and now she was really someone.

'I'm so chuffed for you,' she said. 'Tomorrow, then.'

Jill climbed back into the car and slammed the door.

'All right?' Stoney asked as he pulled away from the kerb.

'Yep. I might even work at this school one day, who knows.'

He gave her a lopsided grin.

As they drove across the island, Jill thought about Susie. There was a confidence in her that she'd never had when they were at school. Back then, her friend had been completely ruled by parents. While Jill was wandering across beaches and fields and thinking about boyfriends, Susie had been a Girl Guide and working on her Duke of Edinburgh Award. Then there had been secretarial college. She'd clearly had some success, judging by the way she now appeared to be a fully-fledged adult, with clothes and shoes to match.

'Does Mick still live in the same place?' she asked, looking for distraction.

'He does. Liness Barn, if you remember.'

'On his own?'

'On his own.' Stoney frowned. 'What you worried about now, little Jilly?'

'Don't call me that,' she muttered. 'I'm nearly twenty-three.'

'Jeez. You go from hot to cold and back again, all in the space of minutes.' He tugged on the car's indicator. 'We're here now so lighten up.'

He parked the Wartburg at the roadside and climbed out. Jill followed. She remembered the uneven strip of tarmac; it led down to her beach. There were no houses, only a row of sandstone barns with a semi-circle of rough ground to the front. This couldn't be the place.

But Stoney was walking towards a wooden doorway, its green paint peeling and a black latch instead of a handle. It wasn't locked, and he shouldered himself in, tilting his head for her to follow. She had to blink a few times, struggling with the grey gloom of the place. There was a living room of sorts, with a filthy brown sofa and two tweed-covered chairs, carelessly placed. In the centre was a large coffee table littered with ashtrays and matchboxes, tobacco pouches and Rizla packets. She could smell dogs and damp. Black mould spread across crumbles of plaster.

Stoney walked away, through another open door at the back of the room. Jill heard him talking to someone, then he appeared at the door with Mick. His skin was harshly tanned, deep grooves surrounding his mouth, giving his face a mask-like quality. He wore a sleeveless leather jerkin and a pair of cut-off jeans. His lurcher, now grizzled rather than brindled, pattered out behind him.

'All right?' he nodded, twisting up his top lip. 'Sit down.'

Jill did as she was invited to do, but something didn't feel right. The atmosphere jumped. Like it was full of buzzing flies. Darting. Trying to escape. And when she peered closer at the contents of the table, she could see tin-foil, metal spoons with brown marks, and the burst-open plastic capsules from medicine, along with half-eaten packets of Spangles and Opal Fruits. She shuddered. What had she got herself into?

Stoney sat down next to her and looked at the older man. 'Make us a brew, lad,' he laughed, 'and I'll light up. What have you got?' He picked up a tin from the table and shook it next to his ear.

'Green,' Mick laughed. 'Careful though. It's hot.'

'Did you get me some?'

'Yep. But it'll cost you.'

'Worth it, I guess?' A sly smile passed between them.

'Oh, aye.'

Stoney cocked his head. 'You getting the brew?'

Mick disappeared into the back room.

Jill wasn't sure what to do. She wanted out of the situation. Less than ten minutes ago, she'd been thinking about becoming a teacher and now, here she was, sitting in a room with two men about to smoke cannabis. She watched as Stoney laid out tobacco on a Rizla paper, then burned and crumbled what looked like a lump of dark green plasticine, laying it along the top. Whatever she thought of him, this wasn't her.

Within minutes, Mick appeared again, this time carrying three mugs. He cleared a space on the table and put them down, pushing one in Jill's direction.

'Haven't got any sugar,' he mumbled.

'It's okay thanks,' she replied, looking at the surface of the tea. She picked up the mug. The tea looked dark and stewed but she sipped it, grateful for the distraction. Stoney held the long cigarette in his mouth and flicked a lighter at it, inhaling deeply. There was the familiar rubbery smell, and it carried Jill back to 1976 as surely as if she'd been there, sitting in a canvas tent in the middle of the hay fields.

He passed it over to Mick, who took it clumsily but drew deeply.

'What about her.' Those black eyes. Like a jackdaw's.

'Doubt it,' laughed Stoney. 'Not our Jilly.'

Jill's face was burning, from the heat of the day as much as from embarrassment. When the aromatic cigarette was offered to her, she shook her head and peered down into her drink.

I've got to get out of here.

'That's good stuff,' Stoney breathed. 'Give us it.' He reached out a hand.

'Greedy,' snarled the older man, taking another deep drag, then he passed it across again. Jill gulped down her tea.

'Did you hear what happened to mi'laddo?' Mick nodded in the direction of the sea.

'Who?' Claggy smoke mixed with Stoney's words.

'That guy from down the boatyard. The one who gets us gear, sometimes.'

'The big guy?'

'Him, yeah. Nearly killed himself, didn't he. Shot-up for the first time with a bad lot of stuff. Foaming at the mouth he was, so his mate told me.'

Stoney ran a hand across his chin. 'Jeez. Was it cheap gear, like?'

Mick raised one shoulder. 'Dunno. Probably, knowing him. Not free with his cash, is he?'

They both laughed at this, and Jill felt foolish. Were they saying they had a friend who'd almost died after injecting something? Is that what shooting-up meant? More than ever, she felt like a child in a roomful of adults. The dog crept across and laid its head on her lap. Watery brown eyes stared into hers. She ran a hand across its bony grey head, and it whined softly.

'Likes you,' said Mick, eyelids drooping. 'Got good taste.'

The dog's ears were velvet soft. Jill rubbed them between her fingers, thinking about what she should do next. The last thing she wanted was to become part of what was going on here. She imagined how Susie would react. *Vouch for Jill Holland? I don't think so.* The cannabis was passed back and forth between the two men, its earthy scent catching in the back of her throat.

Stoney stretched out against a frayed yellow cushion, pressing the palms of his hands to the back of his neck. 'I feel better, now.' A sigh. 'Give us a kiss, Jilly.'

'No.'

Mick sniggered. 'What the fuck use is that?'

'Aww. Is Jilly being all chilly? You always blow hot and cold.' A half-smile at Mick. 'If you get my meaning.'

'Not much of a girlfriend, if you ask me.' Mick had the cigarette again. Chin lifted and forcing out smoke rings.

'Nobody's asking you.' Stoney leaned towards her. 'C'mon, Jilly. Loosen up.'

How does a situation like this end? she thought. *And where do I fit in?* She didn't. She wanted out. Giving the dog a light push to move him away, she jumped up and brushed herself down.

'Stoney,' she snapped. 'Can you drive me home?'

He looked at her through half-glazed eyes. 'Jilly? What you talking about?'

'I want to go,' she insisted, and he caught her tone.

He grabbed at her hand and lifted it to his lips. 'Poor Jilly. In a minute.' A sarcastic laugh. The other Stoney was gone. She yanked the hand away, and a shiver of revulsion snaked its way up her arm.

'Now,' she said coldly, 'or shall I walk?'

He stood up. To Mick he said, 'Won't be long.' Then, taking her hand again, he pulled her across the room and out of the house. She grabbed at the front door and closed it behind them.

'Let go of me,' she cried, but Stoney was dragging her up the tarmac driveway. At the top, he fumbled around in his jeans pocket for the car keys, dropping them and struggling to get them again. When he unlocked the car, Jill stepped away.

'Give me the keys, Stoney,' she growled. 'You're not driving me when you've been smoking that stuff.'

'Fuck off. You're not insured anyway.'

She held out her hand. 'Better than you crashing while half-stoned. I don't deserve this. Your drug habit has nothing to do with me.' The words came out with a force that shocked her. Stoney handed over the keys.

She lifted her eyebrows in mock surprise. Why had he given in so easily? 'Get in,' she told him, 'and say nothing.'

As it turned out, the Wartburg was very similar to her father's Lada, and she had no trouble adapting to the drive. Stoney sat back in the passenger seat, head lolling. He said nothing.

At the end of her street, a wave of relief washed over Jill. She'd never felt more strongly about what she did – and didn't

— want for herself, and this situation with Stoney had been a mistake. He could crash or get pulled over on the drive back to Mick's — she didn't care, as long as she was free of him.

In front of her house, she turned the keys and switched the engine off. They both sat in silence for a moment.

'Swap you,' Stoney said suddenly. A shove at the door, then he climbed out. Jill did the same. Before she could register anything else, he was on her, pushing her up against the back of the car, securing her with one hand and pawing at her with the other, forcing his lips down hard on hers. She tasted the rubbery cigarettes and gagged at the smell of his sweat-soaked hair.

'Get off me,' she choked, pushing her hands against his chest.

He tried again; lips twisted into a sneer. 'Poor Jilly. Not what you want? Shame.'

'It isn't what I want. And I don't want you.' She pushed again and this time he stepped back.

He squinted at her through smudgy green eyes. 'So, you flirt all day with me then say no, right at the last minute. Why am I not surprised?'

Had she flirted all day? No. She hadn't. 'This is your problem, not mine,' she snarled. 'I'll never think anything of you while you're doing drugs.'

She moved towards the house. Her mother was there in an instant. Stoney turned his back and dragged open the car door.

'See you around, Jilly,' he said with a sneer, looking sideways at her, and she watched as he slammed the door and screeched away.

September 2018

The place's fault?

Jill has heard this expression so many times, has wondered whether this was the reason she couldn't let go. And even now, as she stands and watches the glassy green stretch of water, listens to the song of the gulls on the hot still air, she knows the landscape tied her to Andrew Brownstone. It was him and he was it, one embedded in the other. That she hadn't realised his own emotions were spiralling, can only have been because of her youth.

Her feelings for him had been complex. A mix of envy and admiration and just the tiniest sprinkling of sympathy. But she hadn't liked Malcom Gibson, with his hard edges and greedy mouth. He'd always had something to hide. She is sure he would have been disdainful about her wish to become a teacher. Because of him, she knew she had no future with Andrew Brownstone.

Across the water, Jill can see the tall copper coloured building that is the local further education college. She has visited many times in recent years, with groups of teenagers from her school. The college runs an outreach program, designed to sweep floundering sixteen-year-olds away from their youthful meandering and into a life of study and diligence. Sometimes it works. Mostly, the kids engage just to claim the goody bags and access the high-spec canteen. Children aren't left to chance anymore. Accountability exists in the system. She wonders what the outcome for Stoney might have been, had a place like this existed.

While she'd had the chance to become a teacher finally, he was left to the infinite wisdom of Malcom Gibson.

Chapter Sixteen

DECEMBER 1986

'See ya, miss.'

Peter Hall. First in and last out. Jill liked him but wanted him gone. Soft flakes of snow were falling outside, triggering mild panic amongst the teaching staff and utter joy amongst the pupils; she just wanted to get home.

'You get off, Peter. Before it gets too heavy. Homework Monday, don't forget.' But she couldn't help laughing at his toothy grin. He winked, exaggerated, in the way the local boys liked. They thought of themselves as tough hardened men, at age fifteen. She knew the type.

The harsh fluorescent lighting in her classroom jarred white against the soft grey of the outside. School was closing early. She'd have an extra half-day to herself. A pile of exercise books on her desk were waiting to be marked. Science books, some with torn spines, wet and smudgy after experiments and live write-ups. Monday would do. It was her second year of teaching: she was allowed to ease off. Have fun. Kick back. She and Bonnie were meeting up with Susie in a pub not far from their home, and she was looking forward to leaving her teacher-hat behind. Her sister was home for

Christmas, a rare treat now she'd settled in Leeds after her college years.

The classroom door opened again, and Gail Redshaw, Jill's manager, poked her head in.

'Come on, love.' Her piercing, teacher voice. 'Get yourself home.' She lifted her glasses away from her face. 'Good to have a bit of extra time, isn't it? I'm shattered.'

Jill nodded her agreement. The dark December days were some of the hardest she had encountered, even more than the first weeks of her placement at the school. There was tiredness like she'd never experienced, and the sense of living only for the job. The balance was better than it had been, though far from perfect. But every day she thanked Susie for the leg-up.

On the floor lay her leather briefcase: a present from her parents when she'd passed her teaching certificate. The thought always made her smile. They had been so proud. Their daughter, a teacher. She was even starting to believe it herself. Now, she lifted the briefcase onto her desk, and filled it with the things she would need for the weekend. When the brass fastenings clicked shut, she gave a small wink.

Miss Holland, teacher extraordinaire.

The winter coat she had treated herself to, hung on a hook behind her stockroom door. Her usual choice of waterproof anorak had been left at home, in favour of smart black wool, though the anorak would have been better for the journey today. The bus would be leaving in fifteen minutes, and she intended to be on it – there was no guarantee another one would come along, and she wasn't wearing the right shoes for a trek off the island and into town. She shrugged on the heavy coat, twisted up her hair and pushed it down the back of her collar. Then wound her scarf around her neck. The briefcase and her handbag she swung over her shoulder. With a click of the light switches, she left the room.

School was quiet. The children were long gone, the usual

lunchtime banter ditched in favour of home. Jill's court shoes tapped noisily along the corridor linoleum, and she could already smell the familiar scent of Zoflora, drifting on steamy air.

As soon as she could afford it, Jill intended to buy herself a car. Watching her colleagues clambering into theirs, dumping bags of marking on the back seat, made her jealous. How much easier would her life be without the scramble for the bus every morning and evening? It reminded her of the months she'd spent travelling to and from the grammar school back in 1976. A memory too poignant to be enjoyed; the child was long gone.

At the front door, Jill peered out through the glass panels at the weather. The snow had stopped falling, but a thick layer covered the roads and pavements around school. The playing fields were transformed into a vast white desert, and the usual spikes of winter landscape were blurred around the edges.

Outside, the air was heavy with cold and silence. As she walked towards the bus stop, an occasional car crawled by, sending out splashes of wet slush and spattered light. People stepped carefully along the pavements, huddled down in their winter coats, faces starkly pink in the lilac gloom. Jill dodged in between them. The toes of her shoes had darkened. She glanced down. Blew out a sigh. Being near the coast meant any water left a tidemark; she knew this to her cost.

As she trod carefully through the wet slush, she was suddenly conscious of one person. A green parka, hood up, but something about the walk. She stepped aside.

'Sorry.' Then a blinking recognition, a flash of alarm. It was Andrew Brownstone. Stoney. What was he doing here? He peered at her from the depths of his hood.

'Oh,' she said, half smiling. 'Hello.'

The eyes looking back were green and glistening, ringed in brownish-grey shadows. 'Jilly. Long time, no see.'

Jill tried to find words. 'How are you?' was all that would come. What did you say to someone who languished in a part of your life you wanted to forget? But could never forget.

'Been better,' he muttered, harsh and prickly. Not how she remembered his voice.

'I'm about to go for the bus.' She tried to walk past him, but he moved with her, pulling his hood down. His face had altered. The cheekbones were more pronounced and there was a pallor to his skin, freckles almost faded now. Strands of long auburn hair clung together, flat against the bones of his head. Jill stared, open-mouthed, quickly totting up the length of time for this transformation to have taken place. It was almost three years since she'd last seen him. He hadn't aged well. The coat hung off his frame, and he was shivering.

'You working here now?' He gestured towards the building. 'At the island school, like?'

'I am,' she nodded. Then wished she hadn't.

'La-di-da.' His lips twisted upwards.

'What are you talking about?' Jill's sharp retort clouded the air. 'It's not up to you where I work.'

His face crumpled. 'No. Sorry. It's just—'

Jill waited. An awkward silence, reminding her of their first meeting. From behind came the swish of heavy, wet tyres. The bus was pulling along the road. Here was her escape route.

'I'll have to go.' A sick feeling gripped her stomach. 'See you sometime?'

'Whatever,' came the reply. He turned away.

'Could go to the Round House. If you like. For a coffee.' What was she doing? But there was something about him. It tugged at her chest, and she couldn't walk away. The vigour was gone from him. The shine.

'Could do.' The lopsided grin. 'You paying?'

Inside the café it was warm and dank. Stoney sat himself down at one of the circular red tables and pulled out a pouch of tobacco. Jill glanced across at the counter and smiled at the two waitresses, who didn't look very pleased to see them.

'Are we okay to be here?' she called. 'Or are you closing early because of the weather?'

She heard Stoney huff lightly. Then watched as the younger of the two women, sullen faced and dressed in a light-blue tabard, came towards them.

'What did you want?' she muttered. 'Bit late for hot meals.'

'Just coffees. And toast if you've got it. Thanks.'

'Fuck me, Jilly.' Stoney was laughing behind her. 'You've gone all bossy. Who'd have thought it.'

Jill hung her coat over the back of the chair and slid her bags onto another one. What was he talking about? Bossy? If you wanted things done, you did them. The waitress walked away, hands thrust deep in her pockets.

'And a pot of jam if you have any.'

Stoney spluttered and pulled the ashtray towards him. 'God help the kids in your class,' he said, eyes downwards.

Something about him stopped Jill from biting back: the skinny slope of his shoulders perhaps, or the way his fingers trembled around his cigarette.

'What've you been doing with yourself?' she asked, pulling out a chair. His eyes were on her, and it didn't feel good.

'Not much. Just surviving.'

'Still at Seaview?'

'Yep.' He flicked cigarette ash, then shuddered a little. 'Still at fucking Seaview.'

Jill watched him for a moment and wondered if she should ask about his father. But something stopped her. And Stoney was speaking again.

'Before you ask, The Old Geezer is still clinging to life, and still making mine a misery.'

'Why?'

Stoney rested his elbows on the table and rubbed a hand across his face. 'You don't wanna know,' he muttered.

Jill took the warning and searched around in her mind for something else to talk about. Everything she came up with felt inflammatory, and in the end, she settled on the weather, making him sneer all over again, at her smart coat and high-heeled shoes.

The waitress brought their coffee and toast and snapped that the café was closing in another half hour. Jill assured her they'd be gone by then and slipped a five-pound note into her hand, while Stoney sprinkled sugar from a grubby glass pot over his coffee.

'Need the energy,' he laughed when she stared. 'Pass us some toast, will you?'

It seemed to Jill he could do with more than just *energy*. There was something about him, something hovering just below the surface of his snappy bravado. It reminded her of those inflatable swimming rings, when someone pulled the stopper out; he was deflating. And something was causing the puncture.

'Do you still see Mick?' she asked.

'I do.' He wiped toast crumbs from the sides of his mouth. 'His dog died, though. So he doesn't get out like he used to.'

'He could get another. Couldn't he? My mum is thinking of doing the same thing. The boys are pestering.'

'God, Jilly. This isn't bloody happy families. This is real life. You never understood, did you?'

What was he talking about? She had a sudden unsettling thought: he was ill. But wouldn't he have said something? Instead of just biting at the edges of her concern and sending it back, half chewed? She hadn't even wanted to come to this wretched café, with its pine-clad walls and air of misery. Yet here he was, making her feel like a kid who was moaning about a trip to the seaside.

'I am actually happy with my life, as it turns out, Stoney. So don't take the micky out of it, if you don't mind.'

They sat for a while in cold silence. Jill stirred a spoon around in her coffee but didn't drink it. Stoney hoovered up everything else. The waitresses muttered under their collective breaths.

'We'd better go,' she whispered when enough time had passed. 'I have to get the bus off the island, and by the looks of it,' she glanced out of the window at the heavily falling snow, 'they won't be running for much longer.'

'Yeah. Better had. Wouldn't want to get trapped, would you?'

But there was no solace in his tone, no concern. Only a brittle sarcasm.

'Good luck,' she managed to say. 'I'm sure we'll bump into each other again.' Though she wanted anything but.

He leaned back in his chair and looked up at her. His smile gave nothing away.

'Course we will, Jilly.' The chip-toothed grin, not reaching his eyes. 'The island's got you, like it's got me.'

Jill wasn't sure of the emotions flashing through her body. One of them made her want to kiss him. The other was telling her to get as far away from him as it was possible to be.

Chapter Seventeen

DECEMBER 1986

Jill watched her brothers as they sat around the dining table, heads together over homework. Ray wasn't far from the age Stoney had been when she'd first met him. The thought shocked her. Was her brother exposed to the same sordid world? And what about Stoney's friend, Mick? There was a name: a young man leading a boy astray. Her mother would see straight through anything like that, surely. But Annie Brownstone had been doting and attentive. So, why hadn't she been able to do anything? Whatever answers she could find, Jill knew one thing. She didn't want to become tangled in his story again.

Bonnie was busy with heated tongs, creating fat blonde curls that would drop out as soon as they stepped into the damp chill of the evening. Nothing fazed her sister. She'd become a describing-word in their household.

'You should be more *Bonnie,*' their mother would say, if any of them struggled with life. As if.

'Don't be late in, girls,' she was saying as she wiped her hands on a tea towel. 'Your dad doesn't sleep until you're home.'

Bonnie fluffed up her curls and caught Jill's eye in the mirror.

'We're not girls, Mother,' she said, 'and we're only in The Farmer's. It's not ten minutes away.'

Jill was thinking about her new boots. They'd cost a fortune and the black suede would be saturated by the slushy pavements as soon as she set foot outside. Perhaps she wouldn't wear them after all. But her mother was speaking again.

'Jill? What do you think?'

'Sorry. What?' she asked, running a hand across the bones of her face.

Her mother frowned. 'Do you want Dad to pick you up later?'

Bonnie was shaking her head, just slightly, so only Jill could see.

'Erm. No. No need. Susie's Paul will be there, and he'll walk with us, I'm sure. It's only round the corner.'

Susie had fallen in love with a policeman. He was a great guy, wide-faced and healthy, and Jill liked him a lot. He had been born in Carlisle, a city in the north of the county and almost in Scotland, but Barrow had become his patch, and he and Susie were to be married the following summer. She would be Mrs Susie Bates, wife of PC Bates, as she never tired of telling anyone who would listen.

Jill was happy she'd found her old schoolfriend again, and grateful for the strings she had pulled to get Jill onto the teacher training scheme at the school where they both worked.

While Bonnie rummaged around in her shoulder bag, Jill slid her coat on. It was still damp on the outside, but nothing had soaked through the thick wool. She thought about the parka Stoney had been wearing earlier, green canvas saturated with snowmelt. Seeing the decline in him filled her with guilt, but she couldn't have explained the feeling. And now Bonnie was stepping through the front door and beckoning her outside.

When they reached the pub, strings of multicoloured Christmas lanterns, dripping with snowmelt, flashed a welcome. The two windows glowed warmly with yellow light as much as with beaming faces. Jill's feet were soaked after the short walk, and Bonnie's hair was flat and damp.

It was snowing again. Soft white flakes covered the shoulders of their coats and caught in Bonnie's false eyelashes. Jill opened the door and the two of them stepped into an atmosphere of warmth and welcome. Susie waved to them from the bar.

'I'll get the drinks,' she mouthed across the sound of the juke box. Shakin' Stevens' 'Merry Christmas Everyone' blasted out its catchy melody. *Here we go again*, Jill thought. She lifted her hand in greeting. Bonnie went to fix her hair.

People crowded around small wooden tables, drinking and laughing, faces alight with alcohol and heat. Jill unzipped her coat and lifted it off, shaking the last few flakes of snow onto the floor. She crept up behind Susie and laid an arm across her waist.

'Hi. Didn't see you at work today. Is all okay?'

Susie grinned. 'Course. I took the afternoon off and met Paul for lunch. I've picked his wedding suit.'

'You've picked his suit? Is that how it works?' Jill raised her eyebrows.

Susie reached into her purse and handed the barmaid a five-pound note. 'It's exactly how it works in my world,' she said with a laugh, 'and it's only for the evening-do anyway. He's wearing full dress uniform for the wedding itself.'

'Oh, yeah. Course he is.' Would she ever get married, she wondered? Every one of her relationships, apart from with Stoney, had left her cold. And she didn't consider what she'd had with him to be anything other than the fantasies of a spoilt schoolboy. At fourteen, she'd been too young to realise it, but she did now. And wished it different. Yet here he was, pushing into her thoughts, daring to show himself again.

Paul was sitting in a cushioned booth at the back of the pub. Tall and slim, he was a head above everyone else and Jill could see him waving a hand and grinning.

'Hiya,' he said as she sat down. 'Grim out there, isn't it?'

'It is.'

'Where's your sis?' Everyone loved Bonnie.

'She's checking her hair.' Jill sighed. 'You know what she's like.'

Paul smiled at that. 'How're you doing, anyway? How's the world of teaching? Don't know how you do it. Bloody yobs.'

Jill bit back. 'They're not all *yobs*. You only meet the bad ones. And it's not their fault, half the time.'

'Whose fault is it then?' Paul shifted forward in his seat, hands on the table.

'Parents? Friends?' she offered. 'Drugs?'

The atmosphere shifted. 'Drugs? Don't get me started. You wouldn't believe–'

Oh, I would, Jill thought. Here was the chance to find out what was going on with Stoney. That he smoked cannabis, she knew for certain. Its impact, she wasn't so sure about. But she'd have to be careful not to alert Paul to anything but generalised observations. Which would be difficult because the guy had the nose of a spaniel and the brain of an inquisitive border collie.

'There's a kid in my fifth-year biology class,' she said. 'He brags constantly about smoking grass. What does he mean, Paul?' She laughed grimly. 'I'm guessing it's not the stuff you cut from your lawn.'

He slapped his hands against his thighs and let out a loud guffaw. 'No, it isn't.' He shook his head. 'It's the name kids give to cannabis. God knows why.'

'I thought so.' She was trying to act like a misinformed parent. 'It's affecting his schoolwork.'

'It would. Switches the brain off, in my opinion. But,' he held up his hands, 'what do I know?'

'Could it be making him ill? He doesn't look at all well. He's lost weight and he's kind of shaky.'

Paul peered at her. 'I hope you're going to tell his parents, Jill.'

'Oh. Of course.' She needed to be careful. 'I was just interested.'

'Well, they'd better keep an eye on their kid, if you ask me. The soft stuff always leads to the hard, if you get my meaning.' He tapped the side of his nose. 'And then you would see a change in him.' He rummaged around in his pocket. 'You can give them my name and number if they want any help with things.'

Paul Bates. Ever the inflated sense of how important his job was. Jill started to tell him she'd better leave it, then Susie arrived with their drinks.

'You two not arguing again, are you?' A tilt of her head, and Paul winked it back.

'Discussing, you mean.' Jill shrugged. 'Just work.'

'Discussing then,' she laughed. 'No work talk tonight. Not in here, anyway.'

Paul reached for his drink. 'Fair enough.' He flashed a conspiratorial smile at Jill. 'Cheers all.'

Jill and Susie chinked their glasses against his, watching as Bonnie came back, hair fluffed, coat discarded.

'Thanks, Suse,' she breathed. 'I need this.' The drink was swilled down in one gulp, then Bonnie inserted herself into the booth with Paul. 'C'mon, Paulie, keep up,' she laughed, and he downed his drink almost as quickly.

The evening wore on. Bonnie discovered a guy she knew from school, and Jill listened to Susie's wedding talk until her eyelids became heavy and she only wished for her bed. Paul's face was flushed from the heat of the pub, and blurred with fatigue, but he offered to walk her and her sister to the corner of their road, Susie happy to wait inside for his return. Jill accepted his offer, glad to be rounding up her sister. Time to remind her about sharing a house with other people.

'But I'm twenty-two,' she protested, slurring her words slightly. Jill lifted her sister's coat and slung it around her shoulders.

'Well act like it then,' she growled. 'Paul's waiting.'

She took Bonnie's hand and led her outside. A sharp chill lay across the air. Paul leaned against the open door of the pub, hands deep in the pockets of his woollen coat.

'Right then, girls.' Cloudy breath came out with his words. 'Give us your arms.' A nod to Susie, and they were off, stepping between puddles of wet slush, and laughing at Bonnie's loud comments.

When they reached the house, Paul kissed them both and hunkered his way back into the cold evening. Jill looked up at her parents' bedroom window. The light was on, and only flicked off when she put her key in the door. This was their routine. She looked forward to the day when she could get a place of her own, with only her rules and her choices.

'You go up,' she whispered to Bonnie, who was slumped over the telephone table. 'And be quiet. I'll bring us a drink.'

In the darkness of the kitchen, Jill fumbled around for a pan, and working with the light from the fridge, she managed to find milk, and put it on the gas ring to warm. She spooned powdered cocoa into two mugs, then laid her cold hands on the still-warm storage heater, looking out through the kitchen window while she waited. The garden was layered in white, stark against the thick blackness of the evening.

She thought again about Stoney, wondering what was going on in his life. Being at Seaview, living with his dad, he'd alluded to it all, but told her nothing. There had been something infinitely breakable about him, sitting in a café, biting into his toast and sneering at her; a fragility.

And when she remembered that day at Mick's barn, the feel of the place and the evidence of hard drug use, it gave her a sick feeling in her stomach. Liness Barn would be enough to make anyone ill; she'd not forgotten the desperate need she'd seen on the faces of both men.

She leaned against the countertop and ran her hands over her face. She was tired. So tired. Going to work and coming home in the dark, was taking its toll on her well-being more than ever, and she was glad there would soon be a two-week break. The milk hissed and bubbled. She made the drinks, then put the hot pan in the sink and ran some water over it. Tomorrow she would take the chance to catch up on her sleep.

Jill woke the next morning, to a bedroom full of hazy lilac light and Moz grinning at her from the doorway. He was already dressed, in a jumble of sweaters, old trousers and woollen socks.

'Mam says we can go up the fields with my sledge if you take us.' He waited.

Jill groaned and sat up. 'That's nice of her.'

'Please.' The word was stretched to within an inch of its life.

Though she was desperate to stay in the warmth of her bed, something about Moz's pleading cut deeper than he could ever realise. Teenage years should be spent thinking fun and laughter was the whole world. If she could capture those thoughts for her brothers, and help them hold on, she would.

She peeled back the bedclothes and sent Moz to fetch her a cup of tea while she got dressed. A loud cheer came from downstairs, making Bonnie twitch slightly in her bed, then pull a pillow around her head. Jill laughed. Her sister didn't suffer from guilt. She never had.

Outside, the street was silent. Only the footprints of the milkman had caused a flaw in the soft white sheet covering the garden and driveway of the house. Jill's brothers raced away, disturbing the peace like the bands of raggle-taggle Viking raiders from school history books. But they were dragging a sledge behind them instead of a Saxon warrior.

They headed out towards the edge of the housing estate, where gentle green slopes gave way to countryside proper. Today, there were no borders, just a never-ending landscape of snow.

While her brothers charged upwards against the gradient and screeched their way back down again, Jill stamped her booted feet and cheered them on. Being outside never failed to lift the creep of fatigue from her shoulders; something she remembered sharing with Stoney. The endless days billowed with sunshine and salt winds, the open horizon, grounded by home, all of it was interlaced with him. But there had been fear too, the winning emotion, in the end.

By Monday, Jill was feeling refreshed and ready to face the last week before the Christmas holidays. She caught the early bus to the island, hoping to complete her marking before the usual flurry of staff arrivals and pupil problems began.

It was still dark, and the air was bitterly cold. On the bridge, she could see the lights from across the estuary; there would be people getting up, having breakfast, and making themselves ready for the working day. Families just like her own. She couldn't help but smile, remembering Bonnie with the pillow over her head, groaning as Jill put the light on in the bedroom to brush her hair and find her work shoes.

There were no lights on in Seaview.

The bus flashed by, and she craned to see. Nothing. But it was early. Perhaps they kept different hours if no one worked. Not that she had any idea what Stoney did with himself these days, and he was never going to tell her.

When the bus came to a stop outside school, she jumped off, pulling her coat tightly around herself. A cold wind was blowing directly off the Irish Sea, and it cut as sharp as if it were a knife. Her legs, in thin tights, were its first victim.

As she approached, she could see the lights were already on. A plume of warmth hit her as she opened the front door and let herself in to the main building. The caretaker was on his rounds. Jill could smell his brand of tobacco and the inevitable aroma of coffee and disinfectant.

'You're early, lover,' he called, catching sight of her along the corridor.

'Morning, Brian,' she answered, with a wave of her hand. 'Just trying to get ahead of the game. Freezing out there, isn't it?'

He ambled towards her, cigarette in one hand, coffee cup in another. 'You're right there. Gonna be a cold one tonight as well.' He threw a glance at her feet then back up to her face. 'Need more than a skimpy coat, in my opinion.'

Jill cringed a little but put on her best smile. 'You're probably right. I'd better get on though.' She stepped away. 'I've a huge pile of books to see to before the kiddiwinks get in.'

As it turned out, Jill didn't get ahead with her marking. By the time she'd made herself a hot drink and organised her resources for the day, other staff were arriving and chatting, laying out their problems and teaching dramas. The marking was pushed into the after-school slot. At half-past five, she finally put on her coat and began packing for home, hunger gnawing at her stomach and fatigue helping it along. A few days of walking in the daylight and relaxing with books could always reset her body clock, but she would have to wait for the weekend before that was possible.

With her handbag on her shoulder, she tucked her scarf tightly around her neck, glanced around her classroom one last time, then switched off the lights and headed along the corridor.

One or two teachers were still at their desks, marking or just reading. She waved to those that looked up, wondering briefly if they had anywhere to be. There were many staff she didn't know well – only knew by sight really; the job was so intense it gave little opportunity for sharing personal stories. If she ever became a headteacher, she would insist her staff got to know one another, instead of sitting in empty classrooms, wondering if they were doing things correctly. She had suffered terribly in her teens because there had been no one to ask about things. That was never going to happen on her watch.

The cold air cleared her worries in an instant. It cut away any thinking and sent Jill into survival mode. She blew out her cheeks and clutched at the top buttons of her coat. About fifty yards to the bus stop. Even wearing shoes with heels, she could run that far. The longest stretch was the school drive anyway, and it had been cleared and gritted thanks to Brian. She bit her teeth together and set off.

When she got to the gates, she slowed a little. Hunkered down in a hooded coat, back to the wind, was a figure she recognised. Stoney.

'Jilly.'

He stood and turned to her. She blinked through the darkness.

'Jilly. I've been waiting. For you.' His face was deathly pale.

'Why?' There was a sharpness to her voice she hadn't expected.

Be kind, she told herself. 'I mean, why have you been waiting. It's too cold to be hanging around on a night like this.'

'Need money,' he muttered.

Jill held back her shock. Did she hear right? 'What? What are you talking about?' She glanced around. There was nobody else nearby. She was on her own.

'You heard me, Jilly.'

Her name had become a sneer in his mouth. She felt her heart pound against her rib cage, and realised she'd been holding her breath. Taking two gulps of the freezing air, she stepped away.

'I can't give you money. Why are you even asking?'

He reached out a pale hand and grabbed the top of her arm.

'You can,' he said simply. 'You owe me.'

His tug shook up the anger rising inside her; there was no debt to be paid.

'Get off me,' she snapped. 'I don't owe you anything. Why are you even saying that?'

He let her go, shoved her slightly.

'You can't pick me up one minute and let me go the next.'

'What do you mean?'

He flicked his head in the direction of the shore. 'You wanna buy me coffee. Chat, and stuff. Now you want rid of me. Which is it?'

'I don't want to get rid of you. Of course I don't.' Oh, but she did. 'Why do you need money? Can't you earn it, like everyone else.'

'I've got a nasty habit, Jilly. A drug habit. And it needs feeding. Give us a fiver, that should do it.'

A fiver? What was going on? She shook her head. 'How is this my problem?'

'You're the *hoity-toity* teacher. You work it out.'

'In other words, you think I've got money. Is that all you're interested in?'

'Look.' He grabbed at her again. 'I don't want some high-brow conversation with you. Just help me. Please.'

Jill heard the bus come around the corner. A slow, mechanical chug. 'I'm getting on the bus now, Stoney,' she breathed, 'and I don't want you coming to my workplace again.' Fumbling for her purse, she was conscious of him standing right by her. His face. She saw desperation there. Desperation and anger. A lethal mix. In the purse were some notes – fives and tens. Christmas present money. Pulling out a blue five-pound note, she pressed it into his hand. He was ice cold.

'Here. Take this. But don't come near me again.' She spat out the words, hating herself for the contempt she felt.

He looked down at his own hand, clutched his fist around the money. Then started to speak to her again. But Jill couldn't look at him or listen. She stepped away, waving down the bus as it pulled along the road. When it stopped, she jumped on quickly, adrenaline flooding through her body. The conductor approached as she sat down.

'All right, miss?' he smiled. 'Where to tonight?'

His round and cheerful face had a calming effect. She took some deep breaths, trying to understand what had just happened, but knowing she had done the worst thing possible.

Chapter Eighteen

AUGUST 1987

Jill stared at her reflection in Susie's mirror. The hairstyle – chunky curls and a fringe – was not her. Neither was the circlet of flowers on her crown, or the floaty pink dress. Bonnie looked stunning. Same outfit, different girl. She gave herself a wry smile. It was her friend's wedding day, and not the time for sulking or worrying. But the Stoney problem just wouldn't go away: sometimes he would catch her at the school gates, other times, he'd be waiting at the bus stop. They both knew why he was there. And he always went away with money in his hand.

At Jill's insistence, he was trying to cut down on his drug use, telling her he was only smoking heroin, rather than injecting it. She had no knowledge to help her understand, and there was nobody she could ask without drawing attention to the fact. Stoney's appearance had altered dramatically, which worried her the most. There was no fat under his skin, no padding. Just the globe and stick of protruding bones. And the blur of confusion across his face. He had no work, and the little money he did have was soon spent.

Reverend Brownstone still lived at Seaview, but he was ill.

Stoney thought he should be in a nursing home, though this would mean his own expulsion from the house. Refusing to give him money would lead him into minor criminal acts, he told her.

When she had threatened to tell somebody about his demands, he'd countered the threat with one of his own. He would make a scene at her workplace, tell them all how she was responsible for his addiction.

Jill could see no way out. And it was starting to pull her down. What she really wanted to do was shrug him away, laugh at his threats, tell him she didn't care. But every sight of him dragged at her conscience. Had she been complicit in his spiralling addiction? Should she have stuck with him, despite feeling nothing? What would Annie Brownstone have made of that? These were questions she could never smooth over with an answer. Instead, they would ruffle the surface of her world and keep her attention. She'd finally got an interview for a teaching job away from the island. If she was offered the position, she would be gone. But for now, she would keep on pushing a few pounds into Stoney's hand, to keep him quiet.

The bedroom door opened, and Susie walked in, a vision in tiered white sateen. On her short hair was a circlet of flowers. Her skin glowed pink. Jill spun around, away from the mirror, and looked at her friend.

'Like it?' asked Susie, with a wink. She twirled around with a swish and a ruffle.

Words stuck to the back of Jill's throat. She forced them out, but they trembled as they escaped. 'You are beautiful. Come here.'

As she held Susie in her arms, all Chanel and shiny white, a memory floated into the space behind her thoughts: school fields and summer, grassy scents, and the ache of watching her best friend walk away. How had she ever let that happen?

'You and Bon look lovely, too,' Susie was saying. 'Pass me a hanky. I don't want to smudge my make-up.'

Bonnie dug around inside the puff of her sleeve. 'There you go,' she said, handing her a scrunch of white paper. 'Borrow mine. And save your tears for later when I *don't* manage to get off with Paul's brother.'

Susie snorted and laid her hand on her stomach, vivid pink nails standing out against the sheen of the dress.

'Don't,' she groaned. 'It's hard enough to breathe in this corset thingy.' She screwed up her face, making Jill and Bonnie splutter with laughter again.

'And what about you?' Susie continued. 'New job and everything. We're all moving on.'

Jill stepped back, puzzled. 'I haven't got it yet. Interviews are in October. There's ages to wait.'

Bonnie interrupted, bold as always. 'She'll get it. She's clever, our Jill.'

Susie opened her mouth to say more, but a knock on the bedroom door made her turn. Her father, smart in dark grey flannel and a pink tie, stepped into the room. One look at his daughter broke the tension in his jaw, and he beamed at them all.

'Oh, my. Girls. You look amazing. Watch out fellas, that's all I can say.' He held out his hand to Susie, and she shimmered across the room and took hold of it tightly.

'Well, Daddy,' she whispered, 'lead me to the Bentley.'

Jill and Bonnie hooted with laughter.

'What?' Susie winked back at them, then she was gone.

At the foot of the stairs, Susie's mother was waiting with flowers. There were small hand-tied bouquets of pink roses for Jill and Bonnie, and a large trailing arrangement of pink and white, with gypsophila, for Susie. But no words were spoken; Susie's parents glanced at each other, then moved away to let their daughter through the front door.

Across the road, some of the neighbours had gathered, craning to catch a glimpse of the bride. Jill heard their delight as Susie and her father emerged, blinking in the vivid August sunshine. The applause continued as Jill and Bonnie climbed into the dark blue Rolls Royce parked further along the road.

Outside the church, a few passers-by had gathered to watch as the bridal party climbed out of their cars. Jill was already hot, and conscious of the sweat forming under her arms, despite the copious amounts of anti-perspirant she had applied.

The chauffeur came around to the side of their car and opened the door, helped first Bonnie, then Susie's mother, out. And finally extended a hand to Jill, holding her flowers whilst she tried to look elegant and demure.

Standing at the church gates was a man with long dark hair. He wore a black leather jacket and slung across his shoulder was the biggest camera she had ever seen. Bonnie fussed with Susie's dress. Jill stood awkwardly, wondering what to do next.

'You look beautiful.' The man with the camera had come up behind her. She turned around to face him. Was the compliment for her?

'Oh. Thanks. I guess. Feel a bit foolish.' Her hands smoothed down the pink dress.

'Well, try not to outshine the bride,' he grinned. 'It's poor form.' They both giggled.

'I'll try not to,' she whispered, 'but I can't promise anything.'

He held out his hand. 'Stevie Francis,' he said. 'Wedding photographer extraordinaire. At your service.'

Jill couldn't help herself. She took his hand and gave an over-exaggerated flick of her wrist. 'Jill. Friend of the bride, and sister to the glam bridesmaid.'

Where had that come from?

When Stevie brushed his lips lightly across her fingers, she felt a tingle of emotion at her core. Something she chose to feel, something from a fresh place.

'Catch you later, if I can,' he said. 'Jill.'

Then he walked across to Susie and whispered something in her ear. She threw back her head, smiling wildly, and the tension of the moment was broken. His camera began to click at the laughing bride, and as she and Bonnie joined her, he gave Jill a slight touch on the back of her hand.

'Keep smiling. Soon be over.'

'I'll try,' she muttered.

Throughout the ceremony and tedium of set-up photographs, confetti and beaming smiles, Jill watched Stevie. He was courteous but scathingly funny, making even the most hard-faced guests smile and relax. Without his leather jacket, she could see he was slim and broad-shouldered, and she could hardly look away. He chatted with her when he had the chance, and when he followed the wedding cars to the reception on a gleaming Triumph Tiger, she wanted nothing more than to climb onto that bike with him and zoom away.

A loud bell announced that the guests should take their seats, and the red-jacketed Master of Ceremonies took control.

'Please be upstanding for the new Mr and Mrs Bates,' he bellowed, making a babe-in-arms – Susie's niece, Jill thought – match him for noise with its shrieks. The applause began. The bride and groom sauntered into the room, arm in arm, and took their places at the top table. Susie's face glowed, and Jill felt a tightness in her throat, remembering how they'd shared everything in their years at the grammar school. She leaned across from her place to the left of the groom and held out her hand. Susie took it and gave it a squeeze.

'I did it,' she whispered. 'Thanks for spurring me on. You next, Jill.'

'Bonnie next,' she said, nodding at her sister. 'Paul's brother can't stop looking at her.'

Susie gave her a small grin. 'Bit like my photographer. He's staring at you again.'

Stevie was standing on the other side of the room, awkward now, while the guests got settled. He caught Jill's eye and blew a kiss from his fingertips.

The wedding breakfast began. Waiters and waitresses, smart in black-and-white, carried dishes and plates, wine bottles and bread baskets, and the atmosphere surged like a giant wave, with Susie and Paul carried along on its crest. Jill wondered where Stevie was. Perhaps the photographer didn't get invited to enjoy a meal along with the guests, but he would surely be around somewhere. As soon as she'd finished her Black Forest gateau, Jill pulled back her chair, and lifting the bottom of her dress over her arm, whispered to Bonnie that she was going to the ladies.

'Ladies what?' trilled her sister. Jill slapped her arm. Too much wine, too soon.

'You know fine well,' she began, but screeches of laughter and cheers cut her off, as trays full of cocktail glasses were carried in, each drink lit up by a fizzing mini-sparkler.

'My treat everybody,' called Paul, across the merriment. 'Enjoy.'

Jill took her chance and slipped from the room. Stevie was sprawled across an armchair in the hotel hallway, glugging down what looked like a pint of blackcurrant cordial.

He smiled up at Jill, wiping away a dark purple moustache. 'What's happening in there?'

'Cocktail time, I think,' she told him. 'But everyone's already plastered.'

'Happy though.' He put the glass down beside his chair and sat forward. 'You okay?'

She nodded.

'Sit for a bit?' he asked, moving himself to the arm of the chair. It felt so natural, sitting down next to Stevie and chatting to him, and Jill relaxed into his company. He asked her about her connection to Susie and they talked about people they had in common. She told him she was a teacher at the island school, and he told her about the disaster of his own school years. When they heard the announcement for speeches, his smile slid away.

'That's me. Back to work again. Let's talk later.'

Jill reached out to touch his cheek, and the small dimple at the corner of his mouth. 'Let's,' she whispered.

Then he was gone.

During the evening reception, when she and Bonnie had ditched their flower crowns and Susie had gone upstairs to take off her corset, Stevie put down his camera and asked her to dance. Not her favourite pursuit, but holding his hand made her feel she could do anything. They laughed and twirled and made complete fools of themselves, and Jill couldn't get enough of him. At ten o'clock, his photography job was complete. Jill watched as he spoke to Susie for a while, then scanned the room to find her again.

'Come outside for a minute with me?' There was an urgency in his request.

'Course,' she replied, 'want to get a better look at that bike, anyway.'

Jill stepped into the night air. The scent of grass, fresh cut and mixed in with stocks and honeysuckle, drifted across the car park. It was almost dark, but a line of soft lemon light still lay across the horizon, and the faintest threads of cool air crept along her bare arms. She shivered.

'Have my jacket,' he said, lifting it from his arm and laying it around her shoulders. Leather and patchouli zipped across her senses. 'No actually, have everything. Camera. Bike. The lot.'

She looked at him quizzically. 'Meaning?'

'I don't know.' A shrug. 'Something's happened to me, Jill.' His voice, gentle and quiet. 'Somehow, you've got to me. Sorry.' He came to stand in front of her.

Jill ran her arms around his slim waist and rested her head against him for a moment. When she looked up, he kissed her, and it meant something. Really meant something. She hadn't thought about Stoney for hours. It had been a day for thinking about herself.

'I don't know much about you,' he murmured, holding tightly to her, 'but I want to know everything. Can I see you again? Soon?'

She nodded. 'See me now, if you like.'

He moved her away from him, holding her shoulders and looking into her face. 'I have a flat. Nearby. Want to come for coffee? Leave the world behind?'

'I don't have a helmet,' she laughed, nervous now.

'Taxi?' he suggested.

'Taxi,' she agreed.

Jill stretched out in the warmth of the bed. Stevie snored gently beside her; dark hair tangled across a white pillow. Pushing herself up on her elbows, she peered around the bedroom. In the corner was a large dark-wood wardrobe, like the one at her grandma's, and the walls had the texture of lumpy porridge. But the sunshine streaming from the skylight gave the room a lustre that lifted it away from the ordinary. She smiled to herself. Ordinary was the last thing she felt at this moment.

The flat was on the top floor of an old Victorian house, perhaps two miles from the wedding venue, but what lay beyond this room Jill could hardly remember. She noticed the pool of pink chiffon on the floor in the corner. It had been quite a night. She and Stevie had spent some of the time talking, covering new territory, and giving each other context. She told him about her family, about her brothers and their foibles. He told her how he'd set himself up as a photographer five years ago when he couldn't find work. The contacts he'd made were beginning to come good, including the one that led him to Paul Bates, Susie's new husband, though he insisted he would have found Jill eventually. She had laughed at this, then fallen for him just a little bit harder.

She leaned over and kissed Stevie's bare shoulder. He jumped awake.

'Morning,' he croaked, running a hand across his face, now dotted with the faintest trace of dark stubble. 'Did I dream last night?'

'Nope,' she said, pulling up the sheets and twisting back her hair. 'You really did steal the bridesmaid from a wedding.'

He blew out a long sigh. 'Can I just check something?' A touch of her arm. 'My God, you are real.'

'I'm real enough to need a cup of coffee. Do you have any?'

'Can it wait?'

She shook her head. 'It's the final test, and you have to pass.'

'Oh hell.' He swung his legs over the edge of the bed. 'Better do it then.'

'Better had.'

Jill watched his slim back as he rummaged around on the floor for something to wear. He found his discarded boxer shorts and pulled them on, then leaned back to kiss her cheek.

While he was gone, she climbed out of his bed and gathered up her dress and underwear, placing it nearby to save embarrassment later, then dived back under the sheets, wondering what on earth she had done. Susie and Bonnie had been far too drunk to have even noticed she had gone, but her mother would be worried, and she really should telephone her. Perhaps Stevie had a phone, but she couldn't wander around in his flat with no clothes on. Laying across the back of a small bedroom chair was the shirt he'd worn to the wedding. She pulled it on then ventured out of the room. Across a small hallway she could see Stevie reaching into a kitchen cupboard.

'Do you have a telephone?' she called.

He turned and looked at her through the doorway.

'Yeah, sure. It's through there.' He moved his head sideways towards another door, stripped pine, old and knotty.

'Okay if I use it?'

'Course. Like your shirt, by the way.'

Jill pulled at its ragged hem, shivering despite the warmth of the summer morning. The thick woollen curtains in his living room were closed. She trod carefully, weaving between the silhouetted furniture, and pulled them apart. The room contained two huge sofas, low and grey and littered with mismatched cushions, and in one corner was a large television on a glass cabinet, with a video player inside. The telephone was on an orange pine table in the corner.

Her mother hadn't been worried, as it turned out. Bonnie had explained about Jill's flit with the wedding photographer. Nothing got past her sister, it seemed, and when she tried to explain that there was no *flitting* involved, she could hear her mother smiling as she answered. Jill was twenty-four, she said. Did she really need to feel so guilty about staying out all night?

The aroma of coffee cut across her thoughts. She finished the conversation and replaced the phone receiver. In the kitchen. Stevie was laying out a tray with two mugs and a plate of fragrant toast. He lifted the plate towards her.

'Thanks. I'm starving.'

'I aim to please,' he said, winking. He nodded towards the doorway and Jill walked back into the living room and sat down on one of the sofas. The tray of coffee and toast was placed down in front of her, and they were soon chatting and enjoying their first breakfast together.

Something was niggling away at the edge of Jill's consciousness, like a handful of sand in the toe of a plimsol. Guilt, perhaps? Stevie was so different from Stoney. He was the first man she had felt a connection with, and she didn't want to ruin it. Perhaps the problem with Stoney would just fizzle out. Especially if she got this new job. Then he would have to sort out his drug problem himself. How it had become her problem she wasn't quite sure, but she wanted out.

Stevie sipped his coffee.

'How about a ride out on the bike today?'

'Thought you'd never ask. I'd absolutely love to go on that bike with you. Have you a spare helmet?'

'Course I have. And a spare jacket. You can't really ride in a floaty dress though. You'll have to get changed first.' That laugh. It transformed his face.

She giggled. Felt like a teenager again. 'I'll get a taxi home and you can pick me up later, if that's okay?'

But Stevie was getting up from the sofa. He lifted her coffee cup from her hand and knelt in front of her.

'It is okay,' he murmured, 'but I need my shirt back now.' He lifted it over her head and threw it to one side.

'Didn't suit you anyway,' he whispered, nuzzling her ear.

A gasp. 'Not my colour.'

Later, and layered up with thick sweaters and a padded coat, Jill climbed onto the back of Stevie's motorbike.

'Let's have a zoom around the island,' he called over his shoulder. 'See if we can get her up to speed.' He patted a gloved hand across the petrol tank, and grinned.

Jill agreed. Though she'd rather have gone anywhere else. But as the bike chugged away, she felt a pulse of excitement from her belly to her feet. If there was a way to outrun all her worries about Stoney, here it was. Each time Stevie opened the throttle and let the bike surge forward, Jill felt her mood lift a little more. Even crossing the bridge took on a different quality, like she was fourteen again, and arriving on the island for the first time: the stretch of sea, the sky, the light, everything had been washed clean by the exhilaration of a motorcycle ride.

'Tuck in,' he shouted to her over his shoulder. 'Just move with me.'

He clicked through the gears with his toe and let the bike glide into action. Jill gritted her teeth and switched off her thinking. And for ten glorious minutes there was only her and Stevie and the zoom of the wide-open sea.

By the time they'd done a circuit of the island's furthest reaches, Jill was starting to shiver. Even in high summer, the rush of speeding air took heat away from every surface. Her eyes streamed and the skin of her cheeks stung. But her heart was soaring.

At the west shore, Stevie pulled the bike into a lay-by near the swings.

'Enjoy that?' he asked, lifting his visor. 'Let's walk for a minute.' He helped her climb off the bike. 'Your thighs get numb with the cold, don't they?'

'All of me is numb,' she laughed, 'but I loved it. Thanks.'

Stevie fumbled under her chin and undid the buckle of her helmet. Then he was lifting it from her head and kissing her, and she was stunned all over again. With her eyes closed, she let herself drift into the moment: the sky billowing blue, the warmth of the sun across her shoulders, Stevie's leather-and-patchouli smell.

'All right?' He cut across her thoughts with a beaming smile.

'Do you know what?' she said. 'I think I am.'

Something had clicked in her life. The years of trying to prove herself, when every small worry had grown into something much larger, they had slipped away. Perhaps she could finally stop looking back at the things that had happened to her. Carve out a life she had chosen.

Stevie led her towards the water. They stumbled together, crossing first an area of wind-bleached grass, then down the pebbly beach towards the stretch of scattered pools and seaweed. As always, a breeze kept families and children huddled behind canvas windbreaks, and the waves across the shallows were crested with foam and a spraying energy. And further along the sand, standing alone and skimming flat rocks, was Stoney.

Jill felt a flash of alarm. This couldn't be happening.

'Can we get going?' she said.

'Course. You cold?' Stevie slid an arm around her shoulder. 'You've gone all shivery.'

'I've not found my biker-legs yet.' A tense laugh, then she turned her back to Stoney and hurried Stevie away.

September 2018

At the top of the slope, Jill leans against her car for a moment, allowing the atmosphere of the island to slide off her shoulders. Being on the beach has done nothing to calm the squall blowing up inside her. She remembers the sick terror she'd felt on that first day with Stevie, Andrew Brownstone just a heartbeat away. He became a dirty smudge on the clean white pages of her life. Those pages have been turned and turned and turned again as she has tried to rewrite her story, but the smudge always bleeds through.

A Land Rover is pulling up opposite, dark blue, and with three passengers. She squints against the slant of the sun.

'Jill. What're you doing here?'

Stevie.

Jill looks at her husband. He is climbing out of his car and walking towards her. Cool, in a white shirt with the sleeves rolled to his elbows. The atmosphere shimmers.

'You okay?'

'Hi.' Stay bright and breezy, she thinks. 'I was just hand-delivering a letter. Governor business.' She attempts a wink.

'Oh. Right. We're heading over to the shore.' He gestures towards the people in the back of his car. She sees youthful haircuts and the gloss of happiness. 'The Round House shore. Getting some shots on the swings, with a bit of luck.'

She holds her hand above her eyes. 'That'll be nice.'

'Meet us over there if you like. We could have a drink.'

Can she do that? She isn't sure. The last time she'd been to that place had been with Stoney. It had been a long time ago, but the details have stayed with her: the frailness of his body, the dull eyes. The way every word he said sounded like a lie. She hasn't forgotten.

'No. You go. I've got to get back to work.' She leans in for a kiss. 'I'll see you at home.'

Stevie lifts his chin. Shrugs one shoulder. 'All right, darling. I'll see you after.'

Jill waves her fingertips at the smiling couple, then climbs back into her car. As Stevie drives away, he blows a kiss from his open palm. His smile is so much like Phil's. She would die for her son, do anything in her power to keep him from harm. The thought of him being in thrall to an opiate drug makes her feel sick to her stomach.

But by the time she met Andrew Brownstone in that café, he was there, a prisoner of his own making. She remembers buying him a hot drink, them spending a short time talking.

He'd been guarded. Scathing. Making comments about her job. Her coat, even. When all she'd been doing was trying to help him. It had been late afternoon before they'd parted company. She had hated herself for the pity she'd felt. And the clawing guilt.

She has to get her veneer back, her shiny shell. And get off the island. Leave the threat of Malcom Gibson behind. But is he really a threat? There are other people who can link her to Andrew Brownstone, other people who know she had a relationship with him. A brief, teen fling. They'd only tell PC Rose Atherton what Jill already has.

Andrew Brownstone? Yeah. Hung around with him for a little while when we were both at school.

She speeds along the promenade. Doesn't look across the out-going eddies or up at the brilliance of the sky. Doesn't open her window and inhale the brine-soaked breeze. And doesn't look up the flight of stone steps leading to Seaview House. Instead, she breathes herself back into the role of Jill Francis, the world's most consummate actress.

Part III

Chapter Nineteen

Jill smooths down her black skirt. Wearing work clothes, after six weeks of shorts and hoodies, feels like a trap. The heart of her is Californian, Stevie says, although she's never been there.

No children will be in her school today: it's one of those infamous training days. Infuriating for parents, a delight for teachers. But she won't get in the way of staff fun and staff learning. Instead, she'll be attending a case conference for a vulnerable pupil and his family. He's at extreme risk of being groomed by a county lines drug-runner who is operating in the area, and she is damned if she'll let it happen. It's a slippery slope, as she knows only too well.

While her relationship with her husband blossomed in those early days, Stoney spiralled into the murky world of heroin addiction, and for a long time, she helped him feed his habit. There is no denying her part in his struggles, and that is what she will tell PC Rose Atherton when she meets her later in the day. The appointment is set up, and Jill feels better knowing she will at least give her some of the information she seeks. But not everything. She must protect herself and her family.

Stevie walks into the room, dressed down for a day of editing and gardening. He had been surprised to see her standing alongside North Scale's main road yesterday. Especially since she'd always been reluctant to explore the island with him. The cover story hung between them. He'd accepted it, but she has to live with the lie. Another one. Andrew Brownstone has come back into her life, and he is making her into a liar.

'You look nice,' Stevie says, hands around her waist. 'Do you have to go in today?'

She reaches up to touch his face. 'I do. But I won't be late. That starts tomorrow.'

He huffs softly. Buries his face in her hair. 'I don't like it.'

'But you like the money.' Their days of worrying about money are over, thankfully, but they like to reminisce about the early times when every penny counted for something.

'Can't we just retire? Stay in bed all day?'

She wriggles free and turns to face him, placing her hands along his stubbly cheeks.

'Phil would love that,' she groans, 'you know what he thinks of us.'

Their son hates the romance that exists between what he classes as his geriatric parents, hates that they hold hands and kiss. Jill wonders if he's ever thought about where he came from. Emotion drags at her throat. Sadness. And anger. This is her family; she can't lose them. Stevie takes hold of her wrist and sniffs lightly.

'I love the smell of my wife,' he sighs.

'Bathhouse Frangipani and Grapefruit?'

'Sunshine and holidays,' he laughs, 'and the seaside.' He gives her a coy look. They both remember their first holiday together. Phil was the result.

She lifts her jacket from its hanger and lays it over her arm, then slips on her shoes – patent leather and chunky – she can't do heels anymore.

'I will see you at about three,' she tells him. 'I might pop around to see Mum and Dad first. They're just back, I think.'

A memory comes. Her wedding day, and her parents' tears. The promise she made, to never be far away. How will they cope if she suddenly becomes absent from their lives? The thought chills her. Andrew Brownstone cannot have the last word.

'Let's go out somewhere to eat, later,' she says. 'Celebrate the new term. Or commiserate, you decide.'

'Awww. Jilly. Don't go.' He mocks up a sad face.

'Don't call me that,' she snarls, and turns away.

Stevie grabs the top of her arm. 'There is something wrong, I can tell.'

For a moment, Jill wants to react, wants to yank her arm out of his grasp and let everything out. In her mind's eye she can see her younger self in the clutches of Andrew Brownstone, pleading with the world to set her free. If there had been a woman like Jill Francis in her life, back then, she'd have known what to do.

Be the adult you needed as a child. Where has she heard that? She's not sure, but it's how she lives her life, how she'll be at the case conference.

'It's high-stakes today,' she says to her husband, as he lets her arm loose, 'that's all.'

'Everything's high-stakes with you, isn't it?'

'Meaning?'

'Oh, I don't know.' Stevie shakes his head and steps away. 'I'll leave you to it.'

There is nothing Jill can say. A time will come when he'll see her for what she really is. No high-stakes involved. For now, she's going to continue with the trade-offs she's spent years working on. The ones that just might save her from the murky world of Andrew Brownstone.

There isn't as much heat today. The air is sharp and golden, but fresher somehow, and Jill is glad of it. There is torture in watching the summer through a pane of glass, sitting in an office. When the rain pelts down, she doesn't mind so much, but watching the Year Nine children dancing about in the greens and blues of a summer's day, kills her slowly. To be fourteen again, she thinks, but to know what she knows now.

Had she really expected Malcom Gibson to still be living in Liness Barn? He'd probably sold it for a competitive sum of money at the end of the 1980s, when property prices had exploded. Thanks, in part, to the Thatcher years. She and Stevie had benefitted, too. Though he'd never quite understood why she wouldn't view any houses on the island.

Stevie comes to wave her off. He blows copious kisses from his palm, making her laugh, as he knows it will. Since they married, in 1989, there have been few cross words between them, and even those were said over a crying baby or midnight feeds. But he knows nothing about Stoney, and she wants to keep it that way. So, she needs a strategy. And here it is. She will admit to everything that happened between her and Stoney. Except the last thing. And she will manipulate that truth when it comes out. The only threat to it is Malcom Gibson. And he's probably sitting in luxury retirement somewhere, scrolling for local news and making worthless comments.

The case conference tries her patience.

When she arrives at the meeting, she is assaulted by coffee smells suggesting a span of time nobody wants, with added biscuits to stretch it further. The harsh lighting of the room, the droning voices of agency workers who love to talk more than they love the truth; these are reminders of everything wrong with a system that is supposed to be nurturing. She hardly gets a word in, and when she does, she is regarded as an amateur in the grand scheme of this vulnerable boy's life. Yet here he is, scratching at his arms and thin as a lath, in his Nike sports gear.

They've got him already, those dealers, she thinks. Knows. And as always, nothing is resolved and nothing will change, but he will. He'll lose friends, he'll lie, steal, and manipulate, his weight will drop, and he'll be vilified. Then he'll disappear. If there's to be any hope for youngsters like him, it'll come from adults like her. She'll keep asking after him, joking around with him and giving him tokens for breakfast club. And what he won't realise is how much she's doing, where he can't see, to keep him in the eyeline of the system.

In the end, she walks out of the conference, her head thick with suppressed words, her jaw tight. She will look after the boy until every one of her resources runs out, no matter what protocols she is breaking.

Already the afternoon sun is hanging lower in the sky. September weather is her favourite. Horse chestnut trees line the school's long drive, and their leaves are curled, yellow fighting with the summer green. Conker shells scatter the pavement and tomorrow she will have to deal with numerous minor complaints and injuries when their glossy brown treasures are thrown or tasted. It is the same every year, and this thought makes her smile. The autumn routines. May they never change.

The car door closes with a metallic thud. She swings out of her parking place and drives away from school, in the direction of the town centre, where she knows PC Rose Atherton will be waiting, intense and unbending, notebook in hand. If she is to answer any questions, she wants to know who has linked her to Andrew Brownstone. Who has tittle-tattled to the police? Not her own family. Not his family – he had none.

The town has a new police station, replacing the one Jill

has memories of as a child on a school visit. Its frontage looks across to the island. Hundreds of glassy eyes set on cream and grey concrete. Wide at the top, with a narrow ground floor. A gust of Walney Island wind could blow it down. A house of cards, she thinks. But at least there is a car park. And no bars on the windows.

Her jacket is folded on the passenger seat. She leaves it, fluffs up her hair and swings her handbag onto her shoulder. The clumpy shoes are making her feet sweat and she probably won't wear them again. They looked nice in the shop, but she has become used to sandals this summer. Sandals. Navy-blue flats with smart silver buckles; rotted, towards the end, by walks across shingle and salty mud. A simple memory of a childhood summer, but one dragging so many more with it. She is overwhelmed, just for a moment, and leans on her car for support. Then inhales deeply and heads towards the station.

Rose Atherton is waiting for her in the cool white reception area, smart in short-sleeved shirt and slacks. Jill blinks at her for a moment. Surely make-up as heavy as this isn't standard uniform. But she's not at school now, handing out baby wipes to rebellious Year Nines, so she says nothing.

'Hello, Mrs Francis. Thank you for coming in.'

Jill shakes her cold dry hand. 'No problem.' But it is.

'Shall we go through to one of the interview rooms?' Rose Atherton swings her arm outwards, hand suggesting Jill should follow.

They go through a key coded entrance and into an inner hallway, lined with new and heavy light-oak doors, each one closed. It is very quiet, a thick blue carpet muffling their footsteps. Everything smells clean, like fresh paint. It feels restful, not like a police station at all. Another key coded door and Jill is shown into a tidy room dominated by a large metal-framed desk.

Rose points to a chair. 'Please, sit,' she smiles. 'Can I get you a cup of coffee? Or tea?'

'Some water would be good,' says Jill. Her tongue is sticking to the roof of her mouth. She hopes Rose doesn't notice.

'Of course.'

There is a small side-table spread with items of refreshment, and she pours some water from a glass jug and hands it to Jill, then drips coffee from a thermal jug for herself.

This day has been full of the smell of coffee.

'So,' says the policewoman, sitting down opposite. 'Andrew Brownstone.'

A flush of heat creeps up Jill's neck and into her face. She hopes it isn't noticeable. There is a brown manilla folder on the desk, and Rose begins to flick through it.

'You'll have heard a body has been found in the grounds of Seaview House.' A pause. 'Facebook?' She peers at Jill. Clear blue eyes gaze into hers.

'Yes. I have heard.'

Rose Atherton pulls a photograph out from the folder. A computer printout on thin paper. Pixelated and curling. Stoney. Jill blinks. Looks away. But he can still see her.

'We're trying to locate this man. Andrew Brownstone. He lived at Seaview House, as you know. And he may be able to help us identify the body.'

Jill looks down at her hands. They have held and caressed the man they are looking for. The man in this photo. How is that possible? 'I told you before, he only lived there until about 1987 or 1988, I think. Maybe 1990. I haven't seen him since then.' A mixture of truth and lies.

Rose clears her throat, takes a sip of coffee. 'This is our problem. There are no records of this man. He hasn't worked, didn't have a passport. No family. No trace of him.'

'But you've got this photo?' Jill jumps in quickly, then wishes she hadn't.

Rose smooths the corners of the printout with her hands. 'Hmmm. It seems he applied for a passport in–' she rummages through the folder, '1981, but the application was never processed. This is the photo he sent in. Do you know how old he was then?' An innocent question. But how would Jill know? Except she does. And she's trying to tell the fewest number of lies possible.

'He was probably about twenty there,' she says. 'He was eighteen months older than me.'

Rose lifts her chin. 'Did you know him then?'

'I did.'

The policewoman regards her through narrowed eyes. 'How well did you know Mr. Brownstone?'

'We were in a relationship, on and off, for a few years.'

Rose slides the photo back into the folder, then pushes her chair away from the desk, rolling her shoulders slightly. 'It seems, Mrs Francis,' she says, lifting her face to Jill again, 'that you are the only connection we have to this guy. Can I ask you something you might not like?'

'Ask away,' says Jill with a laugh, but it is laughter that comes from a swirling pool of fear, located in the pit of her stomach. And that much must be written across her face.

'Have you any reason to believe the body buried in the garden of Seaview is that of Andrew Brownstone?'

Jill is used to thinking on her feet. She spends every day of her working life doing exactly that. Fast as lightning, she has comebacks for children and staff, even faster for parents.

'He was addicted to heroin,' she says. 'Did you know that? The last time I saw him, he was struggling.' As soon as she says this, she realises it was the wrong call. Rose Atherton has sniffed something out in her response.

'Oh?' She cocks her head. 'And you know this because?'

Oh shit, Jill thinks. *Shit, shit, shit.*

'I saw him on and off during his addiction, and it was pretty obvious.' It's all she can think of, and still fairly near the truth.

'According to our records, Andrew Brownstone's father died in early 1989, and Seaview was closed up around then. It doesn't quite fit with your timings, Mrs Francis.' Rose Atherton is every bit the policewoman now, peering at Jill's face and frowning at her spray of words.

Jill feels a wave of anger, sweeping up from her clenched fists and into her jaw. What have her timings got to do with anything?

'I'm not sure what you mean,' she says smoothly. 'You asked if I thought it was Andrew's body buried at Seaview. How would I know that? I'm just telling you he wasn't a well man, not when I saw him last, anyway.'

The policewoman lets out a long sigh. There is stale coffee on her breath. 'We haven't identified the body, as I've told you. But we have an age for it, and we know roughly when it was buried. It is the *skeleton* of a male, between twenty-five and thirty years of age, and it has been lying in that garden for thirty years at least.'

That word. Skeleton. Jill feels her blood pool, rushing inwards to the centre of her body. Her head feels light, and a sharp buzz starts up in her ears.

'Mrs Francis? Are you okay?'

'There is something I need to tell you.' She takes a sip of her drink.

Chapter Twenty

'You look tired, love.' Jill's mother puts down a plate of toast on the kitchen table and pulls out the chair next to her daughter.

'Stevie keeping you up all hours?'

'Mum.' Jill flinches. Her nerves are too shredded for this. 'Don't ask questions like that. Please.'

Moz sniggers into his cornflakes.

'And you can be quiet,' she snaps. The room falls silent. Denny looks across at her from where he is packing his sports kit. 'Ooooh. Nasty,' he smirks. 'Glad you're not my teacher.'

Ray munches on his toast, head down.

'What time's the interview?' Her mum pours out two cups of tea and pushes one across. 'Drink that. You can't go with an empty stomach.'

Jill nods her thanks. 'I've got to be there for half-nine. Dad said I can take the car.' She wants this job. It will mean getting away from the island for good. Ten miles away, in fact. And far from the demands Stoney is putting on her.

She is sure people are starting to talk. Nothing has been said to her directly. It's just a feeling, but there is something:

Susie driving past while she's talking to Stoney at the bus stop, slowing down her car to stare; the not-quite-relaxed body language developing between them. One of her teaching colleagues had even asked her if everything was okay. Though what he was referring to, Jill had no idea, but it set her wondering.

'Well, come home first and tell us how you got on,' her mother is saying, 'before you go to Stevie's.'

There is something in the way she says *home* that irritates Jill. She sips at her tea. Everything would be so much easier if she could make a home with Stevie. He could drop her at work every morning and she wouldn't feel like such a gigantic *Alice in Wonderland*, living in a house too small. Jill is more than aware of her mother's view on sex before marriage. Old-fashioned it may be, but it bothers her enough to comment continually, which isn't helping anyone. If she knew what happened when Jill had been fourteen, there would be no accounting for the trouble it would cause.

She looks at her mother's rough hands. Years of caring for five children have taken their toll and she wants nothing more than to lift the burden, just a little.

'Mother. We will marry eventually, you know. It's not the same as it was in your day. No one cares if you're not married.'

'I care.'

'I know you do.' Jill stands up, brushing toast crumbs from her new trousers. 'But for now, I've got bigger things to worry about.'

She pulls on her jacket and picks up her handbag. 'I'll see you later.' A kiss on her mother's cheek. 'Wish me luck.'

'Bye, love. Best of luck.'

Jill slams the door and steps out into the brisk wind of an October morning. Puffs of white cloud speed across the blue of the sky and the front lawn glitters with dew. If there is ever a day to feel successful, this is it; she's been trusted to drive her dad's new car, and that feels like an achievement, never mind getting another job. Head of department: unlikely, but she is pleased to have got this far.

The journey to another town is the easy part. By the time Jill pulls into the school's vast car park, she is struggling to breathe. It is anxiety, she knows, but it doesn't make it any less terrifying. Her mouth feels numb, and she can hardly swing her legs out of the driver's seat. But she does. Has to, really. This job is the key to her escape from Stoney. But it is more. It is proof that she, Jill Holland, is worthy. And she so wants to be worthy.

A lady is walking towards her, all brown flared suit and red hair.

She beams at Jill. 'Hello. I saw you pull up. Have you come for the interviews?' She holds out a hand. 'Nina Dawson. Personal assistant to the head. And you are?' She looks down at her clipboard.

'Jill Holland.'

'Which department? We've got four lots of interviews today. We're having a reshuffle.'

'Science.' Jill is totting up in her head. Probably about sixteen candidates then. Terrifying.

'Found you.' Jill becomes a tick on a page. 'If you'd like to come with me, I can show you where you can get a coffee.'

They walk between the parked cars, gathering up a few more candidates as they go. Some are older than Jill, bold, asserting themselves with just a few words. Others look no older than Denny.

Nina Dawson leads them through the corridors of the school and into a large room that reminds Jill of the student common room at her sixth-form college. Coffee and vanilla hang in the air, and some more people perch on low chairs, balancing cups and saucers and gritted teeth.

'Help yourselves to hot drinks, all.' Nina waves her hand, smiling above their heads. 'Tour of the school starts at ten.'

Jill is about to join a group standing near two large hot water urns, when she spies a girl sitting on her own, looking like she is about to burst into tears. One of her hands is resting against a large flat case and the other holds a bunch of something white, scrunched up like tissue.

'I feel your pain,' Jill says as she steps towards her. 'I'd rather have a fourth-form biology lesson at the moment, than be here.'

The girl peers up at her. Says nothing. Jill wonders what she is doing, barging into someone else's thoughts. But then there is a smile.

'Tell me about it. And I've never taught fourth-form biology.'

They both laugh then, and Jill sits down beside her. 'Jill Holland.'

'Kerry Watson. Waiting for her first interview ever. You?'

'I'm after a job in the science department. But it's not my first job. First proper interview though.' Jill waits. 'Shall we get a coffee?'

Kerry lets out a long sigh. 'I really wanted to get one. But I don't know how to work those hot water machines. Didn't want to make an idiot of myself.' She stands up and smooths down her skirt.

'Nice boots,' Jill says. 'Where did you get them?'

What is she doing? Shy, nervous Jill Holland, putting someone else at their ease? And for once, it feels natural.

'They came from Carnaby Street, actually,' Kerry is saying, 'but I'm not showing off. I got them while I was visiting my sister. She works down there. I live in Windermere.'

Jill shows her how to handle the coffee machine, and they chat until Nina Dawson returns and groups them together for a tour of the school. Kerry is being interviewed for a teaching position in the art department – her first post since graduating from art college.

'Good luck if I don't see you again,' Jill tells her. 'And who knows, we could be working in the same school one day.'

Kerry moves in for a hug. 'You too. Fingers crossed.'

———

By four o'clock, the tours and the lunches and the formal interviews are over, and all the candidates are back in the lounge, waiting. There isn't much chat. Just the nervous twitching of legs, eyes on the door when anyone comes in.

Jill knows the drill. Successful candidates are taken out of the room, leaving the others to realise it isn't their time, and to wait for feedback.

Her interview had gone well. She'd had answers to every question and encouraging smiles from the panel. Now, all she can do is wait.

Tension and time stretch.

Any brashness or bold shoulders have crumbled under a desire to be taken on. She had been up against four fellow teachers, older, and three of them male. Heads of department often are. But at least she's been given this chance, and there will be plenty of others, she is sure.

The door opens, and a man in an artist's smock comes in. He casts around the room, then walks over to Kerry. A few words, and she is leaving with him, open mouthed and staring at Jill. They clash at the doorway with a lady in a white lab coat. She'd chatted to Jill on the school tour and now she is walking towards her.

Jill's heart smashes against her ribs. Surely not.

'Miss Holland?'

A nod. And a gasp.

'Come with me, please.'

Is this actually happening? Jill blinks at the woman's back, at the white lab coat. She turns and smiles.

'Congratulations. Miss Fisher is just about to offer you a job in her school.'

Jill is ushered into a room, to find Kerry waiting, along with two other women. Older. Smiles flash between them all. The door flies open and in bursts Miss Fisher; wire thin in blue crimplene, her chunky necklace clacking like a string of children's beads. She points to four chairs semi-circled in front of a huge oak desk.

'Sit, ladies. Please. I'm Christine Fisher.' She joins them. 'But you know that.'

They do.

'I have to say.' Voice as smooth as milk. 'I have been impressed with the quality of candidates I have seen here today. Especially the women.'

They all nod.

'But the four of you stood out. Your experience. Your references. The answers you gave to my panels.'

Four pairs of eager eyes on her face.

'I look forward to working with you all. But let me give you a piece of advice.'

They want it.

'You may or may not get married. May be married already. I never was. It doesn't matter.'

Heads tilted, they listen carefully.

'What matters is your *reputation*, ladies. You must be top quality to get on in this profession. Reputation is all.'

Jill almost falls off her chair. She remembers Lena Clarke, from the girl's grammar school, and her obsession with reputation. What would she have made of all this?

'There will be a time, and it is close I'm sure, when you will need to have papers to prove your reputation is above tarnish, as a teacher. Look after yours. That way, you'll go far.' She clears her throat. 'Welcome aboard. Now, I'm sure you've got questions.'

Silence.

'No?' She gets to her feet. 'Well then. My assistant will talk to you all about giving notice, start dates and the like. Congratulations once again.'

Jill watches as she floats past. What her mother would have called a typical spinster. What Jill wants to call the most amazing woman she's ever seen. And she's given Jill the job. Kerry's arms are around her before she can think any further, and the other ladies are shaking hands as though they will never let go.

When Jill steps back out into the car park of the school, it is almost dark, but she has never felt so full of light. At the end of January, she will finally be leaving the island, and everything it stands for.

Jill stares across the classroom at the detritus left by her third-form biology students. The euphoria of securing a new job has become nothing more than a faint lick of excitement for the future. In the meantime, there are lessons to be taught and exams to be coached for. And thirty lots of fruit-fly larvae to be incinerated.

'Hi there,' Susie calls to her from the doorway. 'You ready? Haven't forgotten, have you?'

Jill's eyelids flicker. She needs to eat and drink but there is still so much to catch up on.

'Hi, Suse,' she replies, dragging herself out of her seat. 'I haven't forgotten.' She eyes the chaos, then adds, 'Shall we go to the canteen instead? It looks cold out there. And it'll be quicker, anyway.'

Susie is well wrapped-up in a thick flannel coat and woollen scarf. She clutches a brown paper bag in mittened hands. 'Put your coat on then, girl,' she says, laughing. 'I want to talk to you in private.'

'Oh-oh. Sounds ominous. Is it something I've done?'

'What? You mean apart from getting another job without even telling me?'

Jill lowers her head. 'We've talked about that. I didn't tell anyone at school when the interview was. You're not being singled out.'

A huff from Susie. But the thought of a blustery sea wind blasting into her face, is enough to make Jill pick up her coat and slide in her arms. Being able to leave the island finally is a huge relief, but there is sadness in it too, like the feel of dusk after the brightest of days.

'Lead the way then,' she says, winding her scarf around her neck and lifting her handbag from its place under her desk. 'Hope you've got coffee.'

Susie pats her bag. 'You know me so well.'

There is a glow to her skin today Jill hasn't noticed before. Life as a married woman and a policeman's wife must be better than she imagines. The thought of living in her own place, with Stevie for company, and a lift to work every day on the Triumph, makes her smile. However tired or moody she feels, he can lift her spirits with one wink of his eye, and his famous cheese-on-toast.

'What's funny?' asks Susie. 'Do tell.' She rolls up the collar of her coat and turns herself towards the classroom door.

'I was dreaming of cheese-on-toast, actually,' she teases. 'My stomach thinks my throat's been cut.'

Susie looks her up and down. 'You should eat more,' she says, a hand on her stomach. Jill sees something in the gesture.

'What's going on?'

But Susie doesn't answer. She is already walking away down the corridor, high-heels clattering against the lino.

Outside, the wind blows sharply, and gulls scream. Jill holds on to Susie's arm and they giggle as if they are schoolgirls again, walking home after double biology, eyeing up the grammar school boys.

At the end of the road is the Irish Sea. Today, it roars in, angry and grey, throwing handfuls of white foam and fine sand onto the wide and pebbly beach. People stand back on a concrete walkway, holding the collars of their coats.

'Are we crazy?' Susie leans forward, clutching her hood. 'Don't answer that.'

Jill pulls her down onto a wooden seat and begins to untangle her own hair with her fingers. 'It clears your head though, doesn't it?'

They watch for a moment, sea-spray like fine rain dampening their faces. Then Susie starts rummaging through her handbag. She pulls out a small thermos.

'Hot drink?' Typical Susie. 'Though I'm a little *off* coffee myself.'

'You are?'

'I am. It makes me feel queasy, now.'

'Are you telling me you're pregnant, Mrs Bates?' Jill stretches her eyes. Susie nods. They look at each other, then scream.

'You guessed right.'

Jill embraces her friend, tears welling up. Where has the time gone? More than ten years ago, they had screamed and hugged each other in the same easy way, but for so many different reasons. She leans back again and holds Susie away.

'I am so jealous,' she cries. 'A baby, Suse. How is it possible when we are hardly even grown up?'

'You want me to explain?' A filthy laugh. 'Well–'

Jill shakes her head. 'No. I just meant– Oh, I don't know. When did we get so old?'

'We didn't. We're young women. And stop being so maudlin. You've got Stevie now. Babies will follow.'

Jill twists off the lid of the flask and pours herself a cup of coffee. Lukewarm but fragrant. There is something about thermos drinks. The taste is so nasty yet so comforting.

'Things are okay between you and Stevie, aren't they?' Susie asks suddenly.

Jill sips her drink. 'Yes. He's great. My mother doesn't approve of me staying at his flat, but she'll have to get used to it.'

Susie pulls a sandwich from the brown paper bag she has been clutching and begins to tear it in half.

'Sardine and tomato. It's all I can eat at the moment,' she says, handing her half in a gesture so reminiscent of their schooldays. But she has stopped smiling.

'Can I ask you something?' she mumbles, her mouth full of bread and brown paste.

'Sure. What?'

'Is Andrew Brownstone still on the scene?'

The sentence hangs in the air for a moment, swirling around with the salt breeze.

'What makes you say that?' Jill looks across to the sea. She already knows the answer to her question.

'Dunno,' comes the reply. 'Thought I saw him hanging around the school gates the other day.'

'Are you asking if I'm seeing him? Why would I be?' Jill hates the lie. But if Susie has seen her with Stoney, then other people will have too. She searches for a distraction. 'Forget Stoney. Tell me all about this baby. You've only been married a few months.' She winks. 'Clever that.'

Susie needs no extra encouragement and is soon babbling about visits to the midwife and decorating spare rooms. Jill drinks her coffee and munches on her sandwich, half listening to the baby talk.

PAULA HILLMAN

Something has to be done about Andrew Brownstone, she thinks.

———————

At the edge of the beach, a lone herring gull catches at the wind and comes to settle at Jill's feet, hope in its eyes. It shakes the energy from its feathers and peers up at her from the side of its face. The cold rocks them both, ruffling the gull's feathers and making Jill pull up the collar of her coat. Evening is closing in around her and Stoney has yet to appear.

When she'd agreed to meet him at the west shore, it had been solely for the chance to warn him about his continual turning up at the gates of her school. It's what she's told herself. The truth feels too difficult to express in words. Its form will only take shape as a picture: she and Stoney walking in the dunes in high summer, heads together, while curlews flock and the bob of sea pinks is bright against the salt marsh. It isn't love she feels – that is reserved for Stevie – it is longing, for the simplicity of the sun-bleached sky, and the sea.

'Jilly?' Stoney's raspy voice cuts across her thoughts. 'Wasn't sure if you meant what you said. To meet. You're not exactly my number-one fan.'

He comes to stand beside her, back arched to hold on to a coat far too large.

'Well, I'm here.'

'You are.'

'Surprised your new bloke let you come.'

Silence hangs between them. Jill does not want Stevie linked to any aspect of Stoney. Then there's the implication in his words; that there was a bloke before.

'I choose what I do,' she tells him, then without leaving him any space to comment, 'which is why I'm here.'

She wonders about the small patches of bare scalp when

the wind lifts Stoney's hair, about the stale smell of him. But can only say, 'Let's walk for a bit?'

'Don't give those much of a chance on the sands.' He gestures towards her feet, eyes glittering with humour. 'Stay on the road, shall we?'

Jill is already slipping off her shoes; the dark water is calling.

'Jilly. Wait up. You'll get holes in your tights.'

'I don't care,' she calls over her shoulder. 'It's been ages since I've felt the sand between my toes.'

Along the horizon is a thin line of pale-yellow light, bleeding upwards into an inky sky. On the surface of the water, moonbeams gleam and dance. And Jill has never felt more alive. But she is here for a reason, and she needs to see that reason through to its end.

Stoney is behind her, shivering now, and way out of his depth, it seems. 'Jeez, it's cold,' he says. 'What we doing here, Jilly? Not for romance, is it.'

A firm shake of her head tells him it's not.

'What, then?'

'I wanted to talk. And not at the gates of my school.'

Stoney lets out a long sigh that ends in a cough. 'Bloody better places to talk than the beach on a Friday night in October,' he mutters. 'Spit it out, Jilly. The pub is calling.'

'You used to love the shore,' she says with a whispery laugh. 'You have to find a way back, Stoney. You have to.'

'And you have to stop preaching.' He turns away, pushing his hands deep into his pockets.

'Here's some more preaching,' she says after a moment. 'You must stop coming to my school. I'll help you out with money. For now. But I'll get into trouble if you're hanging around, waiting for me.'

'You can't tell me where I can go,' he says weakly. 'Christ's sake. Who do you think you are? You sound like my Old

Geezer: still pecking at my head, even though he's on his last legs.'

'My work is who I am, and don't be so bloody nasty about your dad.' She hesitates, then watches as her good sense is dragged away on the salt wind. 'I'll come and see you at Seaview. As long as you promise to stay away from school.'

He is thinking about it, Jill can tell. But he says nothing.

'Stoney?'

A shrill call rises from a rock pool near the water's edge: some kind of wading bird, Jill thinks, and a distraction, though she can't let herself be taken in. There will be no leaving the beach until she has Stoney's assurance. And she knows how hard it is to come by.

'Do what I ask,' she spits, 'or there'll be no more money.'

'God, you really are a bitch, aren't you?' He sounds breathless and Jill hates herself even more.

'I mean it, Stoney.' She has to stay focused.

He flips up his hood and begins to walk away, boots biting into the wet sand.

'Whatever,' he throws back at her. 'But you'd better come. Or I'll be back up your school like a shot. And I'll tell that fella of yours what you're really up to.'

Jill watches him go. More than anything, she wants to give him help. That much, he deserves. Feeding him with money is only plunging him further and further into his habit, but what else can she do? Her own feelings for him veer between contempt and utter desolation, and there is no one to call on for advice.

She has a growing sense of losing control of the situation, of never being able to get it back. If that is the case, she needs to act fast. She will go to Seaview one last time, and then she will close the book on Stoney and his story and begin a new one of her own.

November 1987

The first years can't settle.

Jill tries her best to engage them with the spectacular effects of a burning strip of magnesium ribbon, and the threat of danger in their need to wear the hideous plastic goggles, but they just scuff their feet and gaze out of the window at the draining daylight.

The lure of fireworks and toffee apples and their local bonfire is too much to bear for these eleven and only-just-twelve-year-olds. When the buzzer sounds for the lesson end, a small cheer goes up. She tries to frown them into submission, but they have her sympathies too.

'You doin' owt tonight, miss?' Robbie Forsythe stands by Jill's desk, packing his bag and shrugging himself into his blazer.

'Not sure,' she mutters, gathering up the strewn goggles and tongs from his workbench. 'How about you?'

'We've built a brilliant bommie over on West Shore. There'll be fireworks and everything. Why don't you come?'

He peers at her through pale-blue National Health spectacles. Poor kid. He is looking for a mother figure, and Jill seems to fit the bill. His own mother doesn't care whether he is at the bonfire or not, as long as she can lie on her sofa with a large bottle of Bulmers.

'Teachers go back into their cupboards at night, Robbie. Didn't you know?' She nods toward the open door of her stockroom, and they both giggle.

'Oh yeah. Forgot. Might be able to see the fireworks through the skylight though.' That brash-blond grin, soft-brown eyes, magnified by thick lenses.

'Get home,' she commands, gesturing to the open classroom door. 'And be careful.'

He swings his canvas rucksack onto his shoulder and blows her a kiss.

'Cheeky,' she laughs, though she is awash with envy. To be his age again, with only fireworks to think about.

Her mother is taking the boys to their local display and her dad always works on November the fifth. Stevie is away, shooting the wedding of a couple who have managed to get a registrar to marry them on a Friday afternoon, so they can have fireworks in the photographs. And she has plans for this evening too: they involve her and Stoney. And a visit to Seaview.

When the lesson equipment is finally tidied into baskets for the lab technician to sort out, Jill takes off her white coat, and hangs it up, leaning her head against the door for a moment. Stoney's presence in her life is weighing her down. Why does she feel so responsible for him? He is basically an ex-boyfriend who'd treated her roughly. Roughly? That is an understatement.

It is almost dark outside. She can hear the bangs and whooshes of fireworks and see their bright explosions in the clear November sky. She would rather be over at West Shore with Robbie Forsythe and his gang than heading out to Seaview. She hasn't been to the place for years. Hasn't walked up the stone steps or had tea in the blue room. But it has never been far from her thoughts.

She flicks off her classroom lights and heads out of the quiet school.

The air is sharp with the tang of gunpowder and woodsmoke, overlaid with brine from the incoming tide. She turns her back to the shore and begins to walk along a wide residential street. Most houses are lit up, their windows glowing with the warmth of family life. Back-garden fireworks shoot into the sky, while tethered dogs bark out their panic at the hiss and squeal of it all.

Jill makes her way downhill towards the island's promenade. Towards Seaview. She thinks about Stoney. When she'd seen him last, he had looked sickly-pale. There'd been something like pain in the way he held himself, huddled into an old grey duffle coat which hung off his skinny frame. His addiction has become a tangible presence in his life as much as in hers. The heroin has her in its thrall, just as it has him.

He has mentioned his father is ill. Jill wonders whether he's realised he is ill too. She desperately wants to help him, or at least point him in the direction of help, but has no idea what to offer. Is there help available? She's heard of the methadone program. When her fifth formers studied HIV and AIDS as part of their health curriculum, they'd been horrified to learn about the diseases passed on by the sharing of needles. She'd been loath to admit she knew very little about it herself, and she'd taken in every detail, hoping to learn something that would help. But there hadn't been much.

At the gates of the house, Jill stops for a moment. The place is almost invisible behind a mess of unpruned trees and rotting buddleia. Annie Brownstone always kept the front garden in a neat and trim condition. But she is long gone.

Jill makes her way carefully up the stone steps and onto the front porch. The fish gargoyles stare out at her, and she turns, craning her neck to see the tide. She can just make out its wide black stretch, restless against the dark blue of the townscape. The view takes her back to when she first visited the house, Lucky in tow. She had been worried about that visit, too. But the vibrancy of the place, its sea-light and gleaming wood, its lemon freshness and warmth, everything had drawn her in, seduced her as completely as Stoney's compelling personality. But where is he now?

She knocks at the door and waits. No answer comes. She

tries again, then looks in through the letter box, sees only the gloom of the hallway. She wonders what to do. Is Stoney inside, waiting for her? Or has he simply chosen to go out, making it clear he doesn't have to do what she's asked. Her racing thoughts are interrupted by a shuffling coming from the side of the house, then Stoney appears around the corner, hand lifted in greeting.

'Jilly,' he calls. 'You'll have to come in through the back.'

He looks thin, hunched in an old sweater. Against the dark of the evening, his face is white, his eyes reflecting the moonlight.

'Oh. Have you locked yourself out or something?' she asks, following him down the side path to the back garden. He leads her between broken shrubs and tied black bags, and in through the open door of the kitchen.

'Stoney. I asked you a question.'

A small fire burns in the hearth, and two lighted candles stand on the wooden mantel above. The old fireside chairs are missing, and as Jill's eyes get used to the lack of light, she can see the room contains no furniture at all. Stale food smells permeate the air. Her nostrils flare and she looks towards the sink. It is full of rubbish – foil plates, cardboard boxes and greasy newspaper. She takes in a heap of blankets and a light-coloured sleeping bag. And Stoney's duffle coat.

He is watching her face. 'I live in this room now,' is all he offers as an explanation.

'Where's your dad?' she breathes, eyes round and staring across the room to the open kitchen door. Surely the poor old guy isn't still living here.

'Went into a care home, end of last month,' he replies with a shrug. 'Not that I give a fuck. He never did owt for me. Then the place was emptied. I'm not supposed to be here.' His breath is forming icy clouds, and he steps closer to the fire.

Silence hangs between them. Jill can't think of anything to say; Stoney has been reduced to squatting in his own home.

'Couldn't they let you stay here until you found somewhere?' she asks, holding her coat tightly around her. Who *they* were, she has no idea?

He lifts a roll-up from the ashtray next to one of the candles and leans into the flame to light it, inhaling deeply. Two syringes and some pieces of tinfoil lay alongside. Jill gulps down her alarm.

'Nah.' He gives a small laugh. 'The church owns the place and they wanted me out, and quick, like. But I broke in.'

'Couldn't you have gone to live with Mick or something? Is he still around?'

Another shrug. Jill wants to give him money and leave, but she has things to tell him, things that don't seem appropriate now.

'Stoney,' she whispers into the dim light of the room, 'you can't live like this.'

He gives a soft snort, smoke swirling out of his nostrils. 'No other choice, Jilly.' A tremble in his voice. 'Now. What about you?'

'Never mind about me. There must be people who can help you.' She takes his hand and rubs it. 'You're freezing.'

'Don't start feeling sorry for me.' He jerks his hand away. 'Or does that make you feel better?' The tone of his voice changes: sneering, defensive.

'Why are you always so nasty? I don't have to be here. I've got a life away from you, or hadn't you realised?' Her hands tighten into fists. He isn't going to make her feel bad again.

'But strangely, you're here.' Gentler now. He hangs his head. 'You love me, Jilly. I know you do.'

'Look at me, Stoney. Look.' Gritted teeth. She waits.

He lifts his face, regarding her from beneath gingery-blond lashes.

'I don't love you.' Her voice stretches with emotion. 'I never did love you. I don't even like you. I was just a kid.'

Stoney chews at his bottom lip. Very quietly, Jill slips her hand into her bag and locates her purse. She has twenty pounds: enough to buy some groceries for her and Stevie, and to treat Moz for his birthday.

She holds out the notes to him. 'Take this. Please. Get yourself some food with it. Not that– horrible stuff.'

He doesn't hesitate. With a snatch, the money is gone, pushed into his pocket. 'Say the word, Jilly. Heroin. Say it.' He leans towards her, face forward and breath overlaid with alcohol. She backs away.

'You need help,' she tells him. 'I can't keep feeding your habit. You need to leave me alone and get some proper support.' Moving towards the door, she turns to face him. 'I'm leaving the island, Stoney. Soon. You won't see me again.'

He leaps across the room and grabs her by the arm, knocking her sideways. The element of surprise gives him an edge of strength, despite the withered quality of his body.

'You're not leaving me, Jilly,' he wails. 'You can't leave me.'

She jerks her arm away, sending her bag clattering to the floor. There isn't much fight in him, and she manages to loosen his grip and push him away.

'Don't touch me,' she growls. 'Don't ever touch me.' In those words, are every bit of hatred she's ever felt for Stoney. She recognises the emotion now. She hates what he's made her into. A liar. A girl who had sex at fourteen years of age. His plaything. And now an adult who yearns for her childhood.

As she reaches down to retrieve the bag, there is a moment of hesitation, and she thinks she has won.

'Say what you like, but you'll never get away from Seaview. Or me.'

Jill moves towards the back door. He shoots his last bolt.

'It's me you love, Jilly. Me. There'll never be anyone else.'

But those words don't stop her. She steps out into the sharp night air, breath ragged, hands trembling. Fireworks shoot upwards, somewhere in the distance. Normality. It exists. It is out there.

Stoney follows her into the garden.

'If you don't come and help me, I'll be up at those gates again,' he calls, nasty now. 'That'll be embarrassing for the hoity-toity teacher, won't it? And your fucking leather-clad boyfriend.'

As she faces him, Jill can hardly open her jaw to speak. 'Have it your way,' she hisses. 'And I hope my money kills you, one day.'

She spins around, catching her face on a branch.

'I won't let you forget about me, Jilly.' His voice comes from the shadows. 'I'll be waiting.'

With her hand to her face, Jill storms away.

At the bottom of the stone steps, she stops for a moment, inhaling deeply, and blowing out the air through her lips. The breathing drill again. She needs it more than ever. She runs a hand over her cheek, checking there is no blood. The hand comes away clean.

The bus stop is less than a minute away, and she forces herself to step slowly along the pavement towards it. Towards home. The words she has spoken to Stoney play over and over in her mind. Had she really said those things? To a guy who is struggling with addiction and homelessness? But she hates the hold he has over her, wants to be free of him. What would Annie Brownstone have thought of her actions? The woman who had been pleasant, but so blind? The worst thing about the situation is that no one knows. She can't talk it through, get another perspective, listen to someone else tell her what she already knows.

On the bridge, she stops to look across the channel of black water, inhaling the razor-sharp evening air. This place is in her blood but mingled with it is a poison. A poison named Andrew Brownstone.

January 1988

In the days after Christmas, a hard frost falls. The fields and woodlands on the edge of town are covered in a thick white coating, and the pavements shimmer with ice.

Jill becomes ill.

What starts out as a layer of worry about Stoney being on his own at Seaview, ends up being a full-blown dip in her immune system. Her tonsils feel like shards of glass in her throat, and a fever keeps her in bed at her parents' house for days, leaving Stevie to worry if she's ever coming back.

When she can finally eat and drink again, her mother takes to sitting on the end of her bed, watching while tea and toast are tentatively swallowed. Jill has become a ten-year-old all over again.

'You need to take better care of yourself, my girl,' she scolds. 'You saw what happened to me when I tried to work and keep house as well. It nearly killed me.'

Jill hasn't forgotten: the summer of 1976, the new house on the island and the way their money hadn't stretched quite far enough to keep the family going. The summer she had met Stoney.

'Mother.' Jill starts to argue but can't get enough volume to make her point. 'I'm okay. Stevie does his share.' She begins to cough.

Her mother passes over a glass of water. She waits while Jill takes a sip.

'See, I don't agree with you. Men having to do their share. Everything's upside down with the world.'

Jill finds her voice again. 'So, you don't think I should be a teacher? A head of department, even? I thought you liked telling everyone what your eldest daughter did.'

'I do, love. I'm proud of you. But how will you manage if you're ever married. Can't have Stevie coming home to an empty house.'

Jill tilts her head sideways and looks at her mother, worn out with chasing after five children and never having a break. 'Stevie doesn't come home. He's not even got a traditional job. And anyway, we share everything. You're living in the past. Things are different now.'

'Modern doesn't always mean better,' she snaps back.

Jill is struggling to understand exactly where this conversation is going. It's a bit late for the traditional birds-and-bees talk. Twelve years too late, in fact.

'I really love my job, if you want to know. It's not the part of life I find difficult, not what's made me so low.'

Her mother's eyes narrow. 'Oh?' A bounce of interest.

Here is the perfect opportunity to finally offload the problem of Stoney. Her mother will have some sound advice, she is sure. But when she tries to find the very first words she will use, they're not there.

'I thought I was pregnant.' A white lie to hide the black truth. Her mother's face falls. 'It's okay. I'm not.'

'Jill.' Her mother catches at her hand. 'You should have said.' A tongue pushes into her cheek. 'But wouldn't that have been something.'

'I thought you'd go mad.'

'You'd have had to settle down then, wouldn't you?'

Within a few days, Jill is well enough to take a walk outside with Stevie, but the icy air agitates her cough, and the layers of clothing her mother insists she wears, make her feverish all over again. Stevie frowns at her.

'You all right?'

'I think so. Just tired.'

'Christmas is hard work, isn't it?' He slings an arm around her shoulder. 'All that forced joviality and eating stuff you don't want. Got some great photos of your family though.'

It is true. He fits into the family perfectly. Bonnie is already in love with him, and the boys have made him promise they can have a ride on the Triumph as soon as their heads are big enough to fit snugly inside Jill's crash helmet. Her father enjoys having someone to entertain them, and make their Lego models, and the way Stevie tucks into his food makes him an instant success with her mother.

Jill thinks about the last few days. There has been little joviality in Christmas for her. The time with her family and with Stevie has been wonderful, full of laughter and food, and group games of Monopoly, but thoughts of Stoney won't leave her alone. They creep into every happy moment and crumble it away into the grime of drug addiction. But she's told Stoney it is the end of their relationship, and she must stick to it. So why does she have a claw of icy fear pulling at her stomach? She wants to tell Stevie everything. He would understand. How could he not? But the thought of him knowing what had happened back in 1976, makes her face burn with shame.

Now, here he is, grinning down at her. 'Can't wait for you to be Mrs Francis. There'll be no over-work then. I'll make sure there's only one reason why you're tired.'

She lifts her face and returns the grin. 'You haven't asked me yet. And anyway, you'll soon get bored of me when I'm there all the time.'

He shakes his head. 'Not gonna happen, my darling. Like I said, we'll be together forever, as long as you want me; I'd never force you to be with Stevie the borin' photographer.'

Jill wants to cry. Tears form along her lower eyelids, and she tries to blink them away, but he sees.

'Hey.' He pulls her into a hug. 'I'm not that bad, am I?'

She lets her head rest against his chest, smells the leather of his jacket. 'Ignore me. I just don't want to go back to work.'

'You adore your job. So you keep saying. But we could live on my money, if you've had enough?' He moves her away from him, holding her shoulders. 'Jill?'

'No,' she croaks, shaking her head, 'it's not that. I want to work. I think this bout of 'flu – or whatever it was – has just wiped me out. I'll be okay once I get back to it.'

'I'm glad about that. I always wanted to be married to a teacher. Or a librarian.' A dimple of his cheeks. 'It's very sexy.'

Jill punches him lightly on the top of his arm. 'You pig,' she says playfully. 'I was like that about bikers. There are plenty of those to choose from, so you'd better watch out.'

He holds up his hands. 'Okay. Point taken. I do love you, though. I'm not kidding. So, you will marry me one day, won't you?'

'I will. But let's not get all miserable and worried. It's a beautiful afternoon and I want to enjoy it, with you.'

Stevie takes her hand and tucks it under his arm. 'Come on,' he says, 'let's walk, then we can go home, and I'll cook you something for supper.'

'Fried cheese sandwiches again then,' she laughs ruefully, as he takes her hand, and they step across the crisp white grass.

When Jill is dropped at the school gate on the following morning, she is feeling much better. A night away from her mother's fussing and frowning has lifted her spirits as much as an evening with Stevie, talking and laughing about the future.

And Stoney has been firmly put back in his box, the one she keeps buried in the dark recesses of her mind.

The zoom across the bridge, the fragments of early sunshine glittering across the water, the blast of icy-clean air, it has all served to clear Jill's head. Glancing across the estuary at the Lakeland mountains soothes her, somehow. The island feels like a friend, a companion, and one she will soon be leaving for the last time. But she won't ever forget.

She climbs down and unfastens her helmet, wiping a hand over her face.

Oh, she'll never forget.

'I can't pick you up tonight, darling,' Stevie tells her, reaching down to hook her helmet onto the bike, 'but I'll see you at home. Like the way I said that?'

She does. *Home.* With Stevie. It is exactly the right thing to say.

'Don't worry,' she tells him. 'I'll bring something in with me for tea and I will cook. And it won't involve cheese.' They both laugh, then he kisses her hand and is gone, the Triumph attracting the usual attention with its heavy roar.

With her bag on her shoulder, Jill makes her way down the drive, and through the front door of the building. Inside, the air is warm, with the aroma of coffee and cigarettes drifting from the open office door. Susie is sitting at her desk, her typewriter already loaded up, a steaming mug on a glass coaster next to her. She gives Jill a wave and mouths *see you later*. Jill lifts her hand and returns the greeting, patting her stomach. This gesture causes her friend to swing around on her chair and do the same thing, though Susie's stomach is now considerably larger.

It is good to meet up with staff and her pupils again, despite the comfort of the Christmas holidays, and soon Jill is sparked into action once more.

The day flashes past in a blur of practical biology, girls

wearing too much make-up, boys needing spare school shoes because they've turned up in Christmas Nike or Adidas trainers, and the panic of her O-level chemistry class, when they realised this is the year they'd take their exam.

At lunchtime, she is on duty, which means five tours of the bright but cold playground, breathing in the salty tang from the shore and clutching a mug of Cup-a-Soup.

At the end of the day, when Jill is tidying her classroom, Brian the caretaker puts his head around the door.

'Oh, hi. Good Christmas?' She flashes him a grin.

He doesn't return it, only peers at her from under bushy grey brows. 'It was, lover, thanks. Look. Bit difficult this, but there's a guy down in reception. Asking for you. Bit shady, if you really want to know, but I thought I'd better say. In case you wanted to see him. Shall I take you down?'

Stoney. 'What sort of guy?' Stupid question really.

Brian lifts his shoulders in a small shrug. 'Don't want to say anything bad, if he's a relative, like, but he's about your age with orangey hair, and really pale. Scruffy, like. I've seen him hanging around before.'

'Okay. Well, I'll come down and have a chat. See who it is. No need to come with me, but thanks for the offer.' The last thing she wants is a showdown with Stoney while Brian watches. At least Susie will be long gone. The reception closes at two.

Brian lifts his chin. 'If you're sure, lover.'

'I am.' Too bright. 'I'll pop down now.'

'Right you are.' He hesitates. Jill forces herself to smile, waiting until he's walked out of the room, and she can no longer hear his footsteps echoing along the corridor. Then she follows him.

The reception area is laid out with a semi-circle of low armchairs, covered with grainy oatmeal-coloured fabric. There is a glass-fronted office where the school secretaries reside.

Stoney is sitting down, leaning his elbows on his knees, and smoking a roll-up. The combat jacket and jeans do nothing to help his appearance.

He jumps up as she walks in, all gaunt faced and reeking of tobacco.

'Jilly. You haven't been to see me.'

She puts her hands over her face and inhales sharply.

'What are you doing?' she hisses. 'You shouldn't be here. I told you I wasn't coming down anymore. Besides. I've been on Christmas break; in case you hadn't realised. I couldn't have got away. You're not part of my life, Stoney. I don't even care.' The anger she feels at seeing him in her workplace – *her* workplace – makes her head pound. Her throat tightens. She wants to hit him. Punch at him. Push him out through the door.

'Need money, Jilly. You promised.' He turns to face her, his body trembling. 'Not so good at the moment.'

'You need to go,' she tells him. 'I haven't got my purse on me, anyway. I can hardly go back to my room and get it, can I? People would notice. I'll come down later. Now go.' She storms over to the door and yanks it open. 'Go.'

There is no argument. He pulls the shabby jacket across his chest and shuffles towards the open door. Jill wants to push him through it, but he stops for a moment, squinting at her.

'Don't come up the front of Seaview. People have been looking. We– I've got a secret way in now. Through the back fence. Go to the park woods and you'll see it. You will come, won't you?' His eyelids droop and Jill thinks he might cry. Her arms stretch forward as if to hug him, but she stops herself.

'I will,' she murmurs, touching his hand lightly. And she will also pray for the day when she leaves the island for good.

The island's park has been laid out in a narrow, wooded valley, between two areas of housing. It was originally a place for Victorian shipbuilding workers to take their exercise. There is no boundary, or gate, and Jill can scramble off the main path and up to the back of Seaview without attracting any attention. The evening air is bitterly cold, and her breath hangs in clouds as she picks her way between ground ivy and the runners of last season's brambles. Exactly as Stoney has said, two of the algae covered fence panels encircling the garden have been moved slightly, allowing access. She pokes her head through the gap, wriggling her shoulders, then stepping with her right foot and dragging the left one behind. Her coat snags on the rotting wood, and she has to yank it to free herself. She stops for a moment until the rising panic in her chest starts to calm down. What is she doing? It feels like breaking in, and she's no criminal.

The garden is in a terrible state. Clumps of bracken are strewn across the borders, black and sticky with decay, and overgrown shrubs have fallen in on their own weight, laying like granular shadows in the darkness. Jill walks across the mossy lawn, avoiding pools of half-frozen water. Then she is at the back door of Seaview.

Something feels wrong.

A gentle push gets her into the kitchen. Total darkness. Not even candles, just the sharp smell of urine, mixed in with rotting food.

She steps carefully across the tiled floor, her boots sticking in places. She can see the outline of Stoney's sleeping area, nothing more than a heap of blankets and coats really, and she listens for any sound of breathing. There is none.

A small slice of moonlight shows her the hallway. It is completely empty. There had been a mirrored table and small ottoman, coat hooks and a glossy yucca plant. But not now. Everything is gone. Apart from a pile of unopened letters scattered by the thick red door. She can see into the study, a room she didn't know well. It is also empty. Every piece of furniture is gone. Every sign that the Brownstones ever called this their home. The place is a shell.

She begins to tremble.

She shoulders the door of what she remembers as the blue room, hands flat against the cold wood.

'Stoney. Stoney are you there?' she says quietly, panic welling up. No answer.

The room is as empty as the rest of the house: no artwork, no hi-fi, no navy sofa. Only floorboards beneath her feet. A flash of memory. Lying on the sea-blue carpet, waiting, Mike Oldfield's eerie instrumentals permeating her fear.

The ceiling above her creaks, giving a moment's distraction. She scans across the room, towards the fireplace, silvery light on white marble. And there he is.

Stoney.

Hunched over, head at an unnatural angle, legs extended and feet bare. His thin arms poke from an overlarge T-shirt, and around one of them is a tight strap with a syringe protruding from beneath it. Jill throws down her bag and kneels in front of him. Across his lips are patches of saliva mixed with something foamy. His eyes are closed. The ceiling creaks again.

'Stoney,' she whispers. But she doesn't touch him. Knows not to touch him. He doesn't respond. Where is the auburn-haired boy with the filthy sense of humour? The summer boy who loved animals and yet shot them. This isn't him, slumped there like a bag of old bones.

A tight band of fear grips Jill's body, taking her breath away and leaving her weak to the point of fainting. But she can't allow herself to fall. She must get out. If he is dead, she can't be found here. There can be no explanation for her presence in Seaview. Stepping back, she picks up her bag and looks at him one more time. Nothing. He is gone. A gasp of breath catches in her throat, and she gags. She will not let herself be trapped by this situation. Christine Fisher's words echo through the confusion in her mind.

Reputation is all.

And if that makes Jill a cruel and terrible person, she will live with it. For now, she has to get out. Away from Seaview and everything it stands for.

Treading quietly, she walks back through the hall and across the kitchen, hearing only the sound of her breath, ragged and hollow. Once outside, she takes in some gulps of the cool night air and flees across the garden and out into the park again. Stevie will be waiting. Her new life will be waiting, and she doesn't look back.

Chapter Twenty-One

PC Rose Atherton looks across the table at Jill, her hands pressed together, fingers touched lightly to her chin.

'So, you thought he was dead?' she asks. 'Did you call for help?'

Jill shakes her head. Doesn't say she thought only to save herself.

The policewoman inhales sharply. 'You found your boyfriend dead, and you did nothing? Struggling with that, Mrs Francis.'

'He wasn't my boyfriend. Hadn't been my boyfriend for more than ten years. I told you that.' How pathetic she sounds. Waves of fatigue creep up her arms and legs, and her head feels light. As though part of it is missing.

'You said you thought someone else was in the house. Why did you think that?'

Jill remembers every detail of that night vividly. She has played it over in her mind for many years and has even written it down, despairing that she will never unsee Stoney slouched in the room, needle hanging from his arm. There had been sounds, coming from a room somewhere upstairs – but had she imagined them? When there was no follow up, no news story, no police knocking at her door, she thought perhaps someone had found a rough-sleeping junkie and acted accordingly. Taken him away in a private ambulance and buried the story. After all, drug deaths were on the rise, and heroin addiction was becoming something everyone had an opinion on. Stoney was just another statistic.

'He had a friend,' she murmurs. 'One that got him into drugs in the first place. Mick, they called him, but I think his name was Malcom Gibson. It was a long time ago.' She does not tell Rose Atherton she has forgotten nothing.

'It would have been helpful to know that when we first started the investigation. You told us you hardly knew Andrew Brownstone. Why?' The policewoman rests one elbow on the table and taps her chin with a small forefinger. 'What else haven't you told us?'

Jill is trying to be honest. Rose Atherton now knows more about aspects of her life than even her husband does. Adrenaline is sharpening her wits. There is a fine line between what is said, and what is deliberately left unsaid to cause confusion. She must get it right. There is shame in her avoidance of the truth, not the deliberate wish to mislead. How could this young policewoman understand what it had been like for Jill as a naive fourteen-year-old?

'I've spent the best part of thirty years trying to forget about him and what he did to me. I don't want to think about it… or him. But I never buried him in the garden of Seaview. How could I have?'

Rose Atherton shrugs. 'It's possible. You must know that.'

Of course she knows. The terrible thing she did do; leaving a dying or dead man, stepping away to save herself, is bad enough. And now she will be punished. The years of depression and anxiety have been their own punishment. The nightmares. Stevie wondering what he had done. But she got past that. Found a way to make peace with her actions.

When Seaview had been boarded up, an article had appeared in the local paper, with no mention of a dead body inside. This had been around 1990, and the relief she felt had brought her to tears, though she could tell no one. She had a baby son to focus on then, so Stoney had been buried in the core of her. And now he has been dug up.

'I didn't kill this guy,' says Jill, looking into Rose Atherton's pale blue eyes, 'heroin did. His choice. Mine was to leave him to it. I'll take responsibility for it. But he must take some blame too. Sorry if that sounds harsh, but there it is.' She runs a hand across her face, and sighs. 'What will happen now?'

'We're assuming the body we've found is Andrew Brownstone. We shouldn't assume. There has been no positive identification. We have run tox screening on some remaining tissue samples, but the results are not clear. Nothing to back up your heroin story.' The policewoman opens the brown cardboard file again and begins to leaf through the papers inside.

Jill chews at her nails, and watches.

'Malcom Gibson, you say?' Rose Atherton shakes her head. 'There has been no mention of him.'

Who has done all this mentioning? Jill wonders. 'Did someone tell you about Stoney – Andrew Brownstone – and me? What made you contact me?' She knows there is not much chance of an answer to her question and is surprised when the policewoman begins to speak.

'A DCI Bates has been in touch with us. He works within the Lancashire Constabulary. As does his wife. She saw the photograph of Mr Brownstone we have been circulating on the internal mailing system, and she recognised him. Gave us your name too. Susie Bates? She was a friend of yours?'

Susie. Of course. They had lost touch when her husband

had been promoted. If only she'd heeded Susie's warning all those years ago.

'I haven't seen her for a long time. But yes. She was a friend.' Jill is running out of energy. As though her battery is winding down. Her head slumps forward, and she presses two fingers to the migraine spot between her eyes.

'Look,' says Rose Atherton, blinking at her, 'your information has been helpful, but we are nowhere near wrapping up this investigation. The team would probably like to speak to you. I'm just a mouthpiece really. Would you like to go home, and come back in the morning? You look like you could do with a cup of tea and a rest.'

Jill nods. 'Thank you. Yes.'

The policewoman stands up, smoothing down her black trousers and clearing her throat. 'Follow me. I'll show you the way out.'

They walk together through the quiet corridor, footsteps falling in time. In the reception area, Rose reaches through a glass hatch for a piece of headed paper and a pen.

'What time would you like to come back, tomorrow? After school? I realise it's a busy time for you, but we need to pin down this Andrew Brownstone story.' She writes 4pm and tomorrow's date on the piece of paper, along with her own name.

'So you don't forget,' she says as she hands it to Jill.

'Forget?' A flush of heat spreads across Jill's neck and face. She doesn't want to touch this piece of paper.

'So you remember you've got a date with me. Tomorrow. It's important.'

If this is Rose Atherton's attempt at humour, it isn't working. In Jill's opinion, gallows humour has no place in a police station. But she doesn't say this, says instead that she will see Rose tomorrow at four on the dot, then she pushes at the coded door and lets it swing closed behind her.

Outside, there's a thick bank of lilac cloud moving in from the direction of the sea. The crispness of the air has vanished, and Jill gasps as she tries to take a deep breath. It's as though there's nothing to inhale. She tries again, realising she can breathe, it's just a rise in humidity, but it sets off a burst of adrenaline and before she knows it, she's panting, heart hammering and running towards her car. By the time she's pulling out of the car park, the sky has burst open, sending down rain that covers her windscreen in glittering sheets.

While she drives for home, she can't help remembering rain at the end of another summer, when she'd stood with Andrew Brownstone on the porch of Seaview House, arguing about something: a lift home, she thinks. His mother had taken her, in the end. Annie Brownstone. A woman she remembers admiring for her kindness. It didn't save either of them, in the end.

By the time Jill is parking her car on the drive of her house, she has resigned herself to the fact that this evening with Stevie and Phil could be their last chance for normality. She digs deep in her psyche to find the tools she's used, over the years, to keep people believing she's a commonplace person. And it works. There is kissing and smiles, rummaging in cupboards for ingredients, Phil eating a bowl of cereal while he hovers and she cooks, Stevie clearing the countertops after her. There's conversation and banter, disagreements and huffing, then Phil cuts in.

'Mother. There's a call for you. It's Auntie Bon.'

'Oh. I didn't hear the phone.'

'You're in the zone, tonight, aren't you?' He puts an arm around her shoulder as he drops his bowl into the sink. 'Is all okay?'

'Yep,' she replies, then hands him a wooden spoon. 'Stir this until I get back.'

Bonnie is her unfailingly cheerful self. She's telephoning on a whim, wanting to offload the details of her latest romance. Where Jill has needed deeply rooted relationships and stability, Bonnie craves the breathless freedom that comes from new experiences. Jill has only to ask the right question, and Bonnie will tell all.

When she's finished, and the conversation turns to what is new in her sister's life, Jill finds the lie that everything is okay has trapped itself in the back of her throat and won't come.

'What's happened, sis?' Bonnie is on it straight away. Jill tries to explain, but her story can't be told as words shared over the telephone. Better to make something up and hope her sister will respond as she has before.

'I don't think I'm well,' she croaks, 'and I can't talk to Stevie or Phil at the moment.' She gulps down a ball of choking emotion, then adds, 'Could you come up?' If she can have Bonnie here when tomorrow's visit to the police station detonates the Andrew Brownstone story, she'll find comfort in that.

'Course I will, sis. I'm not working this weekend. I'll come on Friday.'

Friday? The day after tomorrow. Who knows what will be happening then?

'That'd be good,' Jill says. 'We can have a proper catch-up. It'll be wonderful to see you.'

When Bonnie hangs up, Jill walks down the hallway to the front door, and opens it for a moment. The rain has eased slightly, but the sky is heavy and dark. Thunder rumbles from somewhere behind Di's house. She senses Stevie coming to stand just behind her.

'How was Bon?' he asks.

'Fine.' Jill shivers as he slips his arm through hers. 'She's coming up at the weekend. Unpredictable as always.'

Suddenly, there's a silver flash and a strip of lightning splits the sky above them. Jill inhales sharply, her hand on her chest.

'Got the jitters tonight, haven't you.' Stevie kisses the top of her head. 'I'm going to get my camera. Can't miss this.'

Jill nods and turns to follow him. There will be the dinner to finish and the dishes to wash. Then she'll prepare for the return to school of her Year Seven, Eight and Nine pupils tomorrow. She'll greet them all for the first time in the reception area, checking for uniform deviations and distress on any of their faces. And all the while, she'll be waiting for Andrew Brownstone to somehow have the last word.

Chapter Twenty-Two

B y the time it gets to the end of the school day, every joint and sinew in Jill's body is screaming in agony. She wants to open her mouth and let the collected angst escape in a controlled way, before it smashes into her teeth and frees itself. But she doesn't. Instead, she locks panicking Jill Francis away in that same strongbox where Andrew Brownstone resides and pretends she's someone else entirely.

There is a moment, as she's standing in front of a hall full of pupils, telling them about her expectations for the year, when she catches the eye of her newly-appointed art teacher, Ms Watson-Reilly. Kerry. They'd worked together many years ago. After her interview, she and Jill had caught up over coffee in the staffroom. Kerry explained how she and her wife were back from jobs abroad, and she'd seen Jill's advert. Finding out this was Jill Holland, her old colleague, had given her a starry-eyed moment, she said, and she'd applied for the job.

She won't be so starry-eyed by this time tomorrow, Jill thinks.

When the working day is over, and her staff are drifting home, Jill picks up her bag and jacket and steps outside. Yesterday's rain has washed away the last traces of summer:

there's a transparency to the light that comes with the earlier borders of evening. One child makes her way down the drive, ponytail swinging and clad in brand-new sports kit. She's tiny. There's an enthusiasm in the way she bounces along, a challenge to the world that waits for her. Jill remembers that feeling: a fragile strength.

By the time she arrives at her destination, it's nearer to five o'clock than four. If Rose Atherton isn't happy, there's nothing Jill can do; it's not her job to make life easier for the police. If they've had forensic information about this *skeleton*, they'll be building a picture, anyway. She shrugs. Let them paint her into that picture in any way they want; she's too tired to care.

There's a flurry of activity in the main reception area. Jill is eyed with suspicion by a male police officer who seems to be trying to settle a dispute between two adult women and the three children standing with them. Accusations and coarse language fly between them and the officer is shaking his head.

'Can I help,' he calls to Jill, and she wants to say he could probably do with hers.

'I'm here to see Rose Atherton.'

He steps backwards, away from the warring tribe, and pushes open a door.

'Wait in here,' he snaps, but she hears it as a plea. There is no choice but to go where he's sending her.

The door closes with a soft *thunk*, and Jill is alone in what looks like a room for families. There's a box of plastic toys in one corner, and two colourful beanbags. She sits down at a table spread with leaflets: information about anti-social behaviour and railway safety, drug awareness and quitting smoking. She recognises the booklet advertising Project Jack, a local program for juvenile drug offenders. It's an organisation she herself has been involved with for a long time. Payback. That's how she's always thought of her input. She hadn't been able to help Stoney, but she had learnt to help others like him.

The program hasn't been without its problems. Youth offenders were often hardwired by the time they encountered the law, and only wanted to fight, not capitulate.

One glance at her watch tells her Stevie will be starting to wonder where she is. She could send him a message, telephone even, but telling your husband you are at the police station in connection with a death that happened thirty years ago, needs some face-to-face words not a text message. He will have to know eventually. And the story can't be told without mentioning the summer of 1976.

Time passes. The muffled atmosphere of the room is disorientating. It must have special soundproofing because Jill can hear no outside sounds. Only her own heavy breathing. She thinks seriously about just walking out, going home, carrying on. Rose Atherton will track her down, she is sure, and then she'll look guilty, and in a way, she is. Guilty of bottling things up, of putting herself first, of walking away when someone needed her help. But none of those things break criminal law. She didn't kill Andrew Brownstone, so why does she feel as guilty as hell?

The door opens at last, and Rose comes in, balancing two beige plastic cups and a small packet of biscuits. She places one of the cups in front of Jill.

'Sorry. I got caught up with something. There's been a development in the Seaview case. I thought we could have a cup of tea.' She peers down at the surface of the liquid. 'Or it might be coffee; then the team would like to speak with you.'

Jills stomach flips over. The team. Rose Atherton means the detectives charged with finding out what happened to Stoney.

'Erm. Thanks,' she mumbles. 'What development?' Her hand trembles as she lifts the cup and some of the liquid slops onto the table. 'Oops.' She laughs it off but is conscious of the policewoman's focused gaze.

'Someone's come in. With more information.'

This comment throws her. She sips the lukewarm liquid and watches Rose do the same. Neither of them speaks. Either this extra information will see Jill out of the building and free, or it will be damning, and she'll never see the light of day again. She wonders whether she should say anything about the person who's been targeting her house. Waiting around. Asking Phil for information.

A film of sweat crawls its way across her forehead, just below her hairline. She swipes at it with the flat of her hand. Panic grabs at her throat, pounds at her chest and pulls at her hair.

'It's Malcom Gibson, isn't it,' she cries. 'He's made contact. Never mind that he's been hanging around me and my family, he's told you some things, hasn't he?'

Rose Atherton lifts one eyebrow and folds her arms.

'You're jumping the gun, Mrs Francis, but if you've something more you'd like to tell us, before you meet with the others.' She cocks her head in a random direction, then adds, 'I'll be happy to listen.'

Something about her tone is terrifying and Jill suddenly feels cornered. Trapped. Like a rabbit in a snare.

'I need to go,' she cries, jumping up from her chair. She lunges for her handbag, then yanks at the door. The reception area is still crowded with people, some of whom turn and stare. The last things she wants is to pick her way between them. Without thinking too much about where she's going, she veers off down the corridor. Rose follows.

'Mrs Francis. Not that way,' she calls as Jill stumbles about, pushing against locked fire doors. One gives against her shoulder, and she is through. A weeping fig and a row of low armchairs loom up in front of her. And a swing door to the outside. She releases the breath she has been holding and sways towards freedom. Rose Atherton is behind her, shouting something about the doorway.

It will only take her into an internal courtyard, she says, not to the car park. But Jill doesn't care. She needs air.

She glances at a small side table where a man is slumped, a policeman standing alongside him. They are looking at a piece of paper. A form, Jill sees as she moves quickly past. The man turns slightly, leaning towards her. He has dark-grey hair, cropped close to his skull, and there is something recognisable in the shape of his head. Green eyes. They flash at her.

'Jilly?'

Her hands fly to her mouth. Small puffs of breath come out and she realises they are hers.

'Jilly? Is that you?'

Stoney. The same high cheekbones and scattered freckles against paper-thin white skin. A blue anorak, jeans, and hiking boots. Rose Atherton comes up behind her, a hand under her elbow.

'Mrs Francis,' she says, concerned. 'Come and sit down.'

Jill's ears ring, and pinpricks of light flash across her vision. She lets herself be guided to one of the low chairs. Andrew Brownstone and the policeman stare at her. When she can, Jill looks up at them. Her head won't keep still. It shakes as though she is cold.

'None of this makes sense,' she whispers. 'Stoney. How are you here?'

His voice is gravelly and weak. 'No one's called me Stoney for years. Not since–'

Jill wants to hug him. From sheer relief. She's been holding her breath for almost thirty years. Her diaphragm contracts and out tumbles trapped and toxic air, making her slump forward so that Rose and the other policeman jump to her aid.

'I went away, Jilly,' Stoney continues. 'Had to escape from the drugs, and I had to set you free, too. But I did something bad before I left, and it's finally caught up with me.'

The policeman, older and more experienced by the stripes on his shoulder and the white shirt, shakes his head.

'We can't discuss this here. Quiet now.' He holds up a hand to Stoney. His tone reminds Jill of a headteacher she once knew. Uncompromising.

'Don't tell me what to do. I need to explain to Jilly.' A flash of the old Stoney makes her smile. 'Find us a room, or I'll talk to her here.'

A look passes between Rose Atherton and the older policeman. The merest hint of a nod and he steps forward, clearing his throat.

'Follow me please,' is all he says.

Rose helps Jill up from the chair and they walk across the cool white waiting area and into another room. Small, with a table and computer against one wall and two office chairs against the other. The policeman slides the window blind down and Rose leans herself against the table, gesturing to Jill and Stoney to take the chairs. Jill can't relax. She sits on the edge of the chair, hands on her thighs, taking in air through her nose and trying to calm herself. Stoney lifts her hand. She feels sick. His hand is cold and dry. It has explored her body. It has punched her. But she doesn't pull hers free.

'Remember Mick,' he says, not looking at her, 'Malcom Gibson. He died in that house. My house. Seaview. We got a bad fix one night. I was really ill, but he died, Jilly.'

She can't speak. How can she tell him she walked away, thinking he was dead? She'd left the island school not long after that, happy he was gone from her life, but weighed down with the guilt of it. She was the despicable one. Not him.

'I buried him in the garden. Couldn't think what else to do without alerting attention. It was just after Christmas. I remember that.' He chokes on those last words and Jill looks at him. His profile is bony, skin stretched tightly over his skull, but the jut of his chin is so familiar.

'Did nobody ask about Mick?' She feels a wave of sympathy for the guy, though she didn't much like him. 'Someone must have missed him.'

Stoney shakes his head. 'He had no one. That was part of the problem. He was so far gone, Jilly. There was nowt left of him by then. Just skin and bone, he was. And I went away. I had nothing but what I was wearing, but I walked. Lost myself and waited. Thought someone would come searching for me eventually, when Mal's body was found. And they have, in a way. I've been back for over a week now, trying to figure out how this whole fucking mess will play out, trying to manipulate it. In the end, I just walked in here and said who I was.'

Jill feels as though she's been cut adrift from her life. A life spent swallowing down guilt and atoning for any that managed to escape. Who is she now?

Rose Atherton sighs, wanting their attention. 'If what you're telling us is right, Mr Brownstone, there could be charges brought against you. Are you ready for that?'

The older policeman nods towards his colleague. 'I agree with you, PC Atherton. This case is not going to be a straightforward one.' He steps towards Jill and looms over her, extending his hand.

'Thank you for your help, Mrs Francis. We will need to talk to you further.'

Stoney turns to face the policeman, a glacial look passing between them. 'I want to talk to Jill alone. Might be my last chance. Can you give us a few minutes?'

His words bounce around the room. Rose Atherton stands up and looks at Jill.

'Given the circumstances, I expect Mrs Francis would like to go home,' she begins, but Jill cuts her off.

'No. It's okay. I'd like the chance to talk to Stoney, I mean Andrew.' She slides a glance at the policeman. He will have the final say. She is given a slight nod, then he places his hand just shy of Rose Atherton's back and she leads them away, closing the door pointedly behind them.

Jill's knees are touching Stoney's. He is close enough for her to tell he still smokes. The hands in his lap have yellow fingertips, nails bitten down to tiny half-moons. Looking at them makes her want to cry.

'I've been in London, Jilly. Rainham actually. Been working at a bird sanctuary there.'

Confusion floods Jill's brain. Her whole life lived thinking he was dead, when he'd really been saving birds. 'For how long?' This mattered.

'Only the last ten years or so. Had a hard time up till then. Wandering about. Trying to get clean.'

'Did you never think of Seaview? Or wonder about Mick? Why didn't you just phone for help when you found him dead?' She was a fine one to talk.

'The truth? I hated you, but I hated myself more. The stuff that happened between us. It was wrong. But it was like I was addicted to you as much as to the heroin. I walked away from myself, that day. Didn't want the bloody Old Bill stopping me.' He slides his hands along his thighs and the tips of his fingers brush her knees. He leans towards her. 'Sorry if you don't like what I'm saying.'

Jill wants to scream. 'You forced yourself on me. I was fourteen, Stoney. I didn't even know what sex was. Not really. But you obviously did.' She swings her chair away from him. 'And you're trying to say it was my fault? Even your addiction?'

'That's not what I'm saying,' he croaks, 'get off your high horse for a minute and listen, will you. Really listen.'

Her high horse. What is he saying? 'You've got a cheek.' She flies at him. 'I was an innocent. No one would blame me for what I did.'

He looks at her quizzically. 'And what was that? Jilly?'

With her fists clenched, she tells him. 'I came to Seaview

that night. Just after *Christmas*. Found you. Down by the fireplace. Off your head. I didn't think you were alive. And I left you.' These last words are spat out, straight from her heart.

He swings his chair to face the table and sinks his head into his hands. Inhales deeply. 'Jilly. You left me for dead. Not that I blame you. But what did you think would happen?'

'I can tell you exactly what I thought. I wanted you out of my life, and it was my perfect opportunity. Stupid, when I think about it now, because all it did was place you in my life forever.' Tears of anger spill over. 'Why didn't you get in touch somehow. Put me out of my misery?' But it is obvious. He hadn't known she'd seen him. Simple. Yet so profound.

'God. What a shitstorm,' he sighs. 'More so for me, cos I can't deny I buried poor old fucking Mick.'

Jill gets up from her chair. She pulls at the collar of her pale blue shirt and throws back her head. The situation is closing in, and she can't escape.

'Do you know what,' she says.

He looks up at her. 'What.'

'For an intelligent guy, you always were an idiot.'

'And you always were stuck-up.'

But they begin to laugh. Small sniffs at first, then something altogether more throaty, crazy. The laughter of people who have just had a lucky escape. From a life-threatening situation. A car crash or something.

'Did you get married?' Stoney suddenly asks her.

She stops laughing and stares at him. 'You're asking me that?'

'Simple question.' He holds up his hands.

'I did,' she tells him. 'He's the love of my life; we have a son.'

'Right. I think I may have met him.' He runs a hand across his chin. 'You got a blue Ford Fiesta? I saw it, loitering like, outside Seaview a couple of days ago. Tracked it down to an address. Your kid told me no Jill Holland lived there. That's how thick I am. I've been hanging around schools, too. Trying to figure out where you worked. I think I saw you the other day, but I bottled it, in the end.'

'You were trying to see me?' Jill stretches her eyes. 'Christ, Stoney. I'd have had a heart attack.'

He snorts lightly. 'I don't know what I was doing, to be fucking honest.' He puts two fingers to his temple. 'I'm not as sharp as I used to be.'

'I don't believe that,' she says. 'Have you been on your own all this time?' She hesitates. 'What I mean is, did you ever meet anyone else?'

A shake of his head. 'I've never had anyone else,' he says, looking down at the floor, 'couldn't risk it. And I was married to the drugs for long enough, anyway. But I'm clean now. Ten years clean.'

Jill presses her lips together. Good for him. She's only been clean for about ten minutes. A glance at her watch tells her Stevie will be at home, waiting. There is a lightness to her thoughts. Stoney is alive. Has always been alive. She didn't leave anyone for dead. But she will have to be careful.

'I'm really pleased for you.'

And he huffs, just a little.

'No, I am. Honestly,' she says. 'And I will tell the police all about the drug habit you and Mick had. We both know what happened at Seaview. We haven't lied.'

'We'll see. But Jilly–'

'What?' She peers at him.

'I am sorry about forcing you. I thought I could have whatever I wanted, in those days. And you were so fucking gorgeous.'

Her cheeks burn red. 'Don't,' she pleads, like she's a kid again.

'The apology I could make was to stay away, Jilly. Can you

understand? I could give you that, if nothing else. I've never forgotten what you said to me, the last time we met.'

Jill hangs her head. She can't find any words.

'You told me you didn't care,' he continues. 'That I wasn't part of your life. At least you had a fucking life. I had nowt at that point.' He sighs. 'I'm not blaming you, not in any way. The one thing you seemed to want from me was for me to piss off. So I did. I gave you that.'

There is a knock on the door and Rose Atherton appears.

'Mr Brownstone. Mrs Francis. There are things we need to sort out.'

Another woman, older than Rose, and wearing a navy-blue suit and silky shirt, comes into the room behind her.

'This is Detective Inspector Power. She needs to take a statement from you, sir.' She looks at Stoney. 'You can go home now, Mrs Francis. But we will need to talk to you again.'

She pulls out Jill's chair and the older woman sits down, crossing her legs and placing some papers in front of her. She nods a dismissal at Jill and turns to face her charge.

'So, Mr Brownstone,' she begins, 'let's have a think.'

He looks up at Jill and winks. 'See you around, Jilly. Visit me in prison if it comes to that. Will you?' Then, 'Can I have a fag first? I'm gasping?'

Jill pulls her handbag onto her shoulder, a gesture so ordinary, in a room where her life has just changed for ever. Her legs are weak and shaky.

'Let him have a fag,' she says, then she steps out of the room.

Rose Atherton walks with her up the corridor and lets her through the main entrance, and out into the car park. Night is falling. In the western sky she can see a streak of dark blue above the setting sun. Beams of orange light explode across the water. Soft lilac and pale pink. The colours of a September sunset. From the side of the police station, she can see some of the island buildings, silhouetted now, lights twinkling out across the water. Stevie needs to know everything, and she will tell him. This time, she will tell him.

'We'll be in touch,' says the young policewoman. 'Soon, I expect.'

'That's fine.' Jill holds out her hand. 'You have my number.'

Rose Atherton's fingertips brush hers, and it gives Jill a hollowed-out feeling. The one that comes when something wished for is suddenly gained. *Be careful what you wish for*, her mother would say. Is this what she wished for?

A door bangs open behind them. They both turn.

'Wait up, Jilly.'

Stoney. An unlit cigarette between his lips. And a young policeman with a straight mouth, just behind him.

'Hold up, will you?'

Jill smiles. Waits. Then, here he is. Chip-toothed smile and the crackle of an anorak.

'One last look at the island, hey?' He slings an arm around Jill's shoulder. 'Old times' sake, and all that.'

She doesn't shrug his arm away. Not this time. He lights up, and she watches. They look out across the black tide, and they remember.

THE END

Acknowledgements

Seaview House might be the product of *my* imagination, but many other people have helped to bring it to the point of publication, and they have my utmost thanks: my MA tutor, Jane Draycott for applying her laser-like vision to my writing; my daughter, Rosie Hillman for her beta-reading skills and interest; Bloodhound's editor, Clare Law and her structural vision for those final improvements; Bloodhound's Betsy Reavley and Tara Lyons for giving my writing the chance to be out in the world; my patient and supportive husband and fellow-creative, Steve Hillman; my parents and parent-in-law and my son, Frankie, and son-in-law, Tom, who have quietly cheered me on from the side-lines. Those people are my team.

The setting for my novel, Walney Island, is a real place. It has dunes and natterjack toads and its own brand of geranium; it is truly unique Bringing it to life through the medium of story has given me great joy. It is my hope that readers of *Seaview House* feel something of that.

This first novel, my debut, is dedicated to my father-in-law, Raymond Hillman: he was there at the beginning of my writing journey but didn't make it to this point with me. He would be amused that I've used his name for one of my tiny, quiet characters.

A note from the publisher

Thank you for reading this book. If you enjoyed it please do consider leaving a review on Amazon to help others find it too.

We hate typos. All of our books have been rigorously edited and proofread, but sometimes mistakes do slip through. If you have spotted a typo, please do let us know and we can get it amended within hours.

info@bloodhoundbooks.com

Lightning Source UK Ltd.
Milton Keynes UK
UKHW011853310123
416242UK00008B/561

9 781504 083317